617

13.95

Bla... ...bino

Na...

with a...

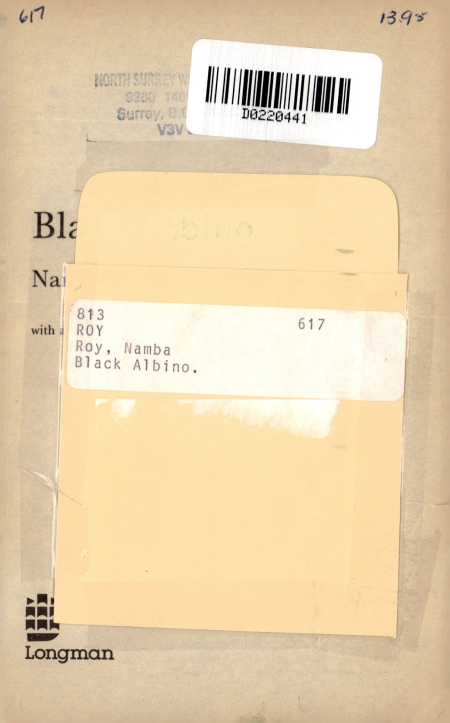

Longman

To the spirit of my Maroon ancestors, to their descendants still living in the Cockpit Mountains of Jamaica, to my wife, whose encouragement, confidence and enthusiasm never wavered, I humbly dedicate this book.

Namba Roy

Longman Group UK Limited
Longman House, Burnt Mill, Harlow,
Essex CM20 2JE, England
and Associated Companies throughout the World

First published by New Literature (Publishing) Ltd,
London, 1961
First published in Longman Caribbean Writers Series 1986
Reprinted 1989

ISBN 0 582 78563 4

Produced by Longman Group (FE) Ltd
Printed in Hong Kong

Front cover photograph of sculpture: Mike Tomlinson. Back cover photograph of Namba Roy both courtesy of Mrs Yvonne Roy.

Introduction

About the author

NATHAN Roy Atkins (who changed his name to Namba Roy) was born in Jamaica on 25 April 1910. We are told 'that his people came to Jamaica under slavery from the Congo and that they subsequently escaped to the Cockpit Country to live as free men, or Maroons, as they came to be called.'[1] Roy spent his childhood mainly in Kingston and in Accompong (in the Cockpit Country), growing up in close contact with Maroon carving, oral history and story-telling. 'Until the age of 11 when his father died, Namba Roy had his father, his uncle and his grandfather as tutors in the traditions of his people. The older men taught the boy the stories and symbols of Africa. Males in his family had been storytellers for over 200 years.'[2] His father and his grandfather were also carvers. 'Namba Roy's grandfather was the traditional carver of his village, a role that was handed down from father to son and was said to have been in his family for 250 years.'[3]

When World War II broke out, Roy joined the Merchant Navy. Suffering from a duodenal ulcer, he was discharged ill in 1944 in England. He remained in England. In 1950 he met Yvonne Shelley, an English actress, who later became his wife. Roy changed his name in 1956. Yvonne Roy has explained: 'by this time we had got one little girl, and he didn't want us to have the name of a slave-owner, so he changed the name from Atkins to Roy by deed poll here in England, and he felt that he would like a traditional family name . . . so he became Namba Roy.'[4]

In uncertain health, Namba Roy struggled to support his family in England. He often worked long hours, leaving home at 5.30am, not to return until 7.00pm; and some of the jobs he took were strenuous for a man in his condition. At night and on weekends he tried to carve and paint and write. He had little money for art materials. As a Maroon he had been taught that 'wood, unlike stone, lives and dies; that horns or tusks from animals are of greater importance as a medium, for the latter are not only born, live and die, but may also be associated with reincarnation.'[5] Ivory was often more expensive than he could afford, and it was difficult to get wood for carving while living in inner London. One piece of his sculpture is carved from a piano leg. He 'began to experiment with synthetic materials like plastic wood, although the fumes from these materials were rather unpleasant. Plastic wood required combining techniques of moulding and carving.'[6] He learnt how to devise support for the material and make it less likely to crack. He used anything he could find: we are told that 'The Water Carrier' was modelled around a discarded Bovril container.[7]

The basic materials for writing were more easily assembled. Roy wrote regularly in the 1950s. His first novel, *No Black Sparrows*, has not been published. *Black Albino*, on which he started work in 1959, first appeared in 1961,[8] only months before the author's death. Namba Roy died on 16 June 1961 in London.

Black Albino *and history*
Black Albino is set in Jamaica early in the eighteenth century.[9] The novel no doubt incorporates information orally transmitted to Namba Roy; but the author, who was the official representative in Britain of Jamaica's Accompong Maroons, also learnt from books and documents. Yvonne Roy has reported:

> He went up to the British Museum. We had a very great friend who was in the Ethnographical Department—Cottie Burland—who introduced us to the people at the Museum so that we could go in into the library and research letters which were written at the actual time of the happenings; and Roy wanted to have a completely authentic account of what had happened there so that his story would be real, and it

would perhaps help people to understand . . . He was so **proud of being a Maroon, very proud, and he wanted other people to be aware of who they [the Maroons] were, what they had done and the place they held in the history of Jamaica.**[10]

The novel's information about Maroons is broadly consonant with historical fact. It notes, for example, that the Maroons came from differing tribes of Africa; and that their culture, a synthesis, was largely Africa-based. But *Black Albino*, though a 'rich bed of **African cultural survivals . . . well sign-posted'**[11], is also alert to creolization. In language, for example: though on the first page of the novel Tomaso is represented as 'speaking in the tongue of the Bantu', a creolized mixture is later indicated as the community's norm:

> out of the many dialects in the language of the Bantu the early Maroons had created a common tongue, easy to understand by any son of Africa. Here and there were improvised words, either created by the old leaders themselves, or culled from the Spanish, and later, the English. (p. 71)

Tahta, who tends the sick, mixes 'his knowledge of bush medicine with that which he learnt from the bakra when he was the slave assistant of his doctor master'. (p. 83) Jacob, one of Tomaso's most trusted lieutenants, is a mulatto who 'could speak broken English well, and because of his mixed blood could pass through the more dangerous parts of the towns without challenge, since he fitted the role of house-slave . . .' (p. 91)

The Maroon community in the novel, like many in history, constantly interacts with the white-controlled plantation society. The Maroons have friends, allies, informants, business associates, down on the plains. The novel mentions, for example, the making of hammocks,

> so useful as a bartering medium with the indentured bakra

or the few fortunate negroes who had obtained their freedom. There were many things precious to the Maroons which these neatly made hammocks could buy — cast-off clothing, grains, salt, fish, and precious metal tools, and perhaps lead for musket shot, or a few charges of powder. (p. 117)

In *Maroon Societies* Richard Price observes:

As long as the wars went on, the need for such things as guns, tools, pots, and cloth (as well as for new recruits, particularly women) kept maroon communities unavoidably dependent on the very plantation societies from which they were trying so desperately to isolate themselves.[12]

They established their communities in almost inaccessible places which were comparatively easy to defend. Tomaso's village is typical, its back 'well protected by the natural precipice which stretched for miles behind and made more impregnable by an area of swampland beneath, fed from time by an overflowing river further away.' (p. 19) The novel's description of the frontal approach is remarkably similar to one in Dallas's history of the Maroons.

Steep, rocky and dotted with trees and clumps of shrubs near its base, with only one negotiable path, narrow and winding, which half a dozen women with stones and boulders from above could hold against an invading battalion . . .'
(*Black Albino*, p. 19)

This passage contracted itself into a defile of nearly half a mile long, and so narrow that only one man could pass along it at a time. Had it been entered by a line of men, it would not have been difficult for the Maroons from the heights to have blocked them up in the front and in the rear, by rolling down large rocks at both ends, and afterwards to have crushed them to death by the same means.
(Dallas)[13]

The novel's historical information is more compelling when effectively dramatized; as in Tomaso's exhortation to his Spirit Men, a speech which illuminates the psychology of guerrilla warfare:

> Strike silently. Let the bakra in the forest look for the one who struck, and find nothing! Let them find death from the trees under which they pass, behind the rocks, at the cave mouths. It matters not if some escape but first they must know what it is to fear. Let them feel that the hills are our mother, the rocks our father, the trees our brothers, the sinkholes, gullies, and even the snakes, our kinsmen. Let them know the night is our friend and the darkness our clothing. (p.168)

What sort of book is this?

Doris Lessing calls *Black Albino* 'an exciting, romantic, historical novel'.[14] Kenneth Ramchand's discussion begins: 'It is a sharp drop from [George] Lamming's intensely wrought novel [*Season of Adventure*] to the wish-fulfilment of Namba Roy's tribal presentation of poetic justice.' Though Ramchand finds detail to commend in *Black Albino*, he considers 'some good moments' marred by '[c]ontinuous exposure to its simple effects . . . and the underlying moral imperatives'.[15] In an important article Edward Kamau Brathwaite contrasts *Black Albino* with *The Secret Ladder*. 'Unfortunately, [Namba Roy] did not attempt . . . more than a romantic tale of "brave warriors" and internecine conflict. Wilson Harris, on the other hand . . .'[16]

Especially if set against such novels as *Season of Adventure* and *The Secret Ladder*, *Black Albino* is indeed a fairly simple book, straightforwardly promoting traditional values. If the writing is occasionally awkward or naïve, it is also nearly always vivid. This is a romantic tale — as much 'a romance', perhaps, as 'a novel' (though the categories overlap).[17] 'The romance characteristically intensifies and exaggerates certain traits in human behaviour and recreates human figures out of this exaggeration.'[18] Some critics make a distinction between

two basic types of prose fiction: the novel proper and the

'romance'. The novel is characterized as the fictional attempt to give the effect of Realism, by representing complex characters with mixed motives who . . . undergo plausible and everyday modes of experience. The prose romance . . . typically deploys simplified characters, larger than life, who are sharply discriminated as heroes and villains . . . ; the plot emphasizes adventure, and is often cast in the form of the quest for an ideal, or the pursuit of an enemy . . .[19]

Dramatizing values

In *Black Albino* values such as love, forbearance, courage, honour and self-sacrifice are dramatized in vivid conflict with their opposites.

Ideal love pervades the book. It is presented not only in the relationship between Tomaso and Kisanka, echoed in Tamba and Manda; but also in Kumse's adoration of Tomaso; in the love between Tomaso, Kisanka and their adopted 'father', Tahta; in the love between Tahta and his 'grandson' pupil, Tamba; in the love between Kisanka and her adopted daughter, Manda; in the loyal love of the Spirit Men for their leader and his wife; in Tomaso's love for his whole community.

As a romantic model of perfection, Tomaso shows extraordinary forbearance in the face of many pressures: he will not let Tahta rid him of the turbulent Lago; he will not accept, not even from his elite corps of warriors, an invitation to divide the tribe. Great courage is displayed not only by Tomaso and his band but also by Kisanka who, though tortured, refuses to betray the liberation; and Tamba who, though fearful, returns to the scene of his cruel rejection. Self-sacrifice is variously enacted or proposed: by Kisanka, Kumse, Manda, Tahta, Tomaso; even, equivocally, by Lago.

Lago—the name suggests Iago, another malevolent man—is the villain, at odds with many of the novel's projected ideals. He is a creature of hate. Though not devoid of courage, he has been found wanting under extreme pressure; he has been more than once a traitor. Repeatedly imaged as snake, devil, monster, 'a thing of evil' (p. 40), he is , from early in the book, a physical and moral cripple. Consumed by jealousy, he does not care to be reminded that once he saved Tomaso's life. But, villain as he is, he is not without a trace of decency. Ashamed of having fathered an imperfect child, at least he lets her live, and he provides for her. When, at the end, he asks a boon—'tell her not that I, whom you call traitor, was her father' (p. 170)—he seems concerned for her happiness. In volunteering for a very dangerous mission, he represents himself as hating still: 'Perhaps my thirst for revenge on the bakra is much mightier than my hatred for thee, blood-brother.' (p. 170) He is willing, for the moment, to neglect his private war. Like a kamikaze pilot, Lago delivers the goods. 'Thus Lago had redeemed himself.' (p. 171) Redeemed himself, incidentally, from being killed at last by Tomaso. The air is heavy with irony.

The fate of the hero, warrior-chief Tomaso, is also often ironic. Though he has suffered greatly at the hands of whites, he does not, like most of his community, generalize from the experience. To most of his community white faces are a nightmare, 'associated with slave pens, beatings, tortures, and death.' (p. 90) But Tomaso entertains the notion 'that there are now some good bakra down there on the plains.' (p. 59) Concerned for his albino son, he knows—and he hopes that others will find—'that the Spirits of Goodness and Greatness make their beds into the bodies of men without first looking at their skins.' (p. 51) A black liberal, he promulgates a law of restraint in the conduct of war against the whites. So when, in spite of assurances to the contrary, young Quame has been fed alive to the ants, Tomaso's humane decree seems insupportable. His honourable resignation only makes things worse. For under the figurehead chief, M'Ango—in Jamaican slang of a few decades ago a man easily handled was 'a mango'—the elders are rarely consulted, the community's agriculture, health and security are foolishly neglected. When fever breaks out in the village, 'due perhaps to contaminated water' (p. 74), the Lago-inspired whispers blame illnesses and death on the albino, the dundoes (dundus), 'the strange picni' who looks white. But the community's hostility to whiteness—'White is evil' (p. 75)—is only one of three main factors which combine to work against Tomaso. The other two—

community neglect and the fact that Lago remains alive—are among the consequences of his own humane decisions.

In *Black Albino* the contest between good and evil is often imaged as actual physical conflict. (This novel, with its vivid characters and plenty of action in an unusual setting, could surely engender an outstanding film.)

> 'What shall it be, my snake-tongued brother?' the chief asked him almost softly. Bull neck knew the crowd's ears were perched to hear his reply.
>
> 'Let is be machetes. Cripple as I am I fear thee not.'
>
> 'Lago is playing safe,' said old Tahta to himself.
>
> 'So be it!' replied Tomaso, and as he said the words a machete was placed in his hands.
>
> Lago had already drawn his from its bark scabbard at his side. As the warriors pushed the people back so as to give the two fighting room, and Lago nervously and eagerly grasped the weapon tightly in his hand, Tomaso looked at his enemy, then threw down his weapon, and to the amazement of all, walked over towards the fire and took up a piece of hardwood which the flames had not yet caught. It was scarcely longer than the discarded machete. (pp. 62-63)

We know Tomaso will not lose. He defeated the devil once before, in spite of an injured hand. As readers of a romance, we know he will succeed against the odds. Similarly, young Tamba, innocent of wrestling, beats the bully Jo, who is older and bigger; and as for Tomaso's tiny task force, they shall overcome. In the world of *Black Albino*, though there are casualties of evil, good can be expected to win.

Lovely Kisanka is a casualty. As promised, however, she is of vital assistance after having died. She warns Tomaso at a critical time. *"Go, Tomaso! Go like the wind to the aid of our people . . . Look well when you reach the hills, My Spirit, or you will fall in the bakra hands!"* (p. 146) It is Kisanka, again, who guides the grief-stricken Tomaso to where the children are. 'I came with my

Kisanka,' says Tomaso. 'She brought me here! But where is she now, Tahta? I can no longer see her!' (p. 204) At the very moment of reunion with his son, the damaged hero is restored to normal. The world is bearable again. Tahta, the wise old man—healer, fighter, devious agent of justice—blows the good news on the eketeh (akete, bull's horn, abeng), 'and after a little while an answering talk came from another eketeh from far away . . . "*We hear you! We hear you! God be praised!*" ' (p. 206)

A tale well told

Black Albino is a romantic tale well told. The language of the dialogue is among the special effects; it is often a thing of ceremony, bespeaking a society built on reverences. People are repeatedly addressed by name or title. 'Greetings Little-Many-Fingers-One! Welcome to the hill of the Maroons!' (p. 41) Even insults are often couched in the forms of courteous address. 'Good-day picni-with-the-old-man's-hair!' (p. 89) 'So! The spirit has gone from thee, O betrayer of women and slayer of picnies!' (p. 159) The many 'thee's and 'thy's, the rhythms reminiscent of the Authorized Version of the Bible; the roundabout, sometimes riddling, often hyphenated, phrases; all help to suggest a vanished age and to remind us that the dialogue we receive in English is purportedly being translated out of an African language. 'Think, Tomaso, has this droppings-of-a-carrion ceased from trouble-making in the village since first he knew the secrets of a woman's thigh?' (p. 9)

Some of the simple narrative strategies work very well: the suspenseful delay, for example, in Nahne's reporting on the new-born child (pp. 22-24); and the artful withholding of genetic information that is taken as evidence of who his father is. But the narrative detail is sometimes subtler than that.

The author is, for example, adept at ironic juxtaposition. At the beginning of the book, Lago suggests that Tomaso, not yet a father, is therefore less than a man; Tomaso promptly defeats him in manly combat; and immediately after Tomaso has returned to the village in triumph, he learns that his wife Kisanka (for the first time, at last) has conceived. Or again: immediately after Tamba's self-questioning monologue, directed at his dog—'Is not my face good to look at now that I have covered it with crushed charcoal?' (p. 94)—his private hideaway is visited by a girl who cannot see he is an albino. Testing her for vision, Tamba cries out as though he has seen a snake. Her panic shames him into friendliness: the ruse had been snake-like, a threatening surprise. Shortly, a new section begins: 'Lago was hiding in the bushes . . .' (p. 102), waiting to surprise Kisanka; Lago, we soon learn, the unpublicized father of the girl; Lago, the character most often called a snake.

There are intriguing areas of suggestion. Kisanka's pimento smell, for example. Lago, who causes the death of Kisanka, is haunted by that pimento smell: a smell associated with a continuing penalty Kisanka pays for having refused to be broken—as Lago will be, and was—by bakra torture; associated also with Tahta, the healer who prescribed the remedy, the avenging psychologist who drives the hapless Lago into paranoid distress. Or take the *cocobeh* episode near the end. It is meaningfully appropriate that children who previously spurned Tamba should, in their time of need, take to following him, and should, believing him to be a leper, choose to acknowledge by physical contact their dependence on him, their acceptance of him. That they prove to have been misinformed about Tamba's actual condition is a wry comment on community attitudes earlier in the story.

The appeal of *Black Albino* does not, in the main, reside in such patterns, meanings, literary effects as may be less than obvious. This book is an enjoyably vivid historical adventure story, a 'romance' with boldly drawn characters and clear-cut moral distinctions.

Mervyn Morris
English Department,
University of the West Indies,
Mona, Jamaica

Notes

1 Pamela Beshoff, 'Namba Roy: Maroon Artist and Writer', *Jamaica Journal* Vol. 16 No. 3, August 1983, p. 34.

2 Marie Stewart, ' "I would like to speak of Namba Roy" ', *Arts Jamaica* Vol. 3 Nos. 3 & 4, July 1985, p. 17.

3 Beshoff, p. 35.

4 Yvonne Roy, interviewed by Mervyn Morris, 19 July 1983.

5 Namba Roy, quoted by Beshoff: p. 35.

6 Stewart, p. 18.

7 Ibid.

8 Put out by New Literature (Publishing) Ltd., a London firm founded in 1960 by a Guyanese author, Peter Kempadoo ('Lauchmonen').

9 When Tomaso is only fourteen *(Black Albino,* p. 43) Cudjo[e] and Accompong, who exist in history, are already effective Maroon leaders.

10 Yvonne Roy, 19 July 1983.

11 Kenneth Ramchand, *The West Indian Novel and its Background* (London: Faber and Faber, 1970), p. 150.

12 Richard Price (ed.), *Maroon Societies: Rebel Slave Communities in the Americas* (Baltimore and London: The Johns Hopkins University Press, 1979), p. 12.

13 R. C. Dallas, *History of the Maroons* (London: Longman, 1803; reissued by Frank Cass, 1968), Vol. I, p. 49. Quoted by Richard Price (Price, p. 6).

14 Quoted on the dust-jacket of *Black Albino* (London: New Literature, 1961).

15 Kenneth Ramchand, op. cit. pp. 149-153.

16 Edward Kamau Brathwaite, 'The African Presence in Caribbean Literature' *Daedalus*, Spring 1974, p. 88. See also *Slavery, Colonialism and Racism* ed. Sidney W. Mintz (New York: Norton, 1974), p. 88.

   Cf. Brathwaite, *Wars of Respect* (Kingston: API, 1977), p. 35; 'There is also a romantical novel of Maroon life, *Black Albino* (1961) . . .' Cf. also Brathwaite, 'Houses', (A Note on West Indian Literature), *First World* March/April 1977, p. 47: 'Namba Roy's *Black Albino* (1961) produced a somewhat romantic but rounded world out of his Jamaica Maroon background.'

17 ' "Pure" examples of either form are never found; there is hardly any modern romance that could not be made out to be a novel, and vice versa,' Northrop Frye, *Anatomy of Criticism* (Princeton: Princeton University Press, 1957), p. 305.

18 Gillian Beer, *The Romance* (London: Methuen, 1970), p. 3.

19 M. H. Abrams, *A Glossary of Literary Terms* (New York: Holt, Rinehart and Winston, 1981), p. 120.

Further reading

Pamela Beshoff, 'Namba Roy: Maroon Artist and Writer', *Jamaica Journal* Vol. 16 No. 3, August 1983, pp. 34-38.

Clinton V. Black, *History of Jamaica* (London and Glasgow: Collins, 1958; revised edn. 1965; illustrated edn. 1983.)

Edward Kamau Brathwaite, 'The African Presence in Caribbean Literature', *Daedalus*, Spring 1974, pp. 73-109. Also in *Slavery, Colonialism and Racism* ed. Sidney W. Mintz (New York: Norton, 1974), pp. 73-109.

Edward Kamau Brathwaite, *Wars of Respect* (Kingston: Agency for Public Information, 1977), partic. pp. 7-18.

O. R. Dathorne, 'Africa in the Literature of the West Indies', *The Journal of Commonwealth Literature* No. 1, September 1965, pp. 95-116.

Rudolph Dunbar, 'Namba Roy — His life — and his work', *Sunday Gleaner*, December 31, 1961, p. 13

Beverley Hall-Alleyne, 'Asante Kotoko: The Maroons of Jamaica', *African Caribbean Institute of Jamaica Newsletter* No. 7, March 1982, pp. 3-40.

Wilson Harris, *The Secret Ladder* (London: Faber and Faber, 1963).

Donald Herdeck (ed.), *Caribbean Writers* (Washington, D.C.: Three Continents Press, 1979), p. 183.

Michael Hughes, *A Companion to West Indian Literature* (London: Collins, 1979), pp. 110-111.

Mervyn Morris, ' "Strange Picni": Namba Roy's *Black Albino*', *Jamaica Journal* Vol. 17 No. 1, February 1984, pp. 24-27.

'George Panton', 'A Real History of Jamaica', *Sunday Gleaner*, April 16, 1961, p. 14.

Richard Price (ed.), *Maroon Societies: Rebel Slave Communities in the Americas* (Baltimore and London: The Johns Hopkins University Press, 1979).

Kenneth Ramchand, *The West Indian Novel and its Background* (London: Faber and Faber, 1970), pp. 149-154.

Kenneth Ramchand (ed.), *West Indian Narrative* (London: Nelson, 1966), pp. 68-69.

Vic Reid, *Nanny-Town* (Kingston: Jamaica Publishing House, 1983).

Victor Stafford, Reid, *The Jamaicans* (Kingston: Institute of Jamaica, 1976; revised edn. 1978).

Carey Robinson, *The Fighting Maroons of Jamaica* (Kingston: Collins and Sangster, 1969).

Marie Stewart, ' "I would like to speak of Namba Roy" ', *Arts Jamaica* Vol. 3 Nos. 3 & 4, July 1985, pp. 17-18, & 23.

One

Tomaso, descendant of chieftains and great warriors of the Bakcongo people, sat with five of his men near the crest of the highest of the mountains known as Twin Sisters.

Some distance away, a young warrior, armed with musket and cutlass, peered down the steep hillside and towards the faraway swampy plains for signs of the enemy, their former masters—for these were runaway slaves.

Tomaso joined in the talk of the moment, speaking in the tongue of the Bantu:

'You speak truly, Tahta. This Jamaica is indeed a strange land, with no lions and no animals with hides to break the point of a spear. Some crocodiles, it is true, and some snakes and wild hogs; but neither the lightfooted antelope, nor asunu, the heavy footed one, whom the bakra named elephant, have ever set foot on this place.' He sighed as he passed his eyes over the wooded hill above him. 'True, there are woods here, and the mighty rocks and steep mountains give good hands to our fighting and hiding from the bakra of the plains; but sometimes I long for the forest so thick and high that the face of the sun cannot be seen beneath and where even the mighty asunu, with teeth as tall as a warrior, must bellow for fear of getting lost.'

Four of the five heads nodded in approval of their young chief's talk. Only one who stood leaning on the tree under which they were resting made no move to join in.

'Perhaps the land seems strange to us because there is so much water around it, Tomaso,' said the old man whom the leader had addressed as Tahta. 'And this water which is all around this place is not like the water in our land. It is like a woman of many moods. I tell you, my brothers, that when I was the slave of the bakra I once went near the water and watched it lying still while my master left me to look after his animal. I went back to care for the animal for a little while and when I returned, my brothers, the water was bitten with madness. It lifted itself and threw its body against the land as if the land had covered it with insults. It was many days and nights before its anger was spent. Never had I seen the waters in our land acting so strange and foolish'. The old man who, like his friends, wore a piece of cloth wrapped around his middle, kept rubbing one of his bare shoulders with his hand as he talked.

'It is not only the land and the water that are strange,' said a harsh deep voice, and as the eyes of all turned towards the speaker, there was a sudden tenseness all around.

The man who was leaning on the tree and had not spoken before could see the effect his simple words had on the company and appeared pleased. He paused long to allow the tension to rise to the full.

He, like his chief, Tomaso, was in his early twenties but he looked much older than the leader. Like Tomaso he was jet black, with the nose and lips typical of the negro race. But whereas his chief's face and body had a fine sheen which gave women the itch to pass the palms of their hands lightly over him, this shortish man with a bullneck on a mighty pair of shoulders had no such attraction. His hair grew high on his head as if it would one day touch the sky. Near his feet were the same type of weapons which all his companions had—musket and Spanish type machete. His loincloth, tightly wrapped, helped to show off his powerful muscles.

At last he seemed to have decided that it was time to feed the fire with more fuel. Looking above the heads of all, he rubbed his face with one of his big hands and began again: 'Yes, my brothers, there are stranger things than this land of few animals and angry waters.' Now his eyes came down from the skies and went to the face of each warrior while his mouth wore a mocking smile. It must have taken the bullnecked one nearly a minute to reach the last face to be scrutinised—that of his chief Tomaso.

Tomaso sat on a stone with his weapons at his feet, his arms folded, and it seemed he was the only one who was cool and unperturbed. He was a handsome man. He was tall and well proportioned and though he looked almost slight in build opposite the bullnecked one yet the width of the chief's great shoulders and the power beneath the shiny black skin of his arms and leg muscles showed even in his most relaxed state. He was dressed like his companions in brown loincloth only, and his only distinction was a band of cloth around his forehead which proclaimed him their chief and leader. Everything about him—his nose, lips, hair, and colour, proclaimed him a full-blooded son of Africa. As he leaned his head to one side, meeting the eyes of the warrior who had just spoken, his calm and dignity did not seem to please this bullnecked one, judging by the sudden change on the face of the latter.

'Take our warriors, O my brothers,' continued bullneck, staring at Tomaso with unmistakable insolence. 'These mountains have seen men who call themselves warriors and who have yet to show their manhood!'

There was a gasp from the warriors for all knew for whom the insult was intended. Tomaso alone remained outwardly calm.

Now the mocking smile on bullneck's face became an ugly leer as he kept his eyes on his chief's face.

'Can one be a warrior when one cannot bring a seed from his loins? Speak, O my brothers?' invited bullneck. He must have known that his companions were angry with him for his words as they sat sullenly watching but it did not deter him.

'Is it not the law of our people to take another woman to mate should a warrior's wife prove barren so that the warrior can prove to himself and his people that he is potent?'

He paused, as if awaiting confirmation but when it did not come he went on: 'I, Lago, rescued women to the number of the fingers of my eating hand from the bakra plantations. Have I not given picnies to two of these in one moon? Yet there is one who is amongst us who may die without a seed from his loins.'

The man who called himself Lago pretended he had not seen the slight stiffening of Tomaso's body. The others saw it and looked from one to the other in the hope that they would find a way of stopping this dangerous talk. It was old man Tahta who tried to warn Lago of his folly.

'I have seen stranger things, O Lago,' said the old man. 'One of these strange things I have seen was a ram goat who tried to fool all the animals in the forest that he was a lion, until one day the real lion came and only the horns of the ram were left.'

Lago gave the old man a scornful look. 'It is the custom of our people to treat the aged with respect, O Tahta,' he said. 'But this custom can be forgotten!'

'I tremble at thy words, O mighty one!' replied the old man with mockery. Lago stared at him; then to the silent Tomaso, his leader, he once more turned:

'Now it has come to my mind that the riddle of the barren ones could be because of a curse; also, it could have been that it is the fault of the woman. What say you, O Tomaso? Can you give the answer to this riddle?'

Slowly Tomaso rose from his seat on the stone. Almost eagerly the bullnecked Lago raised himself from the tree on which he had been leaning. Now they stood facing each other. Lago tensed and his great neck seemed suddenly pushed down between his shoulders. Tomaso, with his arms folded across his powerful chest, stood at ease.

'Once you saved my life, Lago.' His voice was low, almost as if it had no anger.

The bullnecked one laughed scornfully: 'How long must I hear this tale of the saving of thy life, O Tomaso?'

'No warrior can forget so great a debt.'

'When I saved your life as you say I have done, I was but repaying a debt, for did not you rescue me with your own hands from slavery on the bakra plantation? You owe me nothing nor do I owe thee! Come, all can see that this talk of saving thy life is but to hide from a challenge. Are you afraid, Tomaso?'

The men all rose to their feet at the challenge. Now they could not interfere. If they did, neither of the men would forgive them for they knew that these two must decide for themselves.

Tomaso could no longer keep the anger from his face. 'There have been countless reasons for insulting the vultures with thy carcass, O Lago,' breathed the leader as he struggled to control his anger. 'There is also one other reason apart from saving my life why I have spared the birds of the air from bad food.' He stopped and a sad look came over his face.

'Speak, O my brother-with-the-empty-loins! Speak and tell me why I have been spared from the beaks of the vultures?' The teeth of the bullnecked one seemed clamped together as he spoke and the spectators saw that now his hand was almost aiming at the machete lying at his feet. But Tomaso stood still with his arms folded.

'I cannot forget that you and I once took the oath of blood brotherhood, that you and I drank from the same calabash and cut our arms so that our blood mingled together. It is a mighty oath, Lago.' Tomaso's voice became soft now. 'Have you forgotten the words: *Closer than the brother of my father's loins and my mother's womb shalt thou be from this moon into this world and into the land of the hunters also for I have chosen thee of my free will, but the brothers of my mother's womb and my father's loins I have not chosen.*'

As Tomaso paused, everyone, even Lago, looked slightly moved by the reminder.

The leader went on: '*And from this day I cannot slay thee, or thou me, no matter what comes between us, for we are brothers of one blood*. I cannot forget those words which once made us blood brothers, Lago, and so my hands have stayed from thy throat when the evil taunts poured from thy mouth these many moons.'

Lago laughed loudly:

'Ho-ho! Ho-ho! My brother-who-cannot-forget is a warrior who keeps his oaths! My *blood*-brother would never break his promise! Tell me, O brother-who-keeps-his-oaths, has thy Kisanka forced thee to make an oath? And have you kept it? What was the oath or the promise, O my brother? Did she bid thee swear that thy breath will not move over the face of another woman though she, Kisanka, be as barren as a mu . . .'

No one saw when Tomaso sprang forward. They barely saw a flashing hand which struck Lago with terrific force on the side of the head. It was a sweeping blow swung the way one would if one wanted to box someone's ear. But this was no playful blow. Lago crashed sideways on the stony ground, dazed. He raised himself slowly on all fours looking as if he did not know how he got there. Tomaso was now alertly watching and waiting for his opponent to rise. But the wily Lago dived for his machete and was up before Tomaso, seeing his danger, could knock him down again. He did not give the bullnecked one time to use the dangerous weapon however and managed to close with him, grabbing both wrists. It was then that the leader discovered that he had injured himself. The hefty blow he had made hitting the head of his opponent with such force had hurt his hand. And worst of all, this right hand was the one he had to depend on now to wrestle and hold at bay the deadly machete, held in the hand of his enemy. He knew it was not broken by the way he was still able to hold Lago's wrist but the pain was intense and seemed to get worse every second.

As the two men wrestled and tugged on the stony ground, the other warriors looked on anxiously without a word. Sometimes the force which the bullnecked Lago used would send Tomaso back, and more than once it seemed the former would free his hand with the machete. At such times the men would murmur their fear, and it was easy to see that the quarrelsome Lago had no friends around him. At other times Tomaso, in spite of the pain in his wrist, forced the other man to give ground, and there would be an unmistaken look of hope on the faces of all. But they suspected by looking closely at their leader's face that something was wrong with his wrist.

Lago, too, sensed that Tomaso's hand had been damaged by its contact with his head. His hope ran high as he managed to confirm it by watching Tomaso's face as he brought pressure to bear on the particular hand. He felt after that that everything was in his favour.

The sweat made their bodies glossy as they fought in the bright sunlight. Their breathing grew loud, and the muscles of their arms and legs seemed as if they would burst each time they were called into action.

Lago felt Tomaso's hold weakening slightly and made his plans. He would bide his time, then, when he felt Tomaso could stand the pain no more, he would with one wrench break away so that he could use his machete. Tomaso must not die quickly!

After that there would be Kisanka! Kisanka, the woman who not only mocked him but spat in his face before witnesses and made him the laughing-stock of the village! He was certain she had told her husband Tomaso that he had more than once tried to seduce her. It would have been better if Tomaso had challenged him about it. But the man had said nothing and each time he had looked at this blood brother of his, he felt that he was being mocked. It was one of the reasons why now he was so full of hate. Now he had the man at his mercy. Later he would have this proud Kisanka at his mercy. She who showed disgust at the mere sight of him, yet would not go from his mind! He would make her beg for mercy and pity. He would wipe the shame from his face this day . . .

He spoke loudly now: 'I shall give no mercy, Tomaso, prepare for thy going!'

The warriors heard this and their spirits sank low. Lago and his opponent had fought themselves to that part of the ground where the earth was pitted with half buried stones and there was a sudden slope. It was then that the bullnecked one put his plan into action. Inhaling deeply, he suddenly jerked sideways with all his might in an effort to free his hands especially the one which held the machete. Tomaso, appearing weary, must have anticipated such a move, for just as Lago made his great effort to free his hand, the leader, timing the move expertly, let go his hold on both his enemy's wrists. Meeting no resistance against so great a pull, threw the surprised Lago completely off balance, and realizing that he was near the edge of the rockridden slope, he quickly let go the sharp pointed machete and tried to save himself from a bad fall. But now Tomaso got into action. His shiny body flew with the speed of lightning as he tackled the stumbling man. They crashed with a terrific thud on the stones over the slope. Over and over they rolled until they were stopped by a great boulder many feet down. Tomaso, to the joy of his friends, extricated himself from his enemy, and shakily came to his feet, bruised badly. The bullnecked one whose back had hit the boulder lay still on his face. The warriors all gathered around their leader, with no more than a glance for the man who was lying still.

'The spirits were with thee, Tomaso!'

'Aye, Tomaso, thy ancestors were by thy side!'

'That move against the snake Lago was good, O my leader!'

'We rejoice at thy conquest Tomaso, may you live beyond the age of asunu!'

Each man touched the dustcovered shoulder of his leader with respect and affection.

It was Tomaso who first knelt beside the man lying at his feet. The others stood watching as if the kneeling man was handling something untouchable. At last he stood up: 'Tahta, see if this carcass still has life and if he will live.'

The old man looked disgusted and annoyed as he detached himself from his companions and came forward. 'I would rather play the medicine-man to a carrion full of vermin, Tomaso,' grumbled the old one but he obeyed, listening to the heartbeats, then exploring the body expertly with his fingers. It was a long time before he stood up to face his leader.

'Well, Tahta? Has he life?' asked Tomaso.

The old man hesitated so long that it seemed to his companions that he had not heard the question.

'There is yet a little life, Tomaso,' he said at last with genuine regret in his voice. Then he brightened visibly: 'But with coaxing so small that a fly would seem a giant beside it, the spirit of this carrion would go to join its evil ancestors, O my leader!'

'Speak not thus, Tahta,' scolded Tomaso.

The old man went down into the depths of despair: 'Before you rescued me from the bakra plantations, Tomaso, I was a doctor and midwife to the bakra's dogs, horses and pigs. But I had always given thanks to the spirits that the dogs I attended were not carrion dogs of the forest. I had always felt that though there were some unclean animals on this land they called Jamaica I had never been called to doctor them. It seems I had spoken too soon!' He spat towards the man he had just examined and it seemed all but Tomaso were anxious to do likewise.

There was a long silence before Tomaso spoke: 'I cannot let him die.' He too seemed regretful of the stand he had taken, judging by the way he said this.

'But Tomaso, the carrion's back is injured. What good would it do to save the life of such a man, even if he was a true man?'

It was Tahta again, pleading, desperately.

'Think, Tomaso, has this droppings-of-a-carrion ceased from troublemaking in the village since first he knew the secrets of a woman's thigh? Is there a warrior who would not have slain him but for thy intercession? And yet he would have slain thee many times over if the chance came. See, he would not have spared thee this day had he won, though he fought with unfair advantage on his side. Think what such a man will be when he becomes bitter because he can no longer boast of being without blemish and strut like a cock before the hens! I tell thee, O Tomaso, here before my brothers, that if this man breathes after this day, all things on which he breathes will be poisoned. I feel it in my bones and my good spirits whisper in my ears that this Lago will bring sorrow to us all if he lives.'

As the old man stopped speaking the voices of his companions grew loud with their support.

'Tahta spoke truly, Tomaso! I for one would have slain him long ago, were he not thy blood brother!'

'And I, because of his actions to my young sister, would have made him food for the worms long ago but for thee, O Tomaso!'

'And I!'

'I have dreamed of his death many times, Tomaso!'

'Peace, my brothers! Peace!' called the leader, and the voices ceased obediently.

'Listen! Once this man was not full of evil as he is today. Many nights when danger and the spirit of death breathed behind our necks, he did not run, but stayed like a warrior.' The speaker paused to think; then: 'This madness came upon him and changed him. It is the madness of jealousy.' He hung his head in shame as if he were the accused still lying unconscious at their feet. 'You speak of Lago's badness. Who can tell more than I of his snake tongue? Yet until this day I laid no hand on him even when he insulted my wife and would seduce her.' The men around looked away so as not to see the shame on Tomaso's face.

'Had he taken her against her wishes I would have slain him, for all know that is a crime a blood brother cannot commit with his adopted kin without paying the penalty.'

The men, knowing this was the law, nodded in agreement.

Tomaso continued quietly now: 'Kisanka shamed Lago and spat in his face when he tried to insult her before witnesses, then begged me to stay my hand against him because he was my blood brother, claiming that she had avenged his insult with insult. I heeded the woman, for I also remembered how once, when I was wounded and would have been killed or captured, he would not save himself and leave me, though I begged him to do so. It was after he helped me back to the safety of these mountains that I made him my kin.'

The memory of his friendship with the man who was now his enemy seemed to bring new sorrow to Tomaso's face.

It was the old one, Tahta, who spoke next: 'Aye, I remember it all, Tomaso. I also remember that thy woman, Kisanka, almost a child then, saw through that snake. She joined voice with me to plead with thee against the making of the kinship.'

Tomaso held up his hand for silence; then, so as not to shame the aged, he turned to the whole group: 'Yonder warrior on watch must have heard the sound of our mouths and said to himself: *It is bad when warriors fight with women's weapon*. Come, Tahta, see, the man is stirring from his sleep; do not let him die. Quako, climb back to the village for a hammock with poles so that we can carry the injured one home.'

The man Quako jumped to do his leader's bidding while old Tahta, with a despairing sigh and a shake of his grey woolly head, also turned to his task.

When, at last, the bullnecked Lago knew what had happened to him, he looked up at the men around him.

'Slay me!' he screamed. 'Slay me now with the weapons in your hands. Fools! Fools! What warrior would wish to be a broken thing about the village? Slay me, I beg you!' He ended pleadingly, and, but for Tomaso's presence, the warriors would have granted the request. It was then that the injured man turned his face to the other side and his eyes met those of Tomaso looking down on him. He tried to raise himself up in spite of the pain it seemed to cause him. As he rested on one elbow and stared at his leader a look of intense hate came on his face, which caused some of those who saw it to shudder. With teeth clenched and the sweat glistening on his forehead, he managed to growl in a frightening voice:

'Slay me now, O my brother! Slay me! For if I live . . .' He did not finish the sentence, and the spectators watched as he kept his bloodshot eyes on Tomaso, with Tomaso staring back.

It lasted for nearly a minute before the pain of resting on one arm with an injured back became too much for Lago and he fell back into a faint. It was again Tomaso who first went to the sick man's aid while his companions looked at each other, saying with their eyes the fear which came over them. For they knew Lago would seek revenge for what had happened that day, and felt certain that he would not care how many suffered as long as he got what he wanted. Tomaso too must have felt the same foreboding come upon him for he stopped when he was about to raise the man's head and call for help to remove and revive him. But after shaking his head, as if he was saying no to a question or the request of the injured man, he went through with this act of mercy as if his avowed enemy was still his best friend.

Old Tahta would not be consoled however. 'This will be the first of the evil days for the people of these hills!' he murmured sullenly as he lent a hand with the injured warrior.

Kisanka stood at the door of her house on the hill and waited.

From her countrymen's view, there would be three things to prevent her being the most beautiful girl in their midst: she was not plump, and her nose and lips, though flat and full as befitting a daughter of Africa, were not flat and full enough to make her the undisputed beauty of the village. Apart from this, she would have been voted beautiful by any people of any race, with her largish eyes, graceful neck and figure, and a face tapered beautifully to match. Her hair, bunched together by its fine curls, excluded any doubt of her pure African strain, and her skin with the colour and texture of fine black satin, helped also to confirm this. Only when she walked one could see that all was not well, for she limped on the toes of one bare foot, the heel never touching the ground. For clothes, she wore two separate pieces of cloth. One, tied at the waist, reached nearly to the ankles of her bare feet. The other, draped over one shoulder and across her chest, met far below the undraped arm, leaving one firm breast as well as a shoulder bare. She was twenty. Her ornaments consisted of a pair of round wire ear-rings, and around her neck, a string of beads made of seeds from the forest.

. . . Such was the appearance of the wife of the young leader, Tomaso, the woman who insulted the warrior Lago by spitting in his face in public when he tried to be familiar with her.

Now she was waiting like the rest of the villagers for the coming of the stretcher-bearers, for the man whom Tomaso sent for this conveyance for the injured Lago, had told of the fight.

Kisanka saw the crowd lining the path and the group coming up the hill with their burden. But like a good warrior's wife she stood at the door and waited, according to the custom of this comparatively new people called *Maroons*—a custom adopted from the many tribes to which they once belonged before the coming of slavery—that the wife of a warrior should show her faith in her lord whenever he was returning from some dangerous mission by waiting at the door of their house for his arrival, wounded or not; the rest of his kin may rush forward to ask anxiously after his condition should he be wounded; they may cry out aloud if the news is serious. But the wife must wait with dignity after preparing all the things that are to be prepared for emergencies. Only in the case of death will she be expected to lament openly with the rest of relations and friends.

It was also the custom of wounded men on reaching the outskirts of the village to beg those who had helped them this far to leave them to make the rest of the journey unaided so that they may walk with dignity to the waiting arms of their wives. Those who were too badly wounded to walk suffered the indignity of being carried so that if it was humanly possible, all brave warriors could be counted upon to make this request though this was not the law.

The people waiting the coming of the group bringing the injured Lago on the stretcher showed no sorrow, except of course his kin. Even the few friends he had took the news of his injury calmly and almost without a sign of pity, for even they did not like his boastful ways and his unscrupulous pursuit of the women. They sometimes lent ears to his talk against Tomaso because he was the only one bold enough to air his dislike for the way this new leader wanted to change things and bring in new and foolish laws.

'Whoever heard of a chief calling himself a leader, living in a hut like any common person, going out with the warriors on raids, and eating no more than his men?' he had asked his friends once, and they had to agree that this was a bad way to lead the Maroons; and it was said that the Maroons on the other side of the island were adopting this plan of Tomaso's!

'Then take this talk of not slaying all the bakra who are not warriors. Do they not make slaves of our people, slaying those whom they feel will not fetch pieces of silver in the slave market? Would they spare any if ever they reached the mountains?' Lago had asked this, and many had agreed with him that this was foolish talk. 'Yet Tomaso has encouraged such doings! Then take this foolish deed of bringing up to the mountains those who are not young, or those who cannot help to defend the mountains. Tomaso has brought up many such people from the bakra plantations . . .'

He, Lago, had made a mistake and had nearly caused a revolt against himself by objecting when the leader had brought up the greyhaired little man known as Tahta who though his name was good, must have been the father of men, judging by the wrinkles on his face. On the other hand, he, Lago, leading a group of warriors on another plantation raid, had brought back two lovely young women whom he had rescued from the slave pen and who would bring to the Maroons wives for a couple of warriors, and picnies who would grow up to be great warriors themselves.

Now Lago was coming back with something like a broken back! He had tried to get out of his undignified position and walk into the village, even if he had to be helped. This, he thought, would have looked better than being carried by four warriors in a hammock-stretcher, especially so when one of the four bearers was Tomaso himself! He thought it was alright to get wounded in fighting against the bakra, for that was no shame if one had fought well. But to be returning to the village as the loser in a fight with another warrior . . . and to be carried aloft like the carcass of a pig killed in a hunt with the winner as one of the bearers was unbearable!

Try as he did, Lago found that he was too badly hurt to do anything but fall back in his stretcher, groaning, with the sweat like beads on his forehead. But instead of being sorry for bringing this shame upon himself, the bullnecked one used every minute building up more hate and blaming Tomaso for his disgrace. Apart from swearing now and again he spoke no word on the journey, not since he started once more to taunt Tomaso, hoping that he might be killed by the hand of his blood brother.

The wily old Tahta began to speak of how he had seen men die slowly while countless black ants made their dinner on their bodies, the victims so staked out that they could not move a limb to ease their torture. He went on to tell how molasses were rubbed on the victims to attract the ants to the feast, but that a little smell of dried blood would be just as effective for the call to the feast. Even Tomaso found himself shivering at this description of death by Tahta, that every slave or ex-slave knew and feared even more than the roasting of feet, those two being the most popular slave tortures on the West Indian plantations in those days. There was no need to wonder if the injured man was in terror or not especially when old Tahta swore he knew where there was a nest of ants similar in largeness to those to be found on the plains. The hammock-stretcher trembled with the shaking of the occupant's body.

The men with their burden passed through the silent crowd, and apart from his relations, no-one showed any sorrow. Many grumbled because he was still alive after doing something which should have been punished with death.

Tomaso, bruised and tired from the fall and from helping to carry his enemy, walked wearily towards Kisanka after seeing to the dispatch of new warriors to take up duty on the pass for the night. Kisanka watched him coming and her heart beats were like the thumping of a drum but she stood still and waited, as was the custom, and when he reached the door she stepped aside for him to pass.

'Greetings, Little Shadow,' he said softly as he walked through the door of the thatched and reed-wattled two-roomed hut.

The name Little Shadow so thrilled and pleased Kisanka that she stumbled for words to reply. This greeting was not expected as he entered the door, for he usually called her this name when she had finished her work and sat at his feet, fondly leaning against his strong legs.

Kisanka placed the stool in position for her husband to sit and hurriedly brought the warm herb-filled clay pot of water and calabash-bowl to hand, then began to clean the dust and grime from his many bruises. She was relieved to find that he was not badly bruised and wondered if he would tell her of the fight for she would not dream of asking him to do so. It was after she had done most of the work that she noticed his swollen hand. With a gasp she broke the silence: 'I shall run and fetch Tahta for thy hand, Tomaso, for I do not know how to treat such things.' He smiled at her alarm. 'It is nothing, and Tahta is patching up the injured Lago. This must wait.'

Kisanka said nothing but fetched some bark-cloth and pounded herbs which she sprinkled on the split half of a type of flat cactus, warming it over the fire, and getting rid of its prickly spikes. She bandaged the very warm cactus over the swollen wrist as Tahta had done once in her presence. Tomaso assured her that it was already better after her administration, and she smiled with pleasure. When she had at last cleared away all the things, and he had eaten and assured her he did not wish to lie down, she came like a child, asking with her eyes if she could sit in her favourite place, on the beaten ground at his feet, with her arm resting on his knee. His smile invited her and she sat with one leg folded over the other with her face partly away from him.

Tomaso sensed that Kisanka wanted to tell him something though he could not guess what it was. He knew her too well. The request to sit at his feet was so unusual for her to make just after he had arrived. Usually she would let him rest while she found something to do until she was certain he had rested enough and wanted her company.

'Tomaso.'

'Speak Little Shadow.'

She never failed to note the gentleness in his voice, and he the music in hers.

'Soon the shame will go from thy face.'

He did not understand her words; perhaps because he dared not try to do so.

She went on: 'The moon came and went and came again and went and now it is here again and I have not . . . not been . . .' She covered her face from the shame which comes when women try to speak of their peculiar indisposition to those of the opposite sex.

There was a look of bewilderment on Tomaso's face as if he was now trying his best to find the answer to a riddle.

'This was why it was not necessary for me to sleep alone in my hammock these many moons,' continued Kisanka shyly with her hands still covering her face.

A dawning light was beginning to shine on the warrior's understanding. Suddenly the sheer joy of the news she had to tell swept the shame from the girl's face. She turned to meet the eyes of her lord and at that moment her beauty was almost beyond description.

'It shall be a man child, Tomaso! And none shall call thee childless afterwards.' Then almost to herself: 'And I shall rejoice for thy sake more than for myself, for when joy comes to thee my spirit sings like the bird greeting the new fire-which-lights-up-the-sky.'

For half a minute Tomaso was too dumbfounded to speak, then out came a sudden roar of joy so mighty that a hen sitting on eggs in an old basket behind the house screamed her protest as she flew away. The neighbours stopped talking and listened, wondering who could have caused such a roaring noise.

The Chief, forgetting his swollen hand and his many bruises, bent down and lifted his wife in his arms, then made for the door, with the girl blushing invisibly and protesting at the neighbours seeing him with her in his arms, but secretly loving every second of his action.

Like a giant he marched out with his wife clinging to his great neck like a child as he bellowed: 'O people of these hills come out and hear my gladness! Kisanka has conceived. Before many moons I shall be a father. I, Tomaso, shall prove that no curse has been on me and my woman. Rejoice with me, O my people!'

The echo of Tomaso's voice had hardly died before the crowds started streaming up the hill to congratulate the beloved couple. The people shouted the news to each other as they hurried along. It was a great sight to see them pouring out of every corner of the village towards the house of their chief. Kisanka trembled with excitement as she saw the pride and joy in the face of her lord as the crowd grew until the great yard around the house was packed to its capacity.

Tomaso placed Kisanka on her feet now but he would not let her go into the house while the crowd came to congratulate him, for she knew that though they liked her and were happy for her they came mostly because their hero and leader would present them with the long hoped-for child of his loins. Somewhere in the back of their minds they were already planning for the future, and in these plans was the thought that a son of the bravest warrior of the mountain would wear the mantle of his father.

Hastily they planned a celebration for that night. Late as it was, warriors took their old muskets with a few precious bits of lead and powder and made for the places where wild hogs were usually found; drums were drawn tight; wood and water were fetched by the young; food which could be spared was brought. Not long afterwards the echoes of musket fire from the home of the wild hogs told of success from that end, for the Maroons were known through history for their accuracy with the bakra's weapon.

Lago, hearing the commotion from his bed, asked of old Tahta what it was all about. The old fellow, with great joy and not without malice, told him the news. For a while the sick man lay as if he had stopped breathing after one great intake of breath. Then he began to curse. He swore that the child would die at birth. He vowed that it would turn out to be a false alarm. Then he began to threaten what he would do once he was up again. Old Tahta walked out of the hut feeling he might have to break his promise to Tomaso.

When the feast, the dancing and the singing were all over, the exhausted but happy people of the hills swore that never before had they seen such merriment and vowed that the celebrations at the birth of Tomaso's child, especially if it be a manchild, should surpass it.

And on the opposite hillside, the wide-awake Lago still rocked in pain and bitterness and swore that in some way or other he would make this night of gladness turn into a sad day for his enemy and his friends.

Two

The two mountain ranges now famous in Jamaica and Maroon history—the Cockpits towards the west, and the Blue Mountains on the eastern side of the island—were as if they were specially created as places of refuge as well as fortresses for runaway slaves. In each case the Maroons chose that part of the mountain where at least one side, because of its sheer and precipitous nature, eliminated the possibility of invasion from that area.

Twin Sisters were very much like them. Given the name because the two mountains were almost identical in size and structure, they were just as fitted for harbouring and protecting the ex-slaves as their historical cousins.

Tomaso and his Maroons, numbering nearly two thousand souls, had their village near the peak of one of these mountains, with their backs well protected by the natural precipice which stretched for miles behind and made more impregnable by an area of swampland beneath, fed from time to time by an overflowing river further away. The frontal approach to the foot of the Twin Sisters held no invitation for invasion. Steep, rocky and dotted with trees and clumps of shrubs near its base, with only one negotiable path, narrow and winding, which half a dozen women with stones and boulders from above could hold against an invading battalion, the bakra and their militia had discovered more than once how costly in lives it could be to dare the attempt from the plains. Further up the mountains there was jungle growth and places where the land was less rocky and steep but the place which Tomaso's people had chosen for their village was the largest of the near-level area.

Although the militia had suffered great losses each time they tried to invade the mountain stronghold it was not unusual for armed parties to warily probe the defence of the mountain-men periodically, and it was the policy of Tomaso to hold his men in readiness night and day for the sounding of the horn known as ecketeh and then the talking-drum which would warn the village of an invasion. The one weak spot in the chain of defence was the mountain which was not occupied by the Maroons. This, like its sister, had its natural handicaps for the invaders but it was possible to find one or two places which, without defenders, could be scaled. But since such an ascent would begin some eight miles from the village which was their intended goal, and there were not only jungle conditions but chances of running into ambushes all along, the bakra had not tried the invasion. Further there was a great gorge between the two mountains, which the plainsmen judged, by what they saw of the entrance from the plains, to be a deathtrap should one dare to enter its deep, rocky and dark confines, with overhanging rocks or sheer surfaces on both sides hundreds of feet above. They never tried to discover if the gorge ran all the way between the two mountains to the other side of the swampy plains or if it ended abruptly somewhere with the hills. In the first place, it would have been too dangerous to investigate, and in the second they felt that even if there was any possibility of finding a route via this gorge, the accessible place or places would be well guarded.

There were places across the gorge between the Twin Sister mountains which could be crossed. One was situated nearly halfway between them. There the long and dreadful lane came close to a pair of lip-like ledges facing each other. About a dozen chains away the gorge came to an end when both mountains became united by uninviting rocks which towered high above and offered no foothold whatever to any but creepers, crawling animals, and birds, mostly vultures known as john-crows. This place where the gorge almost met by the lip-like narrow ledges was a testing ground for all Maroon warriors of Twin Sisters. For it was possible for one to make a mighty jump from one narrow ledge to the other, providing one was able to forget that to misjudge by a mere inch would mean a fall to some four hundred feet below. Nevertheless, it was a matter of honour for every warrior to make this jump, in spite of the fact that a few reached the land of their ancestors by this route when courage and prowess had not synchronized. A great log was placed across the gap lower down as well so that those who did not wish to risk their lives with the jump could cross over by this means. Far as it was from the village, youths, eager to be looked upon with respect, trained themselves from an early age, first to crawl across the fifty foot gap astride the great round log; then to walk across instead of crawling, a feat which caused many a death; and when they reached the age where they were grown enough to be called warriors, they would go to the narrower Place-of-the-Big-Jump, as it was called, and there prove their courage to the utmost.

Ever since Tomaso became leader of his people, he had arranged guards for every possible avenue of invasion. Many of his officers and elders thought him over-cautious, pointing out that many of these guards could do much with the cultivation of plots so necessary to a people cut off from barter and trade as they were. But the leader, though not wasting his manpower unduly, insisted on guarding these points.

Tomaso was sitting with his company of warriors on the same spot he had been some months before when Lago picked the row and fought with him. But today Lago was not there.

He looked up and saw a woman coming down the narrow path towards them.

'It is Nahne,' cried one of the men, and Tomaso jumped to his feet as he too recognised the visitor to be Nahne, the village midwife. Her visit could have only one meaning —Kisanka!

He could not wait for the old woman to finish the few chains distance between them. As he walked forward with his companions trailing he called out eagerly, 'Greetings Nahne, is it news of Kisanka?'

The midwife suddenly seemed to be more eager to turn tail than to meet the leader and his companions. She was a short stumpy woman with a face full of wrinkles. Her clothing consisted of a long piece of cloth tied at the waist for a skirt and another around her like a shawl, which she kept in place with a knot. Tomaso waited politely for the woman to speak remembering also that she was old and had come a long way. But now they were face to face, and only a couple of yards between them, yet apart from nodding her head in confirmation of his question, she stood looking like a frightened animal. There was fear in her eyes and as Tomaso saw it his heart went almost up to his mouth. He could no longer restrain himself.

'Kisanka, O Nahne, is she well?' he asked trying to keep fear from his voice.

'She is well, Tomaso, and sends greetings.' The voice was subdued and the midwife refused to meet the searching eyes of her chief.

'The child, mother . . . has it come?' He could not keep a tremor out of his voice and his fists opened and closed as he waited for a reply.

'The child has come, Tomaso.'

It was too much for the brave warrior chief and even his companions seemed to have to hold back their anger at the old woman's reluctance to speak because of the respect they held for the aged.

'Nahne, I do not wish to offend thee whom I respect but I am waiting for the news of my wife and my child.'

Apprehension showed over the speaker's whole body. The woman's hand holding the shawl in place was trembling. Tomaso saw it and his spirit sank and yet his thought was for the messenger. He stepped forward and put his strong young arm around her shoulder.

'Nay, do not fear, O Nahne. Thy news has bad things. I see it in the trembling of the hand which holds the cloth. I am ready. Speak, O mother-of-countless-children. I shall not be angry. How could I? It is no fault of thine.' He spoke to comfort the woman though his spirit was heavy with sorrow. He felt that the child must have died at birth and that was why the old midwife was afraid to speak. What else could it be? Had she not told him Kisanka was alive and sent greetings? The woman wiped her eyes with a corner of her shoulder covering, and it seemed she took great courage at Tomaso's words of comfort for she at last looked up in his face. She had no eyes for the dozen or so men around her, who fidgeted as if they wished they were not present to see their beloved leader's downcast look and the face of the frightened old woman.

'Tell me, Nahne . . . was it . . . was it a manchild?' Tomaso's voice sounded hoarse as he asked and his eyes were above the heads of all towards the peak of the mountain where the village lay.

'It *is* a manchild, Tomaso.'

The man stretched his hand and took hold of the old woman's shoulder he had released awhile before. This time his hold was so fierce that she winced from the pain but he noticed nothing.

'You said he *is* a manchild, Nahne! Then he yet lives?' he cried eagerly, catching at the ray of hope the single word gave. He bent his knees so as to see better in her face and as she nodded her head in confirmation he lost control of himself.

'Do you hear, O my brothers? I am a father!'

'We hear, Tomaso! We hear!' shouted the men as if their chief was deaf, waving their hands about and almost jumping for joy, for they loved their young leader.

'No more will Lago be able to mock me!' added Tomaso almost to himself.

'The mountain will shake with the gladness of the people, Tomaso!'

'Aye! The drums will talk good talk, Tomaso, this night!'

'He will be mighty like thyself, O my chief!'

My head grows big at the tiding, O my leader—'

Each warrior had something nice to say, moving forward to press the shoulder of their chief as a sign of congratulation. And yet, as soon as Tomaso had uttered his first words of gladness a chilly feeling came over him, for the old woman, standing humbly to one side, had no look of joy on her face. She had been like a messenger of bad tidings ever since she came and yet he could not see why. She had said Kisanka had sent greetings. This meant that his wife was well after the confinement. The child was alive. It would not have been if it was deformed: being the son of a chief would not have prevented the midwife from doing her traditional duty which even the chief dared not question. On the contrary, being a chief's child would have been all the more reason for a midwife to see that only the physically perfect survived. And yet the old woman stood as if some great evil had shown its head beside the bed of confinement. The men too, after their congratulations, felt that something was wrong and a sudden chilling silence descended on them all.

'Nahne?' The way Tomaso called her brought back the fear on the midwife's face. He saw it and hastened to reassure her.

'Do not fear, O mother-of-countless-children. I would not harm thee even if the fault of the evil news was thine.'

Again the water came to the old one's eyes. 'Thy son is not like thyself, Tomaso, nor like his mother,' she blurted out between sobs.

The startled and puzzled chief shook his head:

'I do not understand this riddle, Nahne, speak clearer, I ask thee.'

The old woman looked up in the face of her chief with pleading watery eyes:

'It is his colour, Tomaso, it is not like that of our people!'

'Do you mean that it is the colour of the bakra, mother?' asked Tomaso, almost unable to control his feelings. Then brightening up he added, 'But no picni has ever been born with the colour of his people, Nahne!'

The old woman looked at her chief with reproof through her tears.

'I have brought countless picnies into the world with these hands, Tomaso. I have seen those whose fathers had been bakra and whose mothers were of our people, but this child's face is whiter than that of a bakra; and its hair is like the cotton that comes from the great cotton trees on the hills.'

They all saw the agony which came on their leader's face, and embarassed, they turned their eyes on their bare toes. The old woman, now that she had broken the news, seemed to feel that promise or no promise, she would be punished. She cowered before the dreadful look she saw on the face of her chief, waiting, it seemed, for sentence to be passed on her, and when, after a long interval of silence, he spoke in a gentle voice, even his companions who knew that his rule was devoid of tyranny or terror, marvelled at his ways.

'Come, Nahne, you and I shall climb the hill and see this

child who has courage enough to have a colour of his own.' He was the only one amongst them who could smile at his sad joke.

'Come, Nahne,' he urged, taking the old woman by an arm. 'We must not keep this little warrior waiting.'

The crowd of men watched the retreating back of their leader climbing the hill with the old woman beside him and shook their heads in admiration and wonder at his courage. For they all knew there was trouble ahead, and guessed Lago would be happy to know one of those rare legendary picnies had been born to the two whom all knew he hated most.

All the way up the hill, Tomaso, impatient to reach the bed of confinement with his young wife and son, had to slow down so as to comfort the old midwife who could not climb as fast as he. All along the journey he had to assure her that she did right in not looking on the newborn as deformed and returning it to the Land of the Spirits.

Even she had not seen an albino before though she had heard of such a birth in her girlhood days in Africa. Dundoes was the name they called such children. She did not know whether it was a bad or good omen to have such a birth in the tribe. Perhaps it was Kisanka, eager to see her firstborn, who prevented her from deciding whether or not the child should live, for the young wife had at one glance seen that her child was not like any other with its chalky white face, and the hair on its head, as well as the eyebrows, also milky white, and realizing what was in the mind of the midwife, had forced herself up to hang over her offspring, protecting it silently with her body, with all the fierceness of motherhood in her eyes. She would not allow the midwife to cut the navel cord, asking for the necessary things and doing it herself, and demanding the herbtinted water for cleansing her offspring with her own hands, while her eyes told the frightened but sympathetic old woman that only death could separate child from mother. She had not protested for she did not know if such a child came under deformity or not. It was only the fear of Tomaso's wrath at allowing it to live and taking such grave news to him which made her tremble.

Other chiefs would not have acted like Tomaso when messengers brought them bad news. It was difficult to reconcile herself with a chief who would eat and sleep with his men, lead them into battle instead of sitting with many wives waiting on him. It was also difficult to think of so young a man so brave and yet so gentle. Had he not rescued her and many of the older people on these hills with his own hand? It was partly this which caused the bad news to stick in her throat when she came to tell him about the birth of his child. It was as if she had hurt him who had done so much for her.

'I could not help it, Tomaso,' she said aloud as they reached the fringe of the village.

'Of what do you speak, O Nahne?' he asked gently, though his mind seemed to be elsewhere.

'Kisanka guarded the young one with her body like a female lion, Tomaso, and I forgot my duty then, for a softness came to my spirit so that even if she could be persuaded I would not ask it of her.'

You have done a great favour by staying your hand, O Nahne, and it is I who shall never forget it!'

The old woman felt cheered for the first time since she carried out her mission. She grabbed the great hand of her chief and pressed it to her withered breast, and the touched Tomaso knew that this old woman would stand by him till death for that was the meaning of her gesture.

He stepped through the doorway of the thatched hut from the bright sunlight and searched with his eyes in the comparative gloom for his wife and their child. She was lying on the low wooden bed, nursing the child. When she saw her lord coming towards her, she forgot her bravery, shown when the life of her offspring was threatened. She hid her face in the cloth-covered straw of the bed and wept. Tomaso laid his hand gently on her shoulder and tried to comfort her, but she was too ashamed to look up into his face.

Gently he took the child wrapped as it was in a piece of cloth. His spirit was heavy as he saw only too well that what the old woman had told him was true. The child was a dundoes — a raceless child with a colour which belonged to neither of his parents. The eyes when he managed to get a glimpse of them were of a strange colour, and the infant kept them closed most of the time. The hair, though like all children of the Negro race was not yet tightly curled, being so young, was almost of cotton whiteness. The face had none of that pink which even children of full-blooded Negroes show at birth, but a whiteness which was completely convincing of its permanency.

Tomaso had seen albinos born to animals of perfectly matched colour, and even birds like vultures had produced their freaks. But he had only heard of the birth of human dundoes in tales. And now he was the father of the one. For he had no doubt whatever that he was the father of the child.

There were a few men and women on the hill who showed traces of the blood of the bakra, but not even the mating of a full-blooded bakra with Kisanka could bring such a colour as this. Kisanka, being lame, had not been able to go a mile from the village since she was brought there. Not even the women who were not lame ever travelled the mountainside down to the dangerous slave plantations twenty miles away. In any case he trusted his woman amongst a thousand men.

As he held the child against his great bare arms and chest he looked down on the helpless little one which came from his body as well as his wife's, and the pride of fatherhood and the love of the parent for his young overstepped all other considerations. He felt the wonder of it all, and the love which is beyond understanding flowed through him and his face lit up. Kisanka watching him silently, still with the water coming from her eyes, felt his mood, and a great wave of love came over her for the man who had chosen her as his mate.

She felt the same emotion as she had one night not so long ago when in frustration at not bearing her brave lord a child after six years, she had gone to a family who had a young comely daughter. The girl had been her good friend ever since she, Kisanka, came to the hills, brought there by the young warrior, Tomaso. She knew the girl, whose name was Kumse, worshipped Tomaso from afar, for apart from being inexperienced, she was shy, and whenever it was time for the leader to come home, she would hastily leave Kisanka's presence. Kumse had told her friend how lucky she was to have such a warrior for a husband, and vowed that no man would know her unless he was like the husband of her friend. Many warriors had asked for this pretty girl, but the parents following the new trend the young Tomaso had encouraged, would not give her into marriage without her consent. They suspected that she was in love with some warrior in secret, but Kisanka knew that this man was Tomaso. One other person had suspected the position—Lago. Kumse had often laughed in his face when he made advances to her, and when he asked her if she was in love with someone else, she nodded her head vigorously but would not tell him who. That was also scored against Tomaso in the mind of his blood brother.

The day before Kisanka had explained to Kumse what was in her mind before she went to see her friend's parents. The girl had blushed invisibly but nodded her head with eyes to the ground, and there was no doubt now in Kisanka's mind. Though to her knowledge, Tomaso had not glanced twice at the girl, Kumse was in love with him. Kisanka had spoken to the parents about what she had in mind and they too, loving their leader like a son, had agreed to Kisanka's request—for it was just in the law of the hills for a man to mate with another woman than his wife if she bore him no children after a long period. That night, Kisanka, with trembling voice, and shame on her face, led an equally shamefaced Kumse by the hand. Stumbling with her words, she managed to tell the dumbfounded Tomaso the reason for bringing her friend Kumse to take her place. Not bearing to say more, she went out of the hut, leaving the two alone. It was night, and Kisanka had wandered into the moonlit hills, torn by the terrible pain of jealousy and despair. The thought that at that very moment, another was sharing the bed of her lord drove her almost to madness, in spite of the fact that it was with her connivance. She had not guessed that she would suffer so much. Into her mind came the strong conviction that it would be best for both of them, as well as herself, if she were to die, for she knew then that she could not stand the sharing of her man with another, in spite of the custom.

She had walked with her mind made up to the lip of the plateau which ended in a sudden drop hundreds of feet below. She was just about to walk into space with her eyes closed and a sob, when a pair of hands gripped her from behind.

'How can a man be away from his shadow, Little One?' the voice soft with love and emotion had asked in her ear, as she was led away from the path of death . . . 'Have I not called thee Little Shadow long before hair came on my face? Must I tell thee once more that my breath shall kiss thy face and none other, though I live many times the age of asunu?' The words came as gentle as the soft nightwind, and as soothing, and as acceptable as the dewdrops on the young leaves of the thirsty dwarf-palm. The water fell down out of her eyes then, as if her head had contained a tiny spring.

Kisanka never asked the embarrassed Kumse what her husband had said after she had left them alone together that night. Yet she never doubted that her lord had gently but firmly sent her friend back to her parents without even laying his hand on her.

Tomaso looked towards her and saw that she was no longer hiding her face but looking at him with her soul showing in her eyes.

'He shall be a child of courage, Kisanka,' he said gently, coming towards her with the child in his arms. 'We shall name him Tamba after my great chief ancestor of whom I used to speak, remember?'

Kisanka looked up with wonder at her lord.

'And you will not send me and the child from thee, Tomaso? Even though I have brought shame on thee, and have not let the midwife take him away?' Her voice sounded even more beautiful because of her anxiety.

'How could you bring shame to me, Little Shadow?' he asked gently. 'Is not the child from my body as well as thine? Aye, even as I look, I can see on his face many things which are mine.' He looked searchingly on the tiny thing: 'Look woman, those lips are like mine. Broad and strong! And his nose! See how it is made? He will have great strength Kisanka, for the wind will go out and come in with great force, and in a little while his chest will be like his father's.'

Kisanka knew her husband was saying these things to comfort her and reassure her. He was telling her there was no doubt in his mind about the paternity of her offspring, and at the same time that she was not to blame for his freak colour. It made the eyewater return in spite of her gladness.

'I would have gone from the village and from thee, Tomaso, if it was thy wish.'

'Hush, Little Shadow! Speak not of such a thing. How many times must I tell thee that no man can live without his shadow?'

He came to the other side of her low bed and gently placed the child in the curve of her arm so that she could continue to nurse him.

'They will throw it in thy face, Tomaso, Lago will mock thee. I feel it.' Each word she spoke brought greater despair in her voice. Tomaso felt too that this birth of his albino son would be a godsend for Lago.

As if to confirm their forebodings a loud mocking laugh came from over the other side of the hill where his enemy now lived.

'Oh-oh! Oh-oh! Oh-oh!' came the harsh mocking sound from Lago, the cripple. Kisanka heard it and began to tremble. Tomaso heard it and his hand clenched as if it was at Lago's throat, and as if the newborn baby feared it he began to cry pitifully. Immediately Tomaso's thoughts went back to his new role of father. He knelt by the bed and gently placed his protective arm over mother and child.

'What? Shall the wife of a warrior tremble with fear at a madman even when her man is at hand to protect her? Shall the young one whimper because he senses the fear of his mother even when the father is by their bedside? Now dry the water from thy eyes, woman! God of my fathers! Is this the day of gladness we planned ever since thy conception?'

Kisanka wiped the water away. 'O, my lord, Tomaso! I am ashamed. It is true that for a moment fear came to my spirit. But the fear is for thee, not for myself. For thee I would gladly die, O my husband.' She looked at him with her big sad eyes, then stretching her hand forward she took hold of one of his and pressed it against her face.

'You must not fret, Kisanka, or Tamba, the young warrior, will drink the milk from thee which will make him ill,' he said.

'I will not fret, Tomaso. Now, there is no fear in me. See the magic of thy words? Even the young one ceased to whimper at thy voice.'

It was true. The baby lay peacefully in the crook of his mother's arm, dropping off quietly to sleep. Even the mother was asleep when Tomaso rose from the bedside and silently went out into the evening sun just in time to see his old friend Tahta approaching.

'Greetings, Tomaso, my son, and to thy fatherhood!' said the old man as he approached. They went towards a shaded tree where thy sat on haunches.

'I thank thee for thy wish, O Wise One, I know it is meant,' replied Tomaso for he knew he could not have a more faithful and trusted friend than Tahta.

Tahta had almost worshipped the young chief since that day that he had brought him to the mountain. The bakra must have been glad to get rid of the old man, Lago had argued from the beginning, and the people had for the first time agreed with him that Tomaso, his blood brother, was not wise in doing this thing. The wise old man knew that a leader of warriors could not afford to show that he lacked wisdom and he was ready to go back down the mountain path to face the consequences. But Tomaso had asked each of his critics if Tahta had been his father, would he have liked to leave the old one to die when the bakra found there was no more work to be got out of him and that he was no longer worth many pieces of silver? Each of the warriors, faced with the question, had looked down on his toes not knowing what to say in reply. Then he had taken the old man by the elbow, and going to the then young Kisanka whom he had not long married, he had said: 'Wife, I have found a father who will take the place of thine and mine.' And when the crowd had seen the young girl taking hold of the old man, and noticed the water which fell quickly from the wrinkled face, they were ashamed, and with bowed heads, went to their homes. They knew they had broken two of the laws of the mountain people. They had insulted one who came to them for refuge, and worst of all, he was an aged person, who, by the laws of every son of Africa, must be respected and honoured. Like embarrassed people everywhere, they had vented their wrath on the luckless Lago, whom they rightly claimed had led them to commit this offence—an offence which made them more guilty in their own eyes when they later learned of the old man's value. For this Tahta had worked for many years with a bakra doctor. The white man had found it to his benefit to teach the old slave many things such as the setting of broken bones, diagnosing illness and even giving medicines for minor complaints amongst the slaves. Such teaching allowed the doctor more time administering to his own people, while his aged assistant was left to answer the calls to the bedsides of his fellow slaves. Tomaso had no knowledge of this when he rescued Tahta, and that the bakra would have paid more than the normal price for a slave to get such a skilled man back on their plantations. And that was not all. The old Tahta was an expert gunsmith and blacksmith, and knew all there was to know about herbs!

After a long silence:

'Tahta.'

'My son?'

'Have you known of such a birth before?'

'I have heard of many such tales, told by our people on the plantations.'

'What is the reason for this, Tahta?'

'There are many talks, Tomaso. Each man has a different reason.'

'It is not like you to speak in riddles to me, O Father-of-men.'

Tomaso's eyes were on the old man now but the other was staring before him.

'I do not speak in riddles, Tomaso. Men put many meanings to things they do not understand.'

'Such as . . . a curse, Tahta?' The chief's voice showed slight anxiety.

'Foolish people say such words, my son, and there are foolish ones to believe them.'

'And the wise ones, father?'

Old Tahta took up a pebble and flicked it away as if he were playing at marbles before he answered.

'The wise ones look in the skies and point to a vulture unlike his companions in colour. They look amongst the goats and point to strange colours amongst the herd. They look at the fruits and pluck one whose colour is unlike that of any other on the tree. Aye, they look at the things of the earth and know that they are fools, for they know nothing. But then it is only the wise fool who knows that he knows nothing, Tomaso.'

The chief brushed an ant crawling on his knee before he spoke again:

'Tell me, O Wise One, will this birth be good news for my enemy?'

'His mocking laughter reached me as I climbed the hill, Tomaso.'

'Aye, Tahta, I heard it too! But who will listen to his bad talk?'

'There will always be ears which will listen to bad talk, Tomaso.'

The two sat silently as a pitcherie perched high on a great almond tree was singing a love song. It was Tahta who broke the silence:

'Lago will strike from now on, Tomaso. His time for revenge is near. This birth has played into his hands.' There was almost fear in the old man's voice.

'I thank thee for warning me, O Tahta.'

The old fellow got wearily to his feet and Tomaso did the same. 'I owe thee much my son, and soon I shall go to the land of my fathers without repaying the debt.' Here he looked straight at his young chief, and his eyes told what he had in mind. Tomaso saw it and shook his head wearily.

'Nay, Tahta, if I must kill my blood brother then it must be my own hand which spills his blood,' he said quietly.

It was embarrassing for the people, less, of course, by far than for Tomaso and Kinsanka.

They came up hill with the gifts they had long planned and prepared to offer congratulations to their chief yet knowing that the child was a dundoes.

There were some women in the village who were whispering that since the child was of so strange a colour it should have been treated as was the custom for deformed infants. There were others who whispered that such a child would do no good to the pregnant women of the village in future, and many more such children would be born by these frightened females.

Tomaso was all for calling off the promised celebrations but he reasoned that to do so would cause joy to his enemy as well as to make all feel that he was ashamed and could not face them. So the fete went on. In the early part of the evening the strained atmosphere could be felt but as the night wore on and the spirits made from their own sugar-cane were passed around, the hunks of roasted wildhogs meat were served, and the drummers found form, singers and dancers got into their strides, and to the annoyance of Lago who sat alone at his doorway listening, the celebration became a night to remember.

But Lago was not downhearted. He knew that such an unusual birth could be made good use of against his enemy, and from that night he became almost happy with his secret thoughts.

It was the ninth day, the important day, when, in the presence of the Nahne, the midwife, the mother and child would leave the confinement-room along with relations and friends according to the custom. Now, for the first time the child would see the light of day.

Some of Tomaso's closest friends were there to see the newborn baby. The Nahne was there, feeling no less excited because she had helped to bring almost every child in the village over the last ten years, for the children all paid great respect to her, almost like a second mother, for was she not the Iyaloda, mother of life?

Old Tahta was there of course. To the old man, Tomaso and his wife were his true son and daughter. The crowd of special friends gathered to the level part of the yard in front of the house. There was no fence, just a path up the hill from the village to the house built on a level patch with the rest of the hill rising right behind it and the high sloping woods on both sides. The sun was now clear of the chain of mountains behind them and the heat was rising slowly.

Tomaso led the way out to the waiting crowd, followed by Kisanka and the midwife, the latter by custom carrying the baby. Tahta who took the place of father and mother to the two since they had no relations, came behind the midwife.

There was a cry of welcome at the appearance of the little procession. Kisanka smiled sweetly at the crowd as they called their greeting to her. Yet all could see that she was very nervous.

Tomaso looked proud and defiant at the same time as he acknowledged congratulations.

The baby, wrapped in a white cloth, could not be seen at first. It was only after the midwife had stuck a small waxlike piece of stuff in the hair just over the pulse of the infant's head, then passed him into the care of his mother before witnesses, that they saw him.

It made them gasp in spite of their preparedness to be polite to the most loved and respected couple of the village.

The gasp had hardly been stifled when another one came to their lips. For coming up the path slowly, with the help of two of his friends, one on each side, was Lago!

It was the first time he had left the confines of his hut since the fight which led to him becoming an invalid.

For invalid he was. Gone was the upright stance, the straight broad-chested figure, dwarfed only by the taller and more graceful Tomaso. In its place was a bent-backed figure looking almost like a hunchback with a slight twist to one side. Every two steps he took forced him to hold on tightly to the shoulders of his helpers and rest, with the sweat from the effort pouring down his hard face. Even his bullneck was no longer impressive. Six months of illness and brooding had taken away the rippling muscles, leaving him gaunt, yet almost more fearsome than before his mishap. It seemed to the onlookers that he was now a man of forty instead of the twenty odd years of age they knew him to be.

The crowd stood silently and helplessly looking as the

visitor approached with his attendants. They knew why he came, and many of the women clutched the children in their arms as if they were afraid that the mere look of this man would harm their offspring. Kisanka held the young child closely to her breasts as she stood beside her husband. There was a flash of the young lioness about her, until, it seemed, she remembered that the lion of the hills, as his admirers named their chief, was there by her side.

Tomaso watched the coming of his blood brother like a man who expected the visit, so calm was his outward appearance. He stepped forward and so contrived to be in front of his wife and the child in her arms. Tahta lined himself to one side of Kisanka while the old midwife took her place on the other side.

'Greetings, O my blood brother!' The harsh bass broke the silence with its mocking sound. The speaker now stood some twelve feet from the chief and his family, with his hands resting on the shoulders of the two men who helped him up the hill.

'What? No greetings for thy crippled brother who, with the help of friends, climbed up this steep path to congratulate thee and thy wife on the birth of thy man child?'

Feigning wonder at such treatment, he looked around on the many people standing silently, and then his malicious eyes came to rest on a young man whom all knew to be a friend of Tomaso and one of his most trusted lieutenants. The man was tall and slim with a colour which made it easy to guess that perhaps as much as half the blood in his veins was that of a bakra. It showed also by his hair which was not straight, but was not the tightly curled hair of the true Negro. His nose was too narrow, but not quite as narrow as that of a white person. This day he wore a pair of tight-fitting trousers barely reaching below the knees, the style and material of which were not unlike that the slaves wore on the plantations. The upper part of his body was bare. He was the only man in the village who could have been called a mulatto, though the colour was not white enough to be thus defined correctly. The young man's name was Jacob, and no-one in the village had ever treated him differently from themselves, and he did not seem to expect

36

it otherwise. His mother was a negress. He never spoke of his father, and the people of the hills never pried. His wife was a girl of the hills and there was no sign of the bakra's blood in her. Now Lago, seeming satisfied at finding the young man amongst the crowd, turned to his chief and blood-brother.

'They tell me thy child is like that of a bakra, O my blood-brother and chief! May not these humble eyes rest on this wonder?', Tomaso sprang forward threateningly towards his tormentor as soon as the word was uttered, and Lago, seeing the look on his chief's face felt frightened for a second. But at the same time he saw that his enemy had halted himself, and he guessed why and took courage.

'Oh-oh!' mocked the invalid. 'My brother who would not kill me when I was whole and needed no one on which to cling for support, abandons his excuses now that both my hands are busy.'

Tomaso was holding himself in check by a mighty effort. Even the great arteries on both sides of his neck were distended and his hands remained clenched.

'I told thee, Tomaso! I told thee I was willing to take thy burden from off thy head.'

It was old Tahta who spoke. No-one doubted the meaning of his words. Lago's eyes flashed fire. His face was ugly with hate now as he spoke:

'Ah, old man, thy master and chief bade thee spare me when it was in thee to send me to the land of my ancestors. And why? Because it makes his spirit glad to look at his blood brother and say with his eyes: *Die, Lago, my enemy! Die! Die when the fireball comes from behind the hills! Die when it goes to sleep under the sea.*'

The crowd looked at the man tormenting himself with self-pity, bitterness, anger and despair; with the sweat on his brow, and his naked torso gleaming in the sunlight with unhealthy moisture; yet not a face showed pity for him, so much had he done to build fear and hatred amongst them. He sensed that the crowd was not for him, and in his fit of rage he was ready to cause misery, suspicion and hate to those who once called him friend, and perhaps death to himself, for there was no doubt in his mind about the risk he was about to run. He looked scornfully at the old man.

'Perhaps, O Tahta, I shall spare a word for thee later, but now I have words for my brother, his wife and his manchild . . . Eh, my leader? It must be thine . . .' He sniggered meaningly. 'Though the colour is that of the bakra, and thy wife as well as thyself is the colour of night without light!'

Now the malicious Lago turned to the light-skinned Jacob. 'Tell me O Jacob, from whom did thy colour come? Was thy father the colour of Tomaso, my brother, and thy mother like my brother's wife Kisanka?'

Surprise at being drawn into the quarrel made the usually quiet Jacob angry.

'I do not care what is said of my father, Lago,' replied the mulatto in the tongue of Africa and the hills. 'But if thy foolish mouth plays with the memory my spirit cherishes for her whom I loved more than life, I shall slay thee, even if thy arms were cut off!'

Jacob had not moved an inch from where he stood nor did his hands move from his side to the cutlass in his waistband. Not even his voice had more than a slight menacing tone and yet every one of the spectators felt certain that Lago would die if he mentioned Jacob's mother again. For a while it seemed the foolhardy man would invite death there and then. But he changed his mind and instead turned to the line he was bent on pursuing. 'I have no quarrel with thee, Jacob—nor with thy people—' A pause, then slowly: 'But perhaps my blood brother might have a quarrel with thee, my friend. Perhaps you have frightened his wife!'

Old Tahta and Kisanka flashed out their hands at the same time to restrain the enraged Tomaso. Kisanka, with only one hand for the leader, held her child to her breast, but Tahta had both his hands on his chief's powerful arm. The two men on whom Lago was depending deserted him simultaneously, so that suddenly bereft of their shoulders he staggered and was forced to ease himself to the ground with the pain, causing him for the time being to desert the garden of mischief and mistrust he had cultivated with his words. The crowd watched him sitting on the ground, half resting on one elbow, breathing quickly, as if he had just arrived running from a long journey. Not a hand went out to help him. Each mind was digesting what he had implied, and wondering how Tomaso would take it. For they knew he was suggesting by his words that Jacob and not Tomaso was the father of Kisanka's child. Tahta's and Kisanka's hands were still on the arms of their chief and lord. Tomaso, with cold fury was still straining forward towards the man on the ground. Then, as he watched his blood brother gasping in pain, he slowly relaxed. On the other side of the crowd, Jacob, whose hand had gone to his cutlass, looked down on the man who had hinted at this treachery, and knew he could not kill a man lying helpless, not even the snake Lago. When he looked up and around him, he knew that the poison of suspicion was in many minds, but he took heart when his eyes met those of his chief and friend. They looked long at each other, then for the first time Tomaso spoke:

'Forgive me, O Jacob, for choosing a descendant of the vulture as a blood-brother. The shame is mine,' he said humbly.

The fair-skinned one looked at his friend with gratitude: 'Nay, Tomaso, my chief! Blame not thyself. Down on the plantations the bakra have a tale which tells of a man-snake called the devil. He was the father of liars. Here we have his son!' Saying this, Jacob pointed to the twisted man half lying on the ground amidst the nodding heads of the people, for they liked and approved the comparison, and accepted Jacob's way of denying the charge Lago had made against him.

It was then that old Tahta and the midwife looked at each other with meaning, then the former stepped forward.

'Hear me, O people!' began the old man in a voice strong enough to reach even the farthest parts of the village. 'As Jacob rightly said, the picni of the snake-man of which the bakra spoke, and whose other name is the devil, is at your feet. But for my part, I believe this picni was born out of the droppings of the snake-man, hence his badness.'

The insult caused guffaws, and ill though the man on the

ground was, he stopped his grimace to answer. 'Old man, once I wanted to die. Now I thank thee, and thy master, for letting me live, even though you have made me into a cripple; for in spite of thee, I shall be strong again and these hands of mine shall be mighty enough to slay thee, as well as my enemy.'

His bloodshot eyes, and the anger and pain which made a monster of his face, caused the people to feel afraid, for he no longer looked like a man but a thing of evil which made their blood run cold. A fit of shivering took hold of the recently-confined Kisanka, and the baby began to whimper like a child in fear.

'I shall finish what I have to say in spite of thy snake tongue, O devil-man!' continued Tahta suddenly lifting the left hand of Tomaso, much to the chief's surprise. 'There are none in these hills who have not known of the mark which the legend says is the gift of the gods to a family of great warriors—the extra finger on the eating hand. There is none but our chief, Tomaso in all these hills who bears such a gift.' The old man waited as the crowds saw for the hundredth time the sixth finger which had caused their warrior chief to be admiringly called by an extra nickname, The-Many-Fingers-One.

'Aye, we all know that the gods gave Tomaso an extra finger at his birth,' said one.

'It is a mark to show our chief is not like ordinary warriors!'

'This is why there are none as brave as he.'

The crowd was enthusiastic, wanting also to show that they had not changed towards him—much to the discomfort of the man on the ground. Tomaso still wore a frown of bewilderment as the old midwife came forward and took the baby gently from his mother's arms,

'Look people!' she cried triumphantly, holding up the tiny left hand of the infant. There, clinging to the side of the little finger was a tinier one, perfect in shape.

Tomaso gasped. For Kisanka had hidden this even from him.

'Now who shall say this is not indeed Tomaso's child?' asked the wise old Tahta.

The crowd burst into a roar of cheering, so that the echoes had a wonderful time.

'A warrior like thee, Tomaso!'

He will be mighty, O chief!'

'Greetings Little-Many-Fingers-One! Welcome to the hill of the Maroons!'

The shouts grew as some of the uninvited felt that they would be no longer intruders and climbed the hill. Now, in spite of the whiteness of the child's face, the people swore how much they could see of Tomaso in his young son. Gone was the embarrassment. More and more they came up the hill to pay homage to the child born with the gift of a sixth finger like his renowned father. And in the excitement the surprised and humiliated Lago sat in the dirt, forgotten. People walked over his legs to be closer to their chief and his heir. Women's clothing brushed past his face without anybody begging pardon. Even children stumbled over his feet and merely looked back without saying pardon as was the strict custom between the young and their elders. And when he could not stand the insults any more and half-crawled and half-walked slowly and without a single helping hand, only a few people noticed his going. All the way down, as the pain in his back grew intense and the anger grew within him, all he could think of was to undo this morning's failure. Now he did not hate only Tomaso, his wife and the old Tahta; he hated the whole village. They had publicly scorned him. He, Lago, the warrior! Even the two women he had rescued from the bakra plantation and given them sons had not spoken on his behalf or tried to help him. He had seen them on the fringe of the crowd as if they were afraid of being identified with him . . . and as if they were ashamed of bearing his children, he thought bitterly. True they had visited him when he first became ill, and dutifully brought or sent him vegetables from their plots, as well as to wash his loin-cloths, fetch water, and keep the room clean, but they never offered to stay with him, and brought his boys to see him only when he asked them. He felt bitterly lonely, but not for a moment would he admit that he had always created enemies, not friends.

It took him a very long time to reach his house, and but

for his hope of revenge, he would have ended his own life. But now his mind was too concerned with his ideas for new forms of revenge to give way to despair. 'I shall repay them for this day also!' he cried loudly as he reached the door of his hut. Then he fell down exhausted.

It was late. Kisanka lay in her own bed with the child at her breast. The lamp, a small clay bowl with nut oil and water in which a tiny slab of chip floated with a bit of wild cotton twisted round for a wick, had a yellowish flame which was barely enough to light up the small room for the occupants to see their way about. To the other side of the partly divided house, Tomaso lay in his hammock.

Kisanka was speaking: 'No, Tomaso, I kept it secret, for if, when first you came to see the child you did not trust me or doubted who was its father, then I would have gone from thy house without showing thee the proof, and I would have taken the child with me. For I could not have borne it if thy eyes had accused me until I showed the extra finger on his hand. But all was well, Tomaso. There was trust that day in thy eyes. There was no doubt on thy face, though the child had no trace of thy colour or mine. It made my spirit glad, Tomaso. I know Nahne, the midwife, had not told thee, for I had made her swear not to do so, and she is a good woman. I told her to tell Tahta also, and he too agreed that you should not know until the time was ripe, unless you came upon it. Today the time was ripe for the telling, Tomaso. Tahta planned it well.'

Tomaso considered a little, then: 'This extra finger has been a mark amongst my people for many generations, Kisanka, as I told thee when we first met. It was always the male amongst my family who had it, and always it was on the same hand, and yet I never thought of seeking this sign; and now I am glad I did not know, Little Shadow, for now you know how big is my trust in thee.'

Kisanka let out a sigh of happiness. 'O, my lord Tomaso, it is no wonder every woman in the village would have been glad to sit at thy feet. And I, a poor girl, who knows not her tribe and has never seen the animal called Asuno, after which they often called thee! For, as I have told thee before,

O my husband, my mother went to the land of the dead before I could ask her of my ancestors, and my father was only a shadow in my mind before they sold him away from the plantation.'

'Hush, Little Shadow!' He got up out of his hammock and knelt by the side of the bed, placing one hand on the head of the white haired infant. As he brought up the other hand to lay on her head, Kisanka grasped it, and passionately rubbed it against her lips, then her cheek, and in the silence which followed, her mind, and his, went back ten years . . .

. . . Tomaso, the grandson of a mighty Bakcongo chief, captured and brought to Jamaica as a slave at the age of fourteen. He had stayed only little more than a year in bondage. As he groomed his master's horses he planned with others to leave for the hills for any of the three mountain hideouts where they told him bands of men once again found freedom. Up in the Cockpit Mountains were warriors who called themselves by a new name, the Maroons, the Isolated. Up in the east of the Island high up among the Blue Mountains were also another band of these Maroon warriors. And to the north on the peak of the almost inaccessible Twin Sisters Mountains was another band of Maroons. These last were not as well organized as the other two bands of Maroons; they lacked a bold leader like the young Cudjo and his blood brother Accompong of the East and West, who later became a part of history. Tomaso, only fourteen, plotted, and around him he gathered a band of fellow slaves who vowed to make the Maroons of the Twin Sisters mountains as strong—or stronger—than those of the Blue or the Cockpit mountains. They began to help picked men and women to escape, providing them with stolen gunpowder and shot, for the empty muskets he learned they had in the hills. The chief was grateful for the recruits and the much needed ammunition, but he lacked leadership. His raids were never led by himself. He lived well while his people had to work for him. He was mostly interested in being a man with great power. Tomaso, fifteen, was the chosen leader of the underground movement down on the plantations after his companions had discovered his ability to lead.

Kisanka was a healthy girl of ten on the plantations on

which Tomaso worked. She was born there. Her mother had died when she was three. Her father was sold to another planter at the same time. The orphaned girl, knowing no relations, and being born on the plantation not knowing freedom, was considered safe by the planters as she grew up to serve at their tables and in their kitchens. At ten she was almost free to travel the distance from one neighbouring plantation to the other without suspicion. She knew Tomaso. At the firesides the slaves whispered how this boy leader had helped to free nearly a hundred slaves within three moons. He was a boy who needed no tribal mark, for he bore an extra finger on his eating hand, and the people said the gods gave it to him.

In a year Tomaso became a legend. Within that year the little girl of ten had offered herself as a messenger to the boy she had worshipped from afar from the day she had set eyes on him. So her dangerous mission began. She was the one who took messages to the other plantations, telling Tomaso's fellow plotters where and when would be safe for the next meeting; telling who were picked to escape when a diversion was taking place, telling when the hillmen would raid the plantation. It was a mighty task for a slim little slave girl of ten, for now the planters were aware that the plotters were on their own plantations, and traps were being laid to discover the culprits. In vain they tried. No-one would talk even if they knew more than that the Extra-Finger-One or the Lion or Asunu was the one who carried off these raids.

But such a secret was always dangerous. A boy with six fingers on one hand was rare indeed. The girl messenger just had time to warn Tomaso that a slave who could stand the heat on the soles of his feet no more, told of the one with the extra finger. Luckily, Tomaso and his friends had anticipated such a danger. That night they escaped by the route along which they had sent nearly two hundred of their fellow-men. It was difficult. Ten men to disappear without being detected! They divided themselves into two parties of five, Tomaso leading one. They were pursued by men with dogs. Two of the slaves were wounded and recaptured. Two were killed, one committed suicide with his homemade knife when he was surrounded. The five which met disaster were not Tomaso's. He, with his four men, outwitted their pursuers by doubling back to the plantation and lying low while their pursuers and the puzzled bloodhounds searched for them in vain. It was some hours before they, reassured by the sound of the returning men and dogs in the early hours of the morning, took the trail to the hills once more. One of the recaptured men threatened with the ants nest punishment, told of the girl who knew the secrets of the plotters. The masters did not act immediately. They waited, knowing that those who escaped would not be satisfied with this. They would return. So the young handsome black girl was watched discreetly day and night. She went on her way calmly, doing the work allotted to her. It was when she had looked around secretively before darting into the cane fields one night that two waiting bondsmen pounced on her, and frogmarched her back to face the masters. She would not tell in spite of all they tried, and afterwards they never ceased to marvel at her courage. After three days of trying—it was useless anyway, for by then the raiders would have learnt that their messenger had been caught—they let her go. They knew also she could not travel far with the sole of one foot in such a bad condition from the torture she was put through. When she was well enough she could be given work such as looking after the young picnies on the estate, or weeding the cane fields with the old women. But she would not fetch anything in the slave market with a lame foot.

It was a month after Tomaso's escape and Kisanka's ordeal when, lying on the floor of the hut which she now shared with two old women, she heard a familiar scratching. At first she would not believe that it was Tomaso as usual. But when she went on her hands and knees to the carefully opened door, she heard his whisper.

She could not as long as she lived forget that moment. He was like a shadow in the starlit night, but still she recognised him as if a light had been turned on him.

'I have come for thee,' he had whispered simply.

'But I am ill—my foot, Tomaso,' she had whispered, thrilled and despaired at the same time.

'You shall ride on my back, little one. Turn only to seize any pieces of cloth that you can, for this is precious.'

She had turned to find the bits of cloth she owned, trying not to wake the two women sleeping in the hut. It was when she had crept past the two that she heard whispers. 'The spirits guide thee, Little One!' said one, and from the other: 'Go good, my child!'

She thanked the old women for their blessing, wiped the water that had suddenly come to her eyes, and limped forward to the waiting Tomaso, but not before he had whispered to the two in the darkened hut: 'You, too, shall sleep in the nest of freedom, good mothers. Wait and see!'

Then he had helped the frail Kisanka on to his back, and they were on their way. They hid in the canefields and on the hillsides close to the route for rest; and on the third day reached the safety of the mountains, without Kisanka once walking as much as a chain on the way.

It was found out later that the lad who talked when he could not stand the heat on the sole of his foot was Lago. But Tomaso did not know; nor did Kisanka. For then Lago was not amongst the inner circle of young plotters, but he had been helping in some small way like most of the young slaves of the plantations, putting stolen things like lead taken from fishing nets, food, bits of rag and salt, in secret places where the raiders could find them. He had been caught with something he was taking to the cache on the instructions of another slave.

Tomaso had kept his word to rescue the two women who shared the hut with Kisanka and had blessed her when she was leaving. One died five years after being rescued and brought to the hills. The other was still alive. She was Nahne—the midwife.

Up in the hills, because of the boy hero's popularity, the chief, an old man, made Tomaso captain of the warriors, and gave him a free hand. Within a year, Tomaso and his band were spoken of in the same breath as the most famous Maroon leaders of the Island.

Lago never knew until now that he had so much capacity for hatred. He hated the old quackdoctor, Tahta who mended him. He made himself believe two things: one, that it was only because of his hated blood brother and chief, that the old man had not killed him slowly; for there was no doubt that Tahta hated him intensely. The other was that he believed that the old man could have made him well without any trace of the result of his fight with Tomaso. Instead of getting straightened as time went on, he discovered that though his back pained him rarely he was getting into a kind of hunched and twisted position as he walked. The thought of being ugly and deformed terrified him. He had seen a hunchback before—when he was a slave-boy on the plantation. Someone had told him that the bump came from a fall, and now it seemed he would be one of these people. He Lago, who used to be straight and upright as a bamboo shoot, and as strong as Asunu the elephant he remembered seeing as child in his own country. No-one could convince him that the wily Tahta had not connived with Tomaso to take revenge on him by making him something to laugh at around the village. That was why Tomaso did not let him die. Death would have been easier than this, he said to himself for the hundredth time. And it was only the schemes Lago had been weaving in his mind night and day which prevented him from attempting to kill Tomaso, his blood brother. For he wanted the man who he claimed made him an invalid to suffer first—suffer in mind as well as body. He wanted to live to gloat over his enemy; to see people hate him as much as they loved him now. Yes, Tomaso must suffer. And his woman! The woman who fouled him with her spittle before witnesses! When he remembered that afternoon when he was shamed, it was hard for him to say whether he hated Tomaso more than his wife. He had not dreamed that she would have done this thing. He had tried to seduce her before, she should have accepted this as a compliment. He had met her coming from the waterhole, she with her women friends, he with his. He had done nothing more than bar her way in jest and had merely stretched his hand to touch her on the breast that was not covered, and then she had spat right into his face in front of his friends. The act had paralysed him so that he was unable to act until the woman had walked away, and when he would have caught her up and slayed her for the insult, his so-called friends had barred his way. And had even threatened him! Why must they be always idolizing this Tomaso! Had he, Lago, not many brave things to his credit? True, there was the time when he talked: but who could withstand even the threat of burning feet, or a feast for the ants, and keep his mouth shut? Kisanka? She must be a witch, that was it! The woman was a witch that was why the bakra's fire could not open her mouth; and that was why she came in his sleep to haunt him. He was sure of it now that he considered the matter. How else could he hate a woman yet long to be near her? She was not beautiful. Only foolish people would think her comely. Her nose was too narrow, her lips were only half-full, and she was not at all plump. Why, there were girls in the village to the number of fingers on his hands who were more comely than this Kisanka. True she was shiny black, and one must admit that her skin was smooth. But were it not for her being a witch he was sure he would not have even looked on her long enough to remember such details. But it seemed the witch had been bewitched! How else could she birth such a child? And she was lame. He had remembered that and so did not make the mistake of hinting that she might have gone down to the plains, even though, without being lame, such a hint would not hold water, since she would have been missed or seen, and the distance to the plains was far too great. He had not, of course, known that the strange colour picni would have the extra finger to prove his parentage. That had been a blow to him, and the wily old Tahta must have guessed his intention and so arranged to keep the news secret until he had had his say. He would one day repay that old bush doctor. He was sure the old man could have made him quite well if he had so wished. But that Tahta would pay. So would Tomaso, Kisanka, and this picni.

Time came and went, and Lago waited . . .

The trees of Twin Sisters never stood naked and ashamed at any time during the years of their lives unless the evil god Hurricane struck them. The aged leaves passed along with dignity and without fuss, and the young ones, full of respect for their elders, took the places of their predecessors without a blare of horns to announce their coming. The earth of the hills and valleys never knew the kiss of frost upon its face, and the animals, with nothing to tell them the time of year, sometimes mated and bred when they should not. The few migrating birds to the island tried year after year to explain to their fellow species, who had never travelled, why they must make the long journey across the great waters from the place where a mighty sheet of whiteness covered all each year, and the trees gave no shelter from the biting cold because they were bare.

'How can this be?' asked the unbelieving birds.

'We do not understand this talk! How can trees live again once they have lost all their leaves? How can this whiteness come to the earth from the sky and stay there for so long? Look! The rain comes from the sky here and the earth swallows all up in a single day. What is this thing called winter you speak of? This is indeed strange talk!'

And the exasperated migrants would shut their beaks in despair with a little disgust as well, knowing that they would never be able to make their feathered friends, who had never travelled, understand.

The ages of the infants on Twin Sisters were always marked by the youngsters' achievements and by the gifts nature bestowed on them from time to time . . .

'Speak Kisanka. I know by the look on thy face that there is news, and that it is good.'

'It is good, my husband chief, of our baby. This day I looked into the mouth of our baby, and lo, there are two.'

'Hush, Kisanka, do not call the name. It is bad to call them by their real name until he has a mouthful.'

'O, I know, lord Tomaso! I know I must not call them by their real name until he has a mouthful.'

'He is growing fast, Little Shadow. He is strong too. Soon he will be walking.'

'He is like thee, Tomaso. He will be brave and strong and you shall be proud one day. Look how peacefully he sleeps.'

'Look Kisanka! Look! He walks! O, he has fallen. He was not hurt. I must have alarmed him.'

'It makes water come to my eyes, husband chief, to see our son stand, and walk by himself. I am glad you were here to see his first steps. Soon he will be a man . . . If only, O, Tomaso! Will the people of the village be cruel to him because of his colour? Now I shall live in fear.'

'Hush, Little Shadow. Am I not here with thee and our son? See, he understands! He is watching thy face.'

'Forgive me, my lord. Fear comes to me only when I am not by thy side. When thy shadow darkens the doorway of the hut, fear flies like a chicken-hawk from thy Little Shadow. How could it be otherwise? Yet it is not for myself that I tremble. All my fears are for thee and this our child. I feel that Lago will find a plot big enough to hurt thee, or the child, my husband. I do not like the way he keeps silent and brooding since the day when he tried to make trouble and failed.'

'Do not let fear take hold of thy spirit, woman. Lago may now see that it is better not to be a maker of mischief. Nevertheless, these eyes of mine watch daily.'

'He called my name this day, husband! At first I did not know the meaning of this word when he kept saying Ka but at last it came to me! It is the ending of my name, "Ka." Now he calls us both. You he calls Ta and I, Ka. Soon he will be a man, my lord, and look how robust is his body! If only he was thy colour and mine!'

'Hush, Kisanka! Hush child! Our son is wise for his age. See how early he walks and talks! What of his colour! Has he not the extra finger to show he is his father's son? Not that such proof was ever needed for me, Little Shadow. Look at his nose, his mouth, and the way he looks. It was as if my head was taken off when I was young and placed on his shoulders. He will be a brave warrior, Little Shadow! Tahta makes a god out of the little one. See how often he comes here with funny excuses on his lips! See how he takes the child and talks to him, and will not go away until the young one is too tired to play! His spirit takes to the little one, Kisanka, and the child's spirit takes to the old one, too! It is a good sign.'

'You speak truly, O Tomaso, my lord. Tahta's spirit takes to our little Tamba, and his to the old man also. He has great wisdom this Tahta, not as great as thee, for none could be as mighty as my lord Tomaso in thought or deed, but he knows many things which he learnt from the bakra, and when you are with the warriors watching on the hillside perhaps the old man will tell our son many things which I could not speak of.'

'You have spoken wisely, Little Shadow. Tahta has great wisdom. There is much I could learn from him, O my Shadow, for age brings wisdom to maturity, and there is none on these hills who knows more about the herbs and doctoring of men in the bakra way. Who knows more about the ways of our people than he? Our son will learn much under him, Kisanka. And fret not about his colour. They will forget the colour of his skin some day when they find that the Spirits of Goodness and Greatness make their beds into the bodies of men without first looking at their skins.'

'O, Tomaso, my lord, did I not say thy wisdom is mighty? Now I have these words of thine to bring me comfort when the pain of his hurt comes heavily on me, for I know by the look on thy face that he shall suffer.'

'Hush, Kisanka, hush.'

Tomaso was dozing in his hammock under a tree at the back of his house when his ears, trained like those of a good watchdog, woke him to say someone was approaching. He sat up quickly to see a face he knew would be coming up the bushy path.

'O, Tahta it is you!' said the chief, showing a smile of pleasure on his face.

'Aye, it is I, Tomaso, my son, and I am ashamed to have called thee from the land of sleep when I know thy eyes are weary from thy night watch by the Place-of-the-Big-Jump. But my inside is full, my chief, and if I do not unload it this night I shall not find sleep.'

Tomaso hastened to climb out of his hammock, and out of a traditional respect for the aged, stood until the old man had settled on his haunches, then he did likewise.

'Mine eyes are always glad to be upon thy face, O Great Father, and the load which burdens thee is my burden also. But need I tell thee this?' asked the young chief, and the old man's face beamed with pleasure and affection.

'No, Tomaso, words are not needed to tell of the entwining of our spirits and yet it is good to hear it from thy mouth.'

They sat silently after that looking at the sundrenched trees before them and the dancing of the leaves to the coaxing of the gentle wind.

'Tomaso.' The old man's voice was full of softness.

'I listen, O my father!'

'I am getting near the time when my spirit craves new lands and old faces.'

'I shall perhaps be there to greet thee, Tahta. This thing called death speaks not only to the aged.'

'That is true, my son, yet death moves his hut closer to the aged than to the young. But I did not bring thee back from sleep to talk only of death's nearness. I owe thee a mighty debt, my son, and it seemed to me that I could repay thee a little of this which I owe if only thy head will nod to say me yes.'

'We have spoken of this before, Tahta.'

'Aye, my son, yet the time is ripe for this talk.'

The silence came, and the two men sat looking out on the beauty of the tropical hills, yet seeing nothing of this. It was Tomaso who spoke at last:

'*He* has been silent since the first time we showed the child to the people, Tahta. The boy is three years old by the bakra way of counting. Could it not be that *he* is no longer looking for revenge?'

A harsh laugh came from the almost toothless mouth of the old one.

'Because there is so much of the spirit of goodness in thee does not mean that there is any in Lago, Tomaso, in spite of the mingling of thy blood with his many moons ago!'

Tahta placed one wrinkled hand gently on the bare knee of his chief:

'Do you think he will forget that because of his fight with thee, he now looks more like a monster than a man? True, by his will to be strong he is even more powerful than before his fall. You have seen how, whenever there is work to do, whether it be clearing the place for a house, or lifting a mighty log in the forest, he always takes the heaviest part of the work. Even I look in wonder at the things he lifts now by himself.

But it is all for a reason, Tomaso, he will plot to shame thee and thy family; and he knows that to succeed thee as chief, he must be strong even if he is almost a cripple. I have watched him ceaselessly, my son, and I feel that he is only biding his time to strike at thee.'

The old quackdoctor was breathing hard now.

Tomaso looked troubled. 'It has come to my mind that he might be waiting for me to bring in some new law or to punish lawbreakers, to turn the people against me, Tahta.'

There was anger in Tomaso's face now as he thought of the insults the children of his blood brother threw at his boy when he once took the youngster through the village.

'The boy of thine means much to me, Tomaso,' broke in Tahta.

'I know thy spirit takes to him and his to thine, Tahta,' the chief replied simply.

'This is why I feel I could repay a little of this debt which I owe thee.' Tomaso held up his hand and the old man waited for him to speak.

'Tahta, whatever little I have done for thee, I have been repaid countless times over. It is I who feel that I am in thy debt for being a father to me and my Kisanka, and now my little Tamba. I pray the spirits will wait a long time for thy coming. As for Lago!' Here Tomaso turned an earnest face to his adopted father and now his words were slow and full of anger. 'It is as I once told thee. If he must die, O Tahta, then in spite of my oath, let it be by my hands.' Then quickly: 'But take my thanks with thee, O Father-of-Men, for I know thy offer was well meant.'

The old man raised himself slowly from his haunches. 'Perhaps I knew what thy answer would be before I came, Tomaso,' he said. 'But I wished for thy sake, for thy Kisanka's, for the people of these hills, and, more than all, for thy Little One, that I would have been given leave. I had it planned—even the spot where we both would fall. It would have been easy to get him there, near the Place-of-the-Big-Jump. We would have jumped together, Tomaso, that snake Lago and I, and after that the hills would be clean and the smell of the village would be kind to the noses of all.' He shook his head sadly. 'Well, you are like my own son, Tomaso, but you are also my chief, and I must obey.'

The next minute the old man was ambling down the bushy path with Tomaso standing watching until he disappeared from view.

It was a hard and frugal life on the mountains occupied by the Maroons. Cut off as they were from barter and trade, they had to depend on their crops of cassava, corn, peas, sweet potatoes and seasonal fruits which every person gave a hand in cultivating. Hammocks, invented by the vanishing Arawak Indians, were made by Maroon women and children.

Tomaso insisted on having the young taught the use of bows, arrows, and spears, in spite of the loads of ancient muskets the Spaniards had given their ancestors as bribes. They made cloth from fine bark, and one in particular called the lace bark was plentiful and under expert hands was as soft as linen when finished.

Just outside the village of Twin Sisters was a clearing used as a market where the people exchanged their goods and which was also used on great ceremonial occasions. It was a very large and level grass covered area capable of holding many times the population of the village. On three sides was almost virgin forest with great hardwood trees standing like giant guards on the fringes. The side which was not extended into the forest was jutted on to a kind of wall-like cliff which the Spaniards had, in their frantic search for gold when they first came to the island, dug in vain. They left behind an artificial cave nearly a hundred feet wide and half that amount in depth, which the new people of the hills found ideal as a place to hold council when rain made open-air sessions impossible.

There was excitement as the crowd came to the great clearing in answer to the call of the drums and eketeh. Tomaso was back! He had gone for a whole week right into the bakra's mouth so as to get news of a lad the slavemasters had captured.

The lad whose name was Quame had been longing to see his brother and sister who were still slaves on one of the plantations. He had, without consulting his elders, ventured down the hills to the plains. Tomaso was not there with the guards but Lago was, and it was he who prevented the guards of the pass from turning the foolish lad back to the hills. And, since Lago was a senior warrior the guards could not oppose him. A week later news came by the usual underground route that the lad was captured by the bakra. The whole village was grieved for they knew by experience that such a capture meant torture for information, then death.

Tomaso, with his trusted lieutenant Jacob, had been away for a week seeking information. Now the call of the eketeh meant that they were back and that Tomaso himself would have something to say to them.

Now as the darkness came the villagers poured into the natural arena lighted up by a great bamboo-fed bonfire. The dry loads of bamboo were eaten up greedily by the flames, for there was nothing the monster loved more than great joints of the hollow wood. Those children who had the good fortune to be allowed to accompany their elders showed their excitement by screaming and chasing each other from one corner of the great clearing to the other while women standing by themselves greeted friends loudly and cheerfully.

Many of the women wore the simple smock supplied to slaves on the plantations while others were dressed in two pieces of cloth, one as a skirt, the other thrown loosely across the right shoulder. But there were many of these women who had no more of the precious cloth of the plains, and these improvised with the bleached heart of dwarf palms, plentiful in the hills, or with bark-cloth, both articles making fine skirts for the wearers.

The men solved their difficulty by wearing loincloths which were not only economical but also ideal for bush fighting. But there were quite a few dressed in the tight-fitting trousers of material worn by slaves on the plantations, and there were even a few who were wearing the flowing gownlike cloth usually seen on Moorish Arabs or some West Africans. The children, boys and girls alike, wore what their parents could afford. From lap-cloths, straw skirts or loincloths to nothing, depending on age and sex.

Tomaso appeared out of the cave-like place situated to one side of the tree lined clearing where he and his Elders had been in conference. The crowd, seeing the tall handsome man, stopped their chattering to throw words of greeting to their chief spontaneously. He answered their greetings, calling to those he recognised by their names as he passed through their midst, until at last he was in the place provided for him, marked by the chief's stool, on which he took his seat. This night he was clad in cloth, tied at the waist and reaching down on one side near to his ankle, while the other side, where both ends of the cloth met, fell some four inches shorter than the other. The upper part of his body was covered loosely by a cloth which was thrown over his left shoulder, across his back, to fasten along with the other material at the waist. The right arm which was bare, gleamed as if it was polished as the firelight caught it in its play.

Now the people waited, barely speaking in low tones, while one by one on each side of their chief, the aged Elders sat on bark mats provided for them. Behind them the warriors, most of whom were dressed only in loincloths, stood with their muskets slung behind their backs, cutlasses on their hips and powderhorns, ramrods and other necessities, hanging by strings around their powerful bodies. Old Tahta, being more than an elder to the people of the village, had his special share of greeting as he appeared beside his chief. There was no doubt of the old man's popularity.

Kisanka was one of the few who was not amongst the great crowd. She had stayed with her four-year-old son, not willing to trust him to anyone.

The firelight danced on the faces of the multitude as they waited expectantly for their leader's announcement.

'I thought my ears were lying!'

Every face around the great fire turned towards the grating voice laced with sarcasm. He pushed his way forward through the crowd without ceremony, and it seemed a chillness descended suddenly on the people, in spite of the blazing fire and the warmth of the tropical night.

Perhaps the magic of the fire made the man look more grotesque than anyone had seen him to be since the accident to his back. But it could not be denied that Lago looked frightening. He had developed a kind of hunch, and because of the way he was bent forward, it seemed his arms and hands had grown longer. His neck had sunk between his shoulders, and his body was twisted as if the upper part was a bit of a misfit on the lower. Yet there was no doubt about it that the bull-necked broad shoulders had become even broader and the muscles of his naked arms seemed more powerful than those of most men of the hills except perhaps Tomaso.

The whole village was now afraid of Lago for one thing or another. He picked quarrels for no reason at all with anyone. His frowning and gaunt face, never pleasant before, was even more unpleasant these days, though many would have sworn that this was not possible before he confronted them with the fact.

Men, women and children avoided him. The men had little to say to him and he to them; the women with child or without, turned back when they saw him coming and it was possible to do so without deliberately insulting him; and when they could not possibly beat a hasty retreat they would stand aside in the narrow paths to let him pass. The children ran terrified from him, and even his own two sons, budding bullies as they were, kept out of his way whenever they could. Even animals, such as pigs and dogs, found it safe to scamper out of his way so as to avoid a kick from his unbelievably hard foot.

One thing about Lago which was now the talk of the village was his show of strength. For whenever there was a chance to show that he had not lost the use of his great arms and shoulders, he would jump at the opportunity. And all had to agree that in this he was a force to reckon with.

Now, as he stood in front of the fire, which the children had been given the special privilege of stoking from time to time, his misshapen figure with the fantastic shadows which the dancing flames cast high on the trees behind him, seemed as if he was something ominous and menacing come from out of the darkness to threaten all with some un-named disaster. Even Tomaso, sitting on the chief's stool facing his blood brother with the fire as a partition between them, seemed to be aware of the un-named fear which came with the man.

Now Lago, sure that he had brought about the maximum of attention dear to the hearts of all show-offs, began:

'My ears told me that my blood brother had ordered the eketeh to be blown, so that he can tell us, his little picnies what we should or should not do.'

The man could scarcely conceal the hate and malice in every word he spoke.

Tomaso, calm and dignified, with his arms folded across his bare chest answered:

'Your ears have spoken truth, O Lago, and all have a right to come when the eketeh calls.'

The calm voice of their chief had a reassuring effect on the crowd, and Lago felt he would have to work hard if he was to turn this new law about to be announced to his own advantage.

'My people, I have caused the eketeh to be sounded for welcome,' said the misshapen one with a sneer, and waited for Tomaso to bandy words with him, but the chief looked beyond and around his blood brother, deliberately ignoring his presence when next he spoke, much to the discomfort of the troublemaker.

'My people, I have caused the eketh to be sounded for two reasons. I have returned with news of the unwise one who went without my permission to the bakra plantations in search of his kin. He is alive!' A great shout went up from the mouths of the people at the news, and Tomaso waited patiently for its abatement before he spoke again.

'My spirit rejoiced when the news came to my ears, my people, for though he did wrong to go without my permission as is the law of these hills, he is but a youth, and I might have done the same in my youth . . . aye, even now were I in his place. He has not suffered torture either which is strange news but good.'

The people gave a deafening roar of happiness at this additional news. And Lago, standing opposite waiting for a chance to make trouble, felt that fate was going against him. The chief held up his hand for silence, then continued:

'I have listened to much, O my people, since I, Tahta, and Jacob, went into the jaws of the bakra. I saw and spoke to men who swore that there are now some good bakra down there on the plains. Some have no slaves. I spoke to one through one of our people who understands the bakra words. This man tells me the bakra have promised that the lad now in their hands will not be tortured or killed. This bakra says many of his people over the great waters are ashamed of this slavery and one day this badness will end.'

As the chief paused, only the mouth of the great fire eating its meal of bamboo could be heard.

'Now hear me, O my people, the chiefs of the other Maroons of the mountains on the other side of the island and I have talked. It has been a long talk and sometimes our blood ran hot with the argument between us. But in the end we parted as brothers promising to do the thing we argued about. I have called the Elders into the Cave-of-Talks as you have heard. I have told them of the talks I made with the leaders of Maroons on the other mountains far away. Then I told them of the law which I have promised to make, just as the other chiefs will do when they reach the villages of their people.' Tomaso raised himself from the chief's stool.

Lago, standing with arms folded, faced his chief across the blazing fire as if he was about to challenge his blood brother to a duel. He wore only loincloth and a loose piece of material hanging over his shoulder. The warm night and the nearness of the bullnecked one to the great fire caused a thin moisture to come out of his body, but there was no shiny, polished glow coming from the uncovered parts as it did on his chief.

There was a tenseness in the air, and no-one sensed it more than Tomaso, for he knew how difficult it was for him to agree to this suggestion for the new law. But their indirect talk with the Man-of-God coupled with his assurance that the boy was not harmed had been in his favour, and in spite of fierce opposition from the Elders, including even Tahta, the majority had agreed. He suspected that it was more out of loyalty than because he was able to talk them into it. Now as he stood before the crowd of more than a thousand—for the population had grown by leaps and bounds over the last four years—Tomaso wondered if even his popularity would be able to carry him through the testing time.

'Hear, O my people, this new law.' His rich voice rang true and firm, not only all over the great clearing, but into the neighbouring hills as well. 'This then is the law: *No Maroon shall set fire to a sugar-cane plantation, or a house if he knows that this fire will eat up women, children, or the aged, though they be bakra. No-one shall slay a bakra if he or she be aged, or if it be a woman who bears no arms. No-one shall slay a bakra child. No-one shall slay a wounded soldier. If any of these soldiers, women, or aged, threatens the life of a Maroon warrior and there is no escape, then it is for the Maroon to defend himself, and this law against killing does not stand. Also, if by setting fire to a cane-field, or a house, a Maroon can save his life or the lives of his people, then the law does not stand. And if a wounded bakra threatens the life of a Maroon, or his people, then it is right to kill him and save himself or his people. These are the only excuses from this law which I shall take. The penalty for breaking this law, which begins from the time it comes out of my mouth, is death.* I, Tomaso, Chief and Leader of the Maroons of Twin Sisters, have spoken.'

While Tomaso was speaking, Lago could hardly contain himself. He was not at the Cave-of-Talks with the elders and warriors, though he had a right to be, but he heard that a law of restraint was about to be made, and feeling that it might give him a chance of discrediting his enemy, decided to choose the great open-air place with the multitude as witnesses, for his verbal, if not physical, battleground. Feeling fit in spite of his deformity, he had made up his mind beforehand to try to force the issue into a physical battle climax.

Now, Tomaso's law was even more difficult for the people to accept without a grumble than he had dreamed of anticipating. There was now a general rumbling from all sides as Tomaso sat down. There was no doubt about the anger and bewilderment on the firelit faces. An elder stood up angrily. He was the brother of the late chief whom Tomaso succeeded, and he had been expecting to inherit the leadership on the death of his kin, but much to his anger, Tomaso, an outsider, took his place. Now he looked around angrily and the sullen crowd stopped their grumbling to listen to what he had to say.

'My people,' he began in a high-pitched voice, 'I have

no part in this law. It is a bad one. Bear ye witness that I am against it.' He sat down quickly as if now that he had had his say his guts had collapsed. He would not look towards his chief. There were many nods of approval for the elder's words.

Lago felt his turn had come. He looked round at the people, turning slowly as he did so, until he had made a complete circle, then he looked across at Tomaso now sitting once more on the stool.

'My brother has courage,' he began with a sneer.

The crowd grew still at Lago's words.

'I said my brother has courage! Courage to make a law such as this come out of his mouth— or is it the mouth of a bakra speaking through that of my blood brother?'

Half a dozen of the chief's warriors touched their cutlasses at their sides ready to slay the man for such an insult, but Tomaso held up his hand, and they stood poised, waiting.

The crowd gasped as the implication of the insult became clear to them. Lago was slightly daunted seeing the men with hands on the handles of their weapons, but as Tomaso waved them back he convinced himself that the other was afraid of public opinion, and continued recklessly:

'How else could my brother speak such folly? Did the bakra not go to our country with their ships and fall upon us though we had done them no wrong? Did they spare our women—our aged—our picnies? Who is among us who has no kin that is a bakra slave, to be sold for pieces of iron, to be beaten and kicked, to be burnt until the flesh smells while the poor slave still lives, to be covered with molasses and staked over a nest of ants? Have we not seen these things? And now my brother comes from the plains full of good spirit for the bakra!' Lago paused for breath while the people nodded in approval of his words, for even Tomaso could not deny these things.

Encouraged, Lago continued: 'Let my brother, whose past is secret, say that there is no such cruelty? Shall we, having won our freedom, sit back and punish those who fight to free our brothers? Would the bakra do this for us? Perhaps now that my brother finds he can also make bakra picnies out of his loins his spirit is no longer with us!'

If a leaf had fallen from any of the great trees around the clearing it would have been heard in the silence. Lago saw the wrath on the face of his chief and knew he had gone too far. He stepped backwards twice without realizing what he had done. Tomaso rose slowly to his feet, and if there was ever a man who could show majesty and dignity in wrath, this was the man now.

Kisanka, had she been there would have been proud of her lord, but she was at home with the child. Her friend Kumse found her heart beating like drums at his magnificence as the chief slowly peeled off the cloth across his shoulder, leaving only the cloth from his waist down. This he made shorter by lifting the hem and tucking it into his waistband, so that now the calves of his great legs were exposed. All this he did slowly and carefully as if he wanted time. Then he looked out on the people around him.

'My people!' he began, 'I shall not ask you to be judges in this quarrel. I only wish to say that this is the secret of my life which he whom I call my blood brother speaks of in mocking tones. My father was killed by the bakra on the slave ship before my eyes, because the captain thought he would not fetch much metal. My pregnant mother died with the child still kicking in her belly when she was struck by the butt of a musket because she could not move fast. I spoke not of these things before, not even to Kisanka, because badness breeds badness, and a leader full of this evil weed cannot think for his people. One more set of words from my mouth . . . I have not betrayed you. To me the colour of the little one sleeping in his mother's arms in my hut, is the same as mine and thine. I see none of the bakra in him.'

Lago knew that the scales were now tipped against him. Tomaso's revelation of his parents and how they died, won the sympathy of the softhearted people. He watched, not without fear, as Tomaso stepped forward and around the fire and stood before him.

'What shall it be, my snake-tongued brother?' the chief asked him almost softly. Bullneck knew the crowd's ears were perched to hear his reply.

'Let it be machetes. Cripple as I am I fear thee not.'

'Lago is playing safe,' said old Tahta to himself.

'So be it!' replied Tomaso, and as he said the words a machete was placed in his hands.

Lago had already drawn his from its bark scabbard at his side. As the warriors pushed the people back so as to give the two fighting room, and Lago nervously and eagerly grasped the weapon tightly in his hand, Tomaso looked at his enemy, then threw down his weapon, and to the amazement of all, walked over towards the fire and took up a piece of hardwood which the flames had not yet caught. It was scarcely longer than the discarded machete.

Lago looked, expecting his blood brother to order him to do likewise, but when Tomaso faced him with the short staff in his hand without stipulations, the bullnecked one's spirit rose and the contempt with which the chief treated him in this choice of weapons before all, touched him to the quick. Tomaso's friends watched with open mouths firmly feeling that their chief had gone mad.

Lago, like Tomaso, had discarded the cloth over his shoulder, so that the chests and arms of both men were now completely bare. Women in panic of witnessing a killing grabbed their children and ran away while others covered their faces with their hands as both men began circling in a crouching attitude. Lago, his face fierce with hate, looked as if he would chop his opponent to pieces once he attacked. Tomaso, moving on bare toes, held each end of the short staff defensively.

Now Lago made a wild swing with his razor sharp machete, but Tomaso, keeping his back to the firelight, could see his enemy's eyes, and anticipated the move, deftly jumping out of the way in time. Again Lago slashed, and this time even Tomaso's speed on his feet could not save him from almost being brushed by the weapon. The crowd gasped.

Encouraged by his success, Lago slashed again, leaping forward as he did so, and the chief could do no more than turn the blow aimed at his shoulder, letting go one end of the wood as he did so. The glancing machete took a great slice off the staff, and Tomaso realized that his weapon could be no longer depended upon and would not stand another blow such as the last.

Lago thought his chance had come when he saw that Tomaso's chosen weapon was almost chopped in two. He pressed his man hard now, while Tomaso was forced to depend solely on the speed of his eyes and feet to save him from a lightning death. The crowd let out a murmur of fear as they saw that the wily Lago, by his constant harassing, had driven his chief closer and closer to the fire. Now he began to thrust at his enemy with the swordlike point of the machete, driving Tomaso back and back, hoping to trap his man for the kill with the help of the fire, but bullneck's anxiety to drive the other into the fire was his downfall for the glare from the great bonfire was only partly blocked by Tomaso's body, and when, as he was certain that Tomaso was trapped and made ready for the final lunge, the chief, with the speed of lightning, brought down the damaged end of the stick on the back of the man's hand holding the weapon. The glare blinded Lago and he let out a yell as the machete fell out his grasp.

Before he had time to retrieve the weapon, Tomaso struck again. The blow which seemed almost light to the delighted spectators, caught the bullnecked one on the side of his head, knocking him down. Dazed, Lago sat up and looked around and above him. Tomaso stood waiting. As Lago tried to get up from his sitting position, Tomaso's bare toes met him under the chin and he sat down again abruptly.

It was plain to the spectators that Tomaso, instead of killing his enemy, preferred to shame him. They began to giggle. Enraged, Lago sat up, turned, and was about to bend over his weapon when a terrific foot from behind set him sprawling face down. The crowd roared, and the women who had run away at the start of the fight, hearing the laughter, returned in haste to the scene. Now it was Tomaso's hand which was punishing the man who was his blood brother. Each time he attempted to stand up Tomaso gave his enemy a terrific slap on his cheek with his huge open hand, knocking the half dazed man to the ground. There was blood from the bruise on the side of his head. His right hand was useless, the thumb was smashed from Tomaso's first blow. He saw the crowd in a kind of blur as he went up and down from the terrific slaps his chief administered. Now his face felt like a great barrel. He wanted to beg for mercy; he opened his mouth, but now he was partly deaf because of the blows to the side of his face and the roar of the crowd, and he wasn't sure whether Tomaso knew if he was begging for mercy or not. Then he realized that he was no longer being slapped down. He half sat, half lay, on the warm earth with his head down, humiliated and beaten. He could not understand why the crowd above him were so quiet. He glanced up and saw that they were still there, standing as if they were a forest of trees when there was no wind.

Tomaso had raised his hands for silence and the crowd had stopped their laughter like one man for he thought he had heard something afar. His ears had not lied to him. It was the distant sound of the talking drum. Now the people also heard it and wondered if it had been speaking all the while and they had not heard it because of their laughter at Lago's downfall. Tomaso's warriors gathered around him, waiting for the translation to come through, so that they could get their orders. Many of the people could understand some of the words and were now trying to follow the message. Tomaso's lips moved as he read it, looking out on the hill above them as he did so. His hands were clenched. He read the words from the mouth of the talking drum a second time.

'*The boy is dead they have killed him.*'
'*. . . The boy is dead. The ants . . .*'

Lago slowly rose to his feet, his injuries and shame forgotten, as he saw the agony on the face of his enemy. The drums on the nearby hill replied:

'*. . . We heard you! We heard you! We heard the boy is dead; the ants ate him.*'

Like a man with the world suddenly thrust on his back, the chief, with drooping shoulders and bent head, turned to face the place where his chief's stool still rested with the elders standing behind it.

'My people,' he began, and now there were no clear and ringing tones in his voice. 'The drums bring us bad news. Quame is dead! Killed by the mouths of the ants.'

A terrible moan came from the multitude at Tomaso's words. It sounded like rushing wind in a treeless waste, and then all was still. In the silence that followed, Lago began to chuckle. It was unearthly, just as if the great crowd standing there had died on their feet and he was the only one left alive.

The chuckle of Lago's turned into a harsh laugh. It woke up the multitude of griefstricken mourners. It woke up Tomaso. He raised his head and looked across at Lago, and the man daubed with dirt and blood stopped his laughter because of the terrible look on Tomaso's face.

Silence now.

Tomaso walked over towards the standing elders and the chief's stool. Taking up the carved seat in both hands he walked back to where he had stood when the message from the drum came. The crowd watched him in silence with mixed feelings.

'Hear, O my people!' he began, 'I, Tomaso, Chief of Twin Sisters, ask you to witness, that from the time the words come out of my mouth I am no longer your chief and leader. I now return the stool I hold in my hand to the elders who long ago, with your consent, gave it to me. Now that I have given up the chieftainship, my successor can revoke the law which I had made this night. It is the rule that the law once made by a chief cannot be revoked by himself. But hear me, O people! This is not the only reason why I shall be your chief no longer. I have been fooled by the bakra, and a chief who allows himself to be fooled forfeits his right to lead his people.' He paused, and there were many in the crowd who could not prevent the water coming to their eyes for they felt that his shame was theirs also. But there were others who disliked this man who tried to change the old laws.

Tomaso continued: 'I shall not divide you against each other, my people, and whoever you choose as your leader and chief, I will serve and obey as long as you have elected him and his orders are just.'

Now he walked with the stool to the standing elders and placed the seat at the feet of the oldest of these.

'May the Great Spirit be with you, O Men of Wisdom!' he said to them; then, taking up the cloth he had discarded for the fight, he made ready to leave.

'Now I go to avenge Quame,' he said, and without giving a glance in Lago's direction, he waved to the many who waved and wished him well and walked out into the darkness with his crowd of tried and faithful warriors behind him.

Lago was no fool. He knew that it would take time for the people to forget his disgrace at the hand of their beloved Tomaso, and even though their former chief was also in disgrace they would not readily accept him. He was young. He could afford to wait. He knew an ailing elder, the brother of the dead chief, who had spoken against Tomaso on the night of the lawmaking. The man would be glad to be chief. And he was already almost dead. His kidney was bad, his face was at times puffy and his ankles were already swollen. The old rascal Tahta had once told him that the old chief's brother would not live very long. So mused Lago.

So when the moon came again M'Ango, brother of the chief before Tomaso, became the new chief, with Lago's full backing.

A week after the boy Quame had been given live to the ants, much to the shame and dismay of the Man-of-God who had pledged otherwise, the slaves of the plantations all over the island were telling a strange tale:

The Spirits disguised, had gone to the house of the Master who had punished the boy by giving him to the ants. They, being Spirits, had turned themselves into ants and gone through the locked door by way of the crevices underneath. Then they had turned themselves into the overseer and one of the fieldslaves. The two then woke the Master, and told him that some of his slaves were caught running away. Being Spirits, they had the power to make the Master follow them to the stable where his horse was already saddled, and being Spirits, they easily kept up with the galloping horse with its rider until they stopped in the woods near a big tree. There the Spirits ordered the Master to come off his horse, which he did, though he shook with fear, for now he knew that he had been tricked by Spirits to the place where he had given the boy to the ants. The Spirits had ordered the Master to lie stretched out into the ants nest and the master had no will-power to disobey, for though he was not staked out like the boy, the Spirits made him feel as if he was tied down. That was why, when they found what was left of him the next day, there were no marks but the teeth of ants.

So ran the tale, and the bakra on the plantations could not get a different version in spite of their efforts. What made them more puzzled than ever was the care which the master usually took to protect himself before he went to bed. And where were the guards and patrol? asked the bakra. After all the Maroons would have to travel some forty miles to do this deed. And the door of the house was still locked the next morning. It could have been through the big window but why should the Master go through the window of his own house?

Tomaso and Jacob returned from their mysterious trip a week after the mystery of the plantation, but the people were told by the drum beforehand that Quame was avenged.

Three

'Ka.'

'Yes, Tamba.'

'Why am I not like thee and Ta?'

'But you are like me and thy father, child.'

'But Ka, look at my arms about thy neck, they are not the same as thine.'

'It is but a colouring, child.'

'But it is not thy colouring, Ka.'

'No no, Tamba.'

'And it is not like my father's colouring.'

'No, child. But . . .'

'Why, Ka?'

'I . . . I . . . cannot . . . Look Tamba, thy face is just like thy father's. Thy head and little body, all is like thy Ta Tomaso's.'

'But my hair is white like Tahta's, Ka, and I am not like my father because my colour is not like his. Why is this?'

'Listen, Tamba.'

'I listen, Ka.'

'Worry not thy father with this question.'

'But he could tell me why, Ka. My father knows everything, more than Grandpa Tahta, more than anyone else in Twin Sisters. Does he not?'

'Yes, child, thy father is full of wisdom.'

'He could lift the whole of this mountain in his hands, could he not, Ka?'

'He is a mighty warrior, Tamba.'

'And if he shouted at Hurrican, the bad wind, would not Hurrican run away and hide?'

'Perhaps he would, picni, perhaps he would.'

'Do they call my father ''The Mighty Asunu,'' and ''The

Lion," Ka?'

'Yes, Tamba, because he is strong and brave.'

'Shall I see an Asunu and a Lion one day, Ka?'

'Perhaps child, if you go back to thy father's country.'

'I have an extra finger like my father, have I not Ka?'

'Yes, Tamba, here it is, a little extra finger just like thy father and his father before him, and like his father's father whose name was Tamba like thine.'

'Shall I be a brave warrior like my father and grandfather Tamba, Ka?'

'You will my child. Now run outside and play with the things Grandfather Tahta made for thee.'

The new chief brought many changes. Lago monopolized the old man's ears, and since the latter was secretly afraid of the bullnecked one, he became merely a figurehead. The people were blinded by the new era which their new leader introduced with nightly festivals, feasting and pageantry. Warriors were taken from watchpoints, traditionally guarded day and night in Tomaso's time, merely to partake in a show or to build new huts, eating places, or booths, either for the chief and his new friends, or to give glamour to forthcoming festivals. Men and women who should have been working at their allotments were encouraged to sit up nightly for some unnecessary ceremonial fete, invented by Lago to gain him popularity, so that many who would have been normally awake before the birds, were still tired and asleep until the sun was in the middle of the sky. Many, especially the young people, praised the new regime for providing them with so many nights of entertainment, and for not being scolded for idleness, as Tomaso would have done. Even the new refugees were neglected now. It was Tomaso's custom to welcome the newcomers personally, and see that arrangements were made for sharing the huts of villagers whom he knew had space and could accept such guests without discomfort to themselves, until he, with the assistance of a crowd of willing hands, could build and present the refugees with their own houses. Next, they would find the new Maroons lots for their vegetables and then there would be a general turnout for the clearing, digging and planting. Even seeds and plants would be presented to them. Then in their spare time they would go to the Cave-of-Talks at one end of the great clearing if it was wet, or out in the open if it was dry, and there they would be given lessons on the new language which was not really new. For out of the many dialects in the language of the Bantu the early Maroons had created a common tongue, easy to understand by any son of Africa. Here and there were improvised words, either created by the old leaders themselves, or culled from the Spanish, and later, the English.

Tomaso, his loyal friends and warriors, watched with dismay as all these customs were either half-heartedly carried out, or neglected. Headmen, whom Lago thought would not be frightened of him, were dismissed, and untried ones took their places. Officers found that they could no longer insist on discipline among their warriors if the former were known to be friends of Tomaso. Wisely, the ex-chief's band of veteran warriors were not taken from him, for Lago knew that none of those fifty-odd would have served under any but Tomaso as long as he was alive, and the bullnecked one and his doting chief knew also that there were no better trained men in guerrilla warfare than these. Tomaso's men did not do the normal watches. Their chosen task was to go down into the plains and rescue slaves from the plantations, to be ready at a signal to travel long distances with great speed, and to endure abnormally long periods of thirst and hunger in doing so. It was said by the people of the hills that there was no part of the great gorge from 'The-Place-of-the-Big-Jump' down, which Tomaso and his band of warriors could not ascend or descend. Always quick at finding apt names for people and things, the people of Twin Sisters named the band the Spirit Men.

Jacob, the light-skinned warrior was next in command to Tomaso, and when he was absent, Tahta, if he could be spared to patrol, would take his place under the ex-chief. For old though he was, Tahta could compete with any of this band of marksmen and it was said that he could out-trot any man half his age. And many of these warriors had learnt the art of bushfighting from this amazing old man.

Tomaso sat on his haunches with the boy Tamba standing between his knees, looking out with his strange eyes on the scene before them. They were at the great clearing where every important affair had always taken place whenever a great level space was required. Kisanka was there sitting flat on the ground beside her lord and their son. A year had passed since Tomaso had abdicated, and now the former disgruntled ones began to discover that the new leadership had not brought them the wonderful things they had anticipated. The village had begun to pay the price of neglect. Food was not plentiful, and though rain had not fallen for a long time they knew this was not the cause. Houses were overcrowded. Waterholes had not been cleaned and made ready to catch the water from the many bamboo gutters Tomaso had had made for conveying precious rainwater from the eaves of each hut to mud and stone-built containers. Many gutters had been blown down by a strong wind months before and had not been repaired. Even the great communal waterholes made with stone and lime, burnt on kilns locally, had not been cleaned. It was the custom for the people to dam the tiny spring which fed these crude reservoirs so that the water ran along another route while they cleaned the accumulation of mud and debris at regular intervals. This had not been done and now that there was a drought, there were only dead leaves and mud almost to the rim of the two great waterholes, and the precious dribble from the partly-dry spring had to be caught day and night by relays of villagers with gourds and great hollow joints of bamboo.

But today was the day for *Junkunu*, and, as the sun moved towards the far away blue horizon which some took to be the sea, the crowds came from all sides into the great clearing. For though they were now weary of festivities, Junkunu came to the village only once every year, and the legend about the ceremony was too great to be ignored.

Tomaso's son, white as a bakra, with cotton colour hair, was a sight which excited the crowd, in spite of their usually good manners. It was rarely that they had the chance to see the strange child with eyes which were unlike any other, and they could not help gaping. Some came to pay their respects to the family, for they were still held in high esteem by the

72

people. Tomaso, proud of his child, would boast as fathers always do of their promising offspring; and of course, even if those who came to greet them seemed a little awed; they had to see the extra finger which the child had just like his father.

More and more people came towards the Cave-of-Talks end of the clearing where Tomaso and his family sat, to pay their respects; and Lago, sitting not far away with his chief, scowled, as he saw that his enemy had not lost his popularity even after his downfall. Something more would have to be done, he thought. But what?

The drums began. Little Tamba had never seen this festival before. He jumped with excitement, and for the first time since his arrival, forgot to feel embarrassed at the multitude of eyes staring at him. His parents, sensitive to his discomfort were glad that the spectacle had taken all eyes to the display before them, though they did not show how they felt at any time during the ordeal.

Tomaso explained to the child how this Junkunu festival came about.

'Long, long ago, before the measuring of time, in the land of their fathers some strange white animals, now known as horses, invaded the land, with riders on their backs. They must have been spirit horses, evil ones, for they were white, and white was the colour of bad spirits. The white horses and riders swept through the land, and after them came drought, famine and death. Even the great trees withered, and others would not bear fruit. All over Africa there was a great cry wherever the horses went. At night they would run on three legs instead of four, and anyone who saw them would die. So it went. Then in one of the tribes was an Old Man of Wisdom. He was so old that even the oldest had never seen him other than as a very old man. He called together the chiefs and elders and said: "Get your carvers to carve a great mask like the skeleton head of one of the white monsters. Paint this skeleton head white, and when it is complete, let your carvers carve the heads of all the animals in the forest. Give these heads to your dancers, and the skeleton head of the spirit monster must be impaled on a pole, and the men who carry the pole must be covered in white cloth — two men, one holding on to the back of the other. Let them dance to a mighty sound of drums and singing, with all the animal-head dancers following behind. Then I will come and invoke my curse upon the evil one, and the people shall throw worthless things at it as it dances. And the white monster spirits will stand afar and see how the people despise even the image of them, and they will be ashamed and depart from the land.''

'The Old Man of Wisdom had spoken truly. That night water poured from the skies. The badness was washed away. The trees blossomed again and bore fruit. The spirits of death departed into the forest ashamed and defeated.

'So ran the legend,' Tomaso told his son. 'And so to this day many tribes in Africa, like us, remember this the Junkunu festival, with the dancing skull and jawbone of a horse leading the procession.'

The young albino looked at the dancing skull and jawbone of some long dead horse as it swayed and pranced around the great arena with the black feet of the two men under the white cloth making a comical show as substitute for the fore and hind legs of the mythical monster.

The day after the Twin Sisters Junkunu festival the rain came.

It was three days after Tomaso's appearance with his family at the festival, that a dozen children and a half a dozen adults took ill with a terrible fever, due perhaps to contaminated water. Within a week the illness had reached fifty, and ten had died. A whisper began to circulate around the village. There was no need to guess who started it:

It is that dundoes child.'

'His eyes bring a curse on all.'

'He is the cause of these illnesses and deaths.'

'We must ask Tomaso to send him away from the village. Banish him. His mother, too. Tomaso may stay, but his evil colour son must go.'

'The chief says it is true. It is the strange picni who is causing this illness and death. Is he not white like the bakra horse of the legend?'

'Like the bakra who made us slaves!'

'White is evil, he must be banished from the village.'

'Here they come, Tomaso, my son! Look at them! Goat-heads who call themselves elders, with mouths which can only speak like the talking-birds who say what their masters teach them to say. Spirit of my fathers! Even at my age I would have liked to meet them with a battleaxe in my hand. I swear, Tomaso, if I had my way, I would waylay them as they come up the path with their mouths and heads full of Lago's words. By my spirit, I would split their coconuts in halves to see if there is much water inside.'

'Hold, O Father-of-Men! Hold! Thy temper will cause thee to do a war-dance in a moment. Let the foolish ones come. You and I, aye, even Kisanka knew that they would be coming bearing the words of Lago. They will say what he wants them to say.'

The five men sheepishly came to a stop as soon as they were a dozen yards from where Tomaso and old Tahta stood. Kisanka came to the door behind them holding the child's hand. The elders seemed as if now they had arrived they wished they hadn't. Each looked at the other hoping to find an opening. Tahta, with acid on tongue, began to mock them.

'The spirits be with you, O dumb ones with heads of coconuts! Has Lago castrated you? For now that I can look closer, I can see that you are not men. Nay, not women either! For women have tongues, and you are as dumb as the stones beneath your frightened feet. Aye, even your feet show fear when they reach the domain of your lord, Tomaso. That is why they will not take you any further, O dog picnies!'

The old man's rage was getting almost out of control now. The men stood looking down on their feet, while Tomaso, with arms folded across his mighty chest looked almost pityingly at them. In their embarrassment they had even forgotten to greet their old chief. This was almost unpardonable on the hills, but Tomaso knew that it was not on account of discourtesy and did not rebuke them. Not so old Tahta.

'You, Jabus, and you, Klube,' shouted the old man,

pointing to two of the five, 'Who was it who took the bands of slavery off your necks? Was it not the chief who you now climb the hill to talk against? Have you no shame? Have you no courage?'

The two men were almost in tears because of their shame.

'We did not want to come, Tahta,' said one. And the breaking of his silence seemed to open the mouths of his companions.

'We have nothing against Tomaso. He has been good to us,' said another. Now it seemed as if it would have been better if they had not spoken for their words made old Tahta dance with rage.

'You droppings of a vulture! You vomit of a sick bush-dog! What has his wife and infant done to you! Are they not innocent of Lago's mischief as their lord? Aye, we know what your new master has sent you to say—that Tomaso must send away his wife and child from the village, for the child has brought a curse on the people. Is not this your message. O coconut heads? And light as this message be, it has taken eunuchs to the number of fingers of my eating hand to take it to Tomaso! And even then he and I must help you to unload it from out of your useless mouths!'

The men were cowed but angry at the abuses.

'Aye, I see the shadow of anger in your eyes, O picni men! Why not show some courage and reach for a weapon?' taunted Tahta.

Now Tomaso placed his hand gently on the shoulder of his raging-mad friend.

'Nay, Tahta! Nay. It is I who should speak to them thus,' said the ex-chief wearily. 'But Kisanka and I have talked of this thing. We shall go. Kisanka and I with our child. We shall seek a home in the friendly hills far from this village.' He looked at the embarrassed deputation. 'Go back,' he said sternly. 'Go back to your master and say you stood like dumb animals before me, unable to give the message he had loaded into your mouths. But I, Tomaso, knowing the words before they were born, even as the lie was hatched from the belly of my blood brother, had made my plans. I, with my wife and child shall go from the village into the hills, but we shall come whenever we wish. And the child shall walk like the warrior's son he is and none shall prevent us.'

The men, glad to be let off so lightly, were ready to beat a hasty retreat.

'We hear you, lord Tomaso. We are sorry about this thing,' said one.

'Aye, we are sorry, Tomaso, but it had to be done,' said another.

'Aye, and my old foot is asking me when I shall send it towards your backside, which would give you the right start down the hillside, O foul nest of carrion-birds!' screamed Tahta, moving forward threateningly.

The men turned and beat a retreat with undignified haste down the hill.

As the committee of elders disappeared, Tahta, embarrassed because he had made the error of swearing before Kisanka and his young friend Tamba, took the child by the hand and walked him towards a clump of woods behind the house.

The minute Kisanka saw that she was alone with her husband, her dignity and self control left her. As he sat on a stool by the doorway and rested his face wearily between his great palms, the girl knelt down before him, clutching one of his arms.

'Let me go, Tomaso. Let me go,' she cried, the water suddenly filling her eyes. 'I will take little Tamba with me far away from here. Then the people will want you to stay. Thy place is here, my husband! Here in this house on the hill right in the midst of your people! Not far away in the forest in a little hut—alone, except for your wife and child, just as if there is shame on your face.'

He tried to stop her flow of words by placing his hand over her mouth, but in her excitement she firmly pushed it aside without knowing what she had done.

'It is I who have brought these sorrows on thee, O my husband, and it is just that I should go. We shall not starve, the child and I. I can use a hoe and plant patches of corn and beans, cassava and sweet potatoes. Have I not done this like the other women when your arms were needed elsewhere? Stay Tomaso! Stay where the people can see your face, and know that you are always near when . . .'

'Hush woman!'

So harsh and strong was the command, that Kisanka who was blinded by the eyewater, had to stare hard through the mist to make sure this was indeed the voice of her husband. And when it was confirmed, she looked a picture of bewilderment, which quickly turned into shame. For through all the years of their courtship and marriage he had never spoken to her as harshly as this. And then she remembered how she had pushed his hand aside when he would have stopped her speaking. She let go of his arm, and now, like a penitent, she knelt with hands in front of her and head bowed, too overcome with shame to speak, so she did not see the tenderness on his face.

'Kisanka, my Little Shadow!'

The gentle tone after his harsh command made the water come once more to the girl's eyes.

'Speak, O my husband,' she replied in a whisper but she did not look up.

'You have never believed me,' he said, still gently, but there was hurt in his tone.

'Tomaso, my spirit, what have I said to make thee feel that there is disbelief between me and thee?'

There was alarm in her voice as she raised her head and placed one hand on his knee, then looking straight into his eyes, she said simply: 'I would rather die than live without faith in thee and thy words.'

He looked back into her eyes, but it was not for confirmation of her words, for he knew by her voice that she meant every syllable.

'And yet, Little Shadow . . . and yet you would speak of going away—alone with our son, while I stay behind?' He shook his head slowly. 'Nay, nay, My Spirit. If I live to the age of yonder fireball; if the snake tongue of our enemy makes mischief as big as these mountains, one on the other, and all was loaded on top of my head, I would not part from thee.' He thought for a little, then continued: 'When the great monster called Death enters the door of our hut, Kisanka, only then shall we part. Now I have spoken.'

She sprang forward and hid her wet face on his great chest,

too grateful and happy to do anything more than to shed more water from her eyes.

They were both sitting holding hands as if they were still courting when Tahta came from behind the house with the little Tamba to say that the warriors known as the Spirit Men which they both led and belonged to, were coming up the hill.

Kisanka rose and took her son into the house with her so as to be out of the way of this man-talk, while the ex-chief waited calmly for their coming. It seemed as they came to the yard and lined themselves up behind Jacob, the mulatto, that they were all there, the fifty-odd men renowned for their courage and endurance.

'Greeting, O Chief!' cried Jacob, stepping forward. 'We have come to ask a boon of you.'

They were as if they came prepared for battle with their arms strung around their powerful half-nude bodies, shining with healthy perspiration.

'Greeting, O Jacob, my brother and friend, and to you, the rest of my brothers also,' replied Tomaso. 'But you have forgotten again that I am no longer chief, and so a boon worthwhile is not mine to give, since I have no authority.' But there was no rebuke in the leader's voice as he said this.

'We have no chief but thee, O Tomaso!' cried Jacob indignantly.

'We acknowledge none but thee, O Chief,' cried the warriors almost together. It was always thus when Tomaso reminded his loyal band of his position, and he knew by experience that nothing he could say would make them change their minds.

'Though I have no boon to give, my brothers,' said Tomaso gently, 'my ears will take in your words just the same.'

'We heard that the snake has struck once more, O chief.'

'That is so, Jacob, my brother.'

'Our feet are ready to stamp on his head and on any who like his talk, my Leader!'

'This is good talk,' cried Tahta before Tomaso had a chance to reply to Jacob's threat of civil war.

'What! O Jacob, what has your wrath done to your head?' asked their leader sorrowfully. 'Must we make war between us, smiting those we are here to rescue and protect?' He turned to Tahta. 'Shame on your words, O Father-of-Men. How could you call this good-talk?'

Jacob and his men looked crestfallen. 'It is true, O Tomaso, my chief, this badness they have done to thee has made us into madmen. And it is hard that we must stand by as if we were chained while all this badness to thee and thine grows bigger and bigger.' Anger and frustration were in Jacob's tone. 'But we have not yet asked the boon, O my Chief, for, knowing the ways of your mind, we came to thee armed with a less difficult thing for thee to give your consent to. This is the boon we ask: that we your special band of warriors be allowed to go with thee, with our women and children, in whatever part of the forest you have chosen in your banishment. Then we shall feel that we are close to our chief and leader, and we have not forsaken him in his time of need.'

Tomaso was so moved by this gesture of love and loyalty that he could not speak for a while. When he did his voice control was not without flaws.

'It is a great thing, this you called a boon, my brothers. It is I to whom you have given something. What you have given has made me strong, and the weight of Lago's lie is no longer heavy on my spirit, for you have shown me that your spirits also have taken some of the burden. I and mine shall feed on this when we are alone. For I cannot accept your offer, O my brothers.'

The men who had been cheered by the thought of sharing the exile of their leader looked at him with dismay because of his last words

'You are warriors, my brothers, but you are also men with wives and picnies,' continued Tomaso. 'What will your wives and families say to this thing?' he asked. 'Are they not like all other women, fearful of danger for their families, if not for themselves? You are men, and you feel there is nothing in this lie, but will your women think so now when they all have sickness and death walking amongst them?'

The warriors looked as if they had not thought of what their women's reaction would be until now.

'We would soon make them see their folly, O my Chief,'

said a stalwart, brightening at his idea of persuasion.

'My woman would not forget it if she said nay,' said another.

'We will take care of that, Tomaso, my Chief!' said a third.

Tomaso held up his hand for silence. 'Nay, nay, my brothers!' he cried. 'It would be one bad thing on the head of another if your women should feel the weight of your hands, or you feel the weight of their tongues because of this. Besides would it not seem that I have taken you away from guarding the hills to plot a war on the new chief? Lago would seize this to make a mighty thing from it, my friends. No, I and my wife and child must go alone.

Now old Tahta, quiet all this while because of the shame he had suffered when he was rebuked, moved up to face his leader.

'Tomaso,' he began quietly. 'Once I was a true father of men: wife, sons, daughters, grandchildren, numbering a family as large as the fingers of each of your hands and all of your toes as well. This slavery came, and this curse has taken all, either by death or to some place I know not where. And when you took me out of the bakra hands and brought me to these hills, I was alone as if I had never had a woman nor a seed from my loins. You brought me here, Tomaso. You gave me life when you defended me, and gave me a son in thyself and a daughter in Kisanka, and now a grandson in the little one. Hear me then, my son, before witnesses. If you should drive me from your side because of this foolish talk, or any other, then my blood will be on your hands, for I swear by Nyankupon, the Lord of the Sky, that I shall go down this night to the village and challenge Lago to a battle to the death.'

All listened with respectful silence as the old man with watery eyes had his say, giving a glimpse of his life they had not known before. At last Tomaso spoke.

'This is indeed a day of baskets of badness and cartloads of goodness!' he cried. Turning to old Tahta, he placed his hand on the old man's shoulder, then he called:

'Kisanka!'

The girl answered the call and came from inside the house holding the hand of their child.

'Kisanka, this badness by the tongue of my blood brother was no badness at all,' Tomaso shouted to his wife. 'Just now, all these, my brothers, came to ask to share in our banishment, with their wives and children as well. This I could not accept because it would not be just to their wives, if not to themselves, also. But our Father Tahta has sworn to be with us or die, and since his spirit is now part of ours, how could we let him die?'

Kisanka, graceful as ever, with her fine curls combed into one sweep upwards, and held there by a piece of barkcloth, showed her gratitude. 'It was a great offer to make, O good Warriors,' she said. 'Now my sadness will not be so big, for my husband has true friends.' She turned to Tahta. 'My head grows big at hearing of your oath, O my father!' And perhaps it was because her eyes were getting misty why the girl hurriedly retreated into the house holding the hand of little Tamba.

'You have dug the ground from under our feet, O my Chief,' said Jacob when Kisanka had disappeared. 'We still have one hope that we pray will bring a nod from your head.'

'Speak, O Jacob, my brother,' replied the ex-chief.

'Let us each and every warrior and none else, be the builders of your new house, the diggers of your garden, and the makers of the path to the place of your choice. And that we, the warriors, shall always be honoured with thee as our leader.'

'Like Kisanka's of a while ago, my head grows big at your offer, my brothers, and a house built by your kind hands, and a garden planted with your sweat will be a mighty gift. As for being your leader, I can promise this: I shall not give this up, unless it be your wish.'

The men gave a shout of joy at Tomaso's words, and those in the village, hearing the noise, felt ashamed, but were mostly willing to satisfy their consciences with the thought that their ex-chief and his family had friends.

Only Lago and his puppet chief felt angry and worried by the cheering which came from the house of their enemy.

The exiles chose a place higher up in the hills a mile from the village. The Spirit Men, true to their word made a path through the thick growth right to the door of the isolated house—a house with three rooms with an annex for Tahta. Within two weeks, Tomaso and his family, living in a hurriedly erected leanto near the site, were able to move into their new, comparatively palatial home, and in a month, path, house and vegetable patch were complete.

Kisanka was pleased at the result of the warriors' effort, but when they all went, and only Tomaso, herself, and Tahta, remained with the child, she could not help feeling the shame of being away from the frequent laughter, singing and general noise of the village, and at night as the fireflies darted through the thick trees around the house, and the toads in some hole between fern-covered rocks bawled in the way of their kind, she thought how deep must be the wound of her brave husband, and blamed herself for his downfall. For it seemed to her that every one of Tomaso's troubles came into being because of her. She began to brood, searching in her mind for ways in which her man would be accepted by the people once more as chief, and the young child accepted by all as a normal child instead of someone to be feared.

Tahta was always busy at the bedside of the sick, mixing his knowledge of bush medicine with that which he learnt from the bakra when he was the slave assistant of his doctor master.

But as the sickness decreased and the dying became less, he spared himself time to be with his 'grandson', teaching him all his little brain could take; and it seemed to the old man that there could be no brighter pupil than the boy. He noticed Kisanka's restlessness at times, and when she complained of continued headaches as the trouble for this, he prescribed a remedy he had formulated for her when he first knew her and she had suffered from pains in the head. It was the leaves and dried seeds of the pimento boiled together with a couple of other herbs, and which, when used to wet the hair, acted like bay rum, and because of the pimento leaves had a similar smell as that which is made with bay leaves. Kisanka used it daily as she had done for years until the child's birth, not only because of her headaches, but also on account of the strong but pleasant smell which it gave to her hair.

In the meanwhile, Lago made good use of the lessening of illness and death from the strange fever in the village, claiming that this was because they had driven out the ex-chief and his child with the bakra colour and strange eyes. And, of course, there were many who believed him. But Tomaso would let none feel that he was afraid of their opinion. At times, when he was home, he would take his son by his hand through the village and back, and though little children from afar shouted some things which the child could not understand, no adult, not even Lago, dared to come out openly. Women hurried by paying their respects, and worrying afterwards about the abrupt way they had treated their former chief. Men who were not among Tomaso's special warriors would look defiant as they spoke to the father and praised the growth of his son. While the leader's own warriors would show their disgust and disbelief of the child's hoodoo by lifting the youngster to one of their naked shoulders while they walked and talked gaily through the village, and in each case, it was only Tomaso's insistence which prevented these men taking father and son to their homes.

Jacob, knowing the child suffered loneliness in isolation, took his life in his hands to bring back a little pup with black shiny body and white paws, from one of his periodic missions on the plantations, to present to the son of his friend, much to Tamba's great delight, and the gratitude of his parents.

While Lago ruled through the ailing chief, the wily Tahta did his utmost to spread mistrust between the sick man and the man who was using him whenever he was called to the chief's bedside, which was often enough. And although Lago suspected the old bushdoctor of making mischief, he knew that to bar the best *doctor* in the village from visiting the sick, would be to bring him under suspicion; so here bullneck's hands were tied.

And Tahta, knowing that the longer he could help the chief to live the less good it would do Lago, did all in his power with doses of bush medicine which did seem at times to help the affected kidneys. Within a few months after Tomaso went into exile, the chief, though still in fear of Lago and doing what he was told, showed that he did not trust his sponsor any more in many ways, and only fear of the chiefmaker prevented open defiance.

'Mother Ka!'

'Speak, my child.'

'I threw another of my old teeth on the roof of the house to Brer Rat, and I asked him to bring me new ones each time they came out, remember, Mother Ka?'

'Yes, Tamba, when I was a child I did the same, and so did thy father, and Brer Rat did bring us new teeth.'

'Some of my new ones are coming up now, Mother Ka. Look into my mouth.'

'Yes, child, I can see them, they will be nice strong teeth when they have finished growing.'

'Mother Ka.'

'Yes, my child?'

'You promised long ago that when Brer Rat gave me my new teeth, you would let me go to the village to fetch water if our waterhole went dry. Now it is dry. Can I go?'

It has come! The thing which I feared all this while! He will be hurt by the way they will treat him if he goes alone, yet how can I prevent it? His father has said the child cannot be hidden from this badness about him all the time. But how shall I bear it? 'Did I promise, child?'

'Yes, Mother Ka. Long ago I sat on thy lap and asked when I would be allowed to go to the village to fetch water for thee, since you are lame, and you said when my new teeth came.'

'But I did not remember you would still be so small, Tamba, and the journey is long to the village waterhole.'

'But I would not mind it, Mother Ka. I would run all the way down to the village.'

I cannot find any reason for stopping him. O, I wish his father was here! The spirit of fear will ride on my shoulder when he goes, for I know they will not treat him well.

'Grandpa Tahta says there are many picnies of my size in the village who fetch gourds of water for their mothers. Perhaps I shall see some of them, Mother Ka, then I shall make friends. Can I play with them a little before I return with my gourd of water?'

He has forgotten the colour of his face, poor child.

'Perhaps tomorrow I will let thee go, Tamba.' *His father might be here by then; or the rain might come.* 'And if I let thee go, and the children of the village are not nice to thee, because you—you are a stranger, then you must come back to mother as fast as thy feet will carry thee.'

'Oh, but I went with my father to the village, Mother Ka, and it was good. A warrior took me on his shoulder and carried me through the village.'

'But, Tamba, there are many who may not be like the good warrior; even picnies.'

'But they will like me when I speak with them, Mother Ka, and tell them of my own little house which I built all by myself in the forest behind the big almond tree, and about Bangie, my dog. And perhaps they will wish to come up here to see my house and my dog and we shall play games.'

'So you still wish to go, Tamba?'

'O, yes, Ka. I shall be happy when I fetch thee the gourd of water and show thee that I am growing up to be a big boy.'

It is no use. He has his mind on doing this thing, and it is better to let him know now. But the pain of waiting!

'Well, go then, my son. Will Bangie go with thee?'

'No, Mother Ka, let Bangie stay with thee till I return.'

He walked and trotted all the way down to the village, excited at the prospect of meeting others of his own age and making friends, eager to boast as children always do about things they feel are worthy of praise and admiration.

His upper body was bare, and the lower half was clothed only in narrow loin cloth of bark. His face had escaped from its cherublike roundness of babyhood, but not altogether. He had a definite and suddenly pointed chin. His nose was flat at the bridge, and somewhat wide like his father's, and his lips were full. His white woolly hair was allowed to grow fairly high on his head. In the bright light he squinted slightly and sometimes his strange coloured eyes were apt to seem out of focus. With his bark encased gourd hanging by a strong handle from his young shoulders he trotted along. Strangely enough, in spite of his colour handicap, he was far from an ugly child. His new upper front teeth would show a neat little space between them when he laughed, and his voice was clear and strong. But there were few, who were ever present to see that the child was normal in every way but his colour.

Now as the boy went forward, the thought of the many things Tahta had taught him, assuring him that there was no other child in the village with so great a knowledge of woodcraft, made him feel he would win friends, since he was willing to share all his knowledge with them. Now he was on the outskirts of the village and his heart beat with the tramp of his firm bare feet. From afar, the picnies spotted him and became attracted because of his colour. They began to follow at a distance, and he suddenly became conscious of the difference between them. He walked on now, aware of hostile glances at him over fences as he passed, and these were from adults as well as children. A sudden coldness came over his young body, though the sun was shining and the day was as warm as usual. He glanced back, and now saw with alarm that there was no look of friendship in any of the faces behind him. Out of the little stockade-like fences they came as he passed, to swell the band of hostile children following him. He had no illusions now. His dream of friendship had evaporated, leaving him with bewilderment. He went forward with his heart battering itself from the fear which took hold of him. The crowd of children came silently on behind him. Adults hurried out of his path as if a plague was on his face—resentful and speechless.

'Dundoes!'

A young voice from behind screamed out the word, and the boy, though he had never before heard himself called by the name, instinctively associated it with his colour. It made him almost halt in his tracks and look around wildly as if he was seeking some way of escaping. He went on, with his nerves keyed up almost to breaking point, but he would not look back even when the sound of bare feet on ground told him that the hosts of children were getting larger and nearer.

'Picni-with-the-old-man's-hair!' shouted a voice.

The albino winced as if someone had struck him with a stone.

'Black bakra!'

'Spirit!'

'Picni-with-the-old-man's-hair!'

'Dundoes!'

'Black bakra!'

The noise was deafening now. They screamed out the names, one after the other. The fear in the strange child's heart was great now that the crowd grew into a mighty band. They ran past him so as to walk backwards in front of him wounding him with their hated names. They tried to block his path, but gave in when he came near.

'Black bakra!'

'Spirit!'

'Dundoes!'

'Picni-with-the-old-man's-hair!'

They laughed at the bewilderment and shame on his face. They mocked the whiteness of his skin and the pinkish colour of his eyes, but all through the attack, there was fear in their eyes. Fear of this stranger who was like no-one they had ever seen before, and whom, it was said, had caused the illness and death of many of the kin and perhaps the parents of many amongst the crowd. They forgot that he was the son of Tomaso. The father was not with the boy so it was impossible for them to associate him in their minds with this strange monster.

'Dundoes!'

'Duppy!'

'Black bakra!'

'Picni-with-the-old-man's-hair!'

They screamed out the names they gave him, and it seemed to the child that the whole world of children was following him. They pulled at the gourd he carried, and by the time he had reached the waterhole, they were exhausted from their efforts at mocking him. As he bent down to fill his gourd, they picked up handfuls of mud and flung it over his bare white body. His strange eyes flashed, but he must have seen how hopeless it was to fight so many, for he lifted his full gourd and held it close to his chest. Then he turned his face towards the hellpath once more. By this time they were hoarse with their cries and insults, and when some of the adults came out to see what the commotion was about and saw that it was the child whom it was said brought the curse to the village, they did not call off the tormentors, for they hoped that he would learn his lesson and never return to their waterhole. Yet there were some who would have taken the boy's part because he was the child and the son of the brave Tomaso, but they were afraid of the wrath of Lago. Had he not told them they should have nothing to do with that child of misfortune? Did he not say the boy's eyes alone could, by one stare, cause disaster to any one? So they either pretended they had not seen the mob of picnies tormenting the little dundoes, or they called or dragged away their own children and left the others to enjoy themselves.

'Dundoes!'

'Black bakra!'

'Duppy!'

'Picni-with-the-old-man's-hair!'

He walked between rows of his tormentors neither looking to the right or to the left, clutching his little gourd of water to his white naked breast. His eyes full of fear and shame, his lips fighting hard to keep from trembling.

'Black bakra!'

'Dundoes!'

'Duppy!'

They were now mad with excitement. The child was filled with terror. They wanted him to break out into a run, but he kept on walking though without knowing that he was staggering along the path because he was partly blinded with eyewater. The road seemed endless. He did not know why he would not run. He felt it would be quicker, for he was a good runner, but he still walked on with children before, beside, and behind him.

'Greetings Dundoes!'

'Greetings Duppy!'

'Good-day picni-with-the-old-man's-hair'!

He did not know they had left him. He walked uncertainly along the narrow path up the hill, still blind by unwelcome eyewater. He did not remember that he still had his gourd of water. He did not know how far he was from the crowded village. At last he came in sight of his lonely home. His mother, waiting anxiously for his coming, saw her son clutching his gourd to his breast, now with dried, vacant eyes, and feet which took drunken steps along the narrow path, fouled and mud-spattered from head to toes. Her spirit cried out in resentment against the injustice of a child born with such a handicap as this in a village where a white face had always signified the enemy. That was what Tomaso had said. The people of the hills had learned to look upon a white face with fear and hate. It was their nightmare—white faces, associated with slave pens, beatings, tortures, and death— and now converted into another sign of ill omen. So her man had explained when they had first greeted his son with hostility. But why must she be the unfortunate one to bring such a child into the world? A child so wonderful, so loving, yet, because of his colour, must be tormented as if he were bearing the curse of all the bad bakra on the plantations on his back! Look at his little face, twisted in pain. Look at his eyes, seeing nothing but what he had endured down there in the village.

'Spirit of my fathers! God unknown and of countless faces, why must this curse fall on the head of my only child? Have I done wrong in saving his life at his birth? O the pain comes again to my belly when I look this day at my little one! What can I say to comfort him? I cannot ask him of his suffering, and his little lips tremble, but he does not speak.'

The boy spoke not a word as his tearful mother met him and took the precious gourd with water out of his numb hands. Kisanka said to herself as she watched the vacant and strange eyes of her whitefaced son: 'He will not go back to the village or to its waterhole. I am glad. He has learnt of the badness of man's spirit; he has tasted the bitterness of a herb which he had not grown or cooked himself. Now he will not go beyond these doors for he will not wish to expose himself to murderous claws of hate.' As if the boy knew the thought in his mother's mind, he slowly turned to her and said: 'Tomorrow, I shall bring thee some more water, O my mother.' The dumbfounded mother could only turn her face away as the water welled up like a spring in her eyes.

She could not tell at that moment whether she was glad or sorry that she had birthed a warrior worthy of Tomaso his father.

Tomaso and a handful of his picked warriors were away on the dangerous mission of bartering and planning the escape of the next batch of runaways from the plantations. Jacob, the mulatto, was among them; so was Tahta, for in spite of the old one's age, he could travel the great distance between the plantations and the mountain hideout almost as fast as his young companions. These two were indispensable on such an errand for Jacob could speak broken English well, and because of his mixed blood could pass through the more dangerous parts of the towns without challenge, since he fitted the role of house-slave who usually went from place to place on their masters' business. And if needs be, the ex-slave had a document to show that he truly was one of those trusted chattels. The soldiers who would scrutinize these documents were usually barely able to write their own names and most of the time were unable to do even such a simple task. So, although the document did not really apply to Jacob, he was safe. Tahta, being old, could play the role of beggar and discarded slave with little fear of exposure, especially as the plantation slaves all looked to the Maroons all over the island as their saviours, and rarely betrayed their brothers of the hills unless they were tortured. These trips sometimes lasted for a week, and if the expedition was successful, the hillmen would return to the village full of information, precious powder, and lead for their muskets and perhaps such items as salt, iron-made tools and bits of cloth. So neither the father of Tamba or old Tahta were present to see the boy's first ordeal.

Kisanka hardly slept the night after her son's terrible experience. She wondered what Tomaso would have done had he been home. Would he have have allowed the child to go again to the waterhole on the morrow after what he had suffered that day? Would she be doing the right thing if she were to forbid him to go? Her only hope it seemed was that the child would not wish to go after all. She would say nothing to him, she decided, and he might abandon his voiced intention. As the hours for fetching water approached the following day, Kisanka watched her offspring with anxiety. Rain had not come to the hills for months now, and the waterhole dug by Tomaso and his friends and fed by water from the thatched roof carried to its destination by a number of bamboo gutters, was dry and cracking at the bottom. Hence the whole population who found their own water supply exhausted turned to the only spring located at the foot of the village. There was no other route to the waterhole from Tomaso's place except through the village.

Tamba, who had been more quiet than his mother had ever seen him, came from the backyard with the empty gourd in his hand, just when his mother had been hoping that he would not go. Her heart came to her mouth. She stood looking down on her boy, she black as ebony with the regal stance of a queen, with one breast and shoulder bare and the loosefitting cloth, covering the other breast and shoulder, tied at the waist to flow gently and almost Grecian-like down to her ankles, with her hair drawn this day tightly above her head and bound with a piece of bark cloth halfway to the top. She had lost none of her beauty. Indeed, her longish face and sad big eyes seemed to be even more attractive by her anxiety at this moment.

The boy, white, with some freckles on his face, hands and shoulders, completely out of the setting one would design for such a colour, stood with his gourd now lashed into a cage of bark, his face wearing a frightened but stubborn look, his clean young limbs covered only by the small piece of cloth around his middle.

'I go now, Mother Ka,' he said, in a slightly strained, half defiant voice.

'Tamba,' Kisanka felt desperate: 'Will you let us go together? Yes, little one, let us go together! I have not gone to the village with thee since thy babyhood.' *Why have I not thought of this before. Surely he will accept, they dare not treat him as they did yesterday when I am with him.* 'I shall be able to carry the big gourd, and the waterjar on my head, little one, then we shall have much water.'

For a second or two the child's face lighted up, for he was

as proud of his mother as he was of his father, and he longed to walk by her side feeling that he was there to protect her. Kisanka watching him closely, felt her heart leap for joy as she saw the fleeting look on his face. Then suddenly a sad vacant stare, such as she had seen the day before, came back to his face, and she knew even before he replied that she had lost her fight to help him.

'Mother Ka.' The voice at that moment was that of a man instead of a six-year-old.

'Speak, little one.' A sort of film came over the eyes of the mother and she looked away over her boy's head out at the open door and the trees bathed in golden sunlight.

'I would like to go alone. Can I?'

Kisanka did not know that once before, long ago, a Mother had a similar problem with her Son, though the reason for the problem was not the same. Perhaps had she known it would have comforted her. As it was there was nothing to comfort her—not even the thought of knowing she had birthed a child living up to the ancestral name his father gave him. Tamba—The Courageous!

'The spirits go with thee, child,' said the woman; and without another word the boy turned, and with his gourd slung by the bark strap over his arm, he walked down the hill towards the village.

Prejudiced as the people were against the strange boy, they had to admire the courage which brought him back to the scene of torment of the day before. The children, feeling that their victim insulted them by his return, vowed within themselves to vie with each other in tormenting him. They would let him run this time. Lago's two sons, known as the greatest pair of bullies amongst the children of the hills, had missed the sport on the first day that Tamba had his ordeal, and mourned their misfortune all afternoon. Now they were there to join in. Thanks to their father they hated this boy even before they first set eyes on him. Now he was within their grasp! They led the mob with glee.

Kisanka saw her son coming at last. There was dirt on his knees, and when he came nearer she saw that on the side of his head was an ugly bruise which stained his woolly white hair, and like the day before, he was fouled with mud. But in his terror-filled eyes came a gleam of pride as he handed the gourd filled with water, to his mother. She looked, and there was no stain of eyewater on his face like the day before. He stood before her, his mouth twisted slightly, as he said unnecessarily: 'I did bring thee the water, Mother Ka.' Then added: 'And I did not run.' But the breaking of the silence was too much for even so great a little man and warrior. He lost control, and rushed forward, burying his little face into his mother's bosom, as sobs loud and uncontrollable shook his young body. And, as if the Great Being, knowing the child's spirit and wishing to save it for the present from further trial, sent the long awaited rain from the skies, before the water from the eyes of mother and son had completely dried, and the empty waterhole was filled to overflowing before the evening was far gone.

'The Great One has heard my plea,' whispered Kisanka. And she walked hand in hand with her son to the open door and into the welcome downpour.

There was a small fireplace beside the leanto built against a great almond tree. Tamba went there and carefully rubbed all over his white face with crushed charcoal, talking to himself as he did so. After a while he began working on his hands and arms to the elbows, but he went no further. Then he turned to his goat Bahbah, and Bangie for their opinion.

'Tell me, Bangie, how do I look? Is my face like that of my mother and father now? What do you think, Bahbah? Do I look like the picnies of the village? Why can't you stop eating nothing and look at me properly, Bahbah? You are always eating. Sometimes something, sometimes nothing! And you, Bangie, you just sit on your legs and tail leaning your head to one side and then the other with your tongue always hanging out. Why do you look at me like that? Is not my face good to look at now that I have covered it with crushed charcoal? You are better to talk with than Bahbah, for she only cares about food!'

Bangie sat back looking anxiously at his master's face as if he was not sure he had seen right.

'I know what I shall do since I cannot get an answer from

you, Bahbah and Bangie. I shall pour the water I have in my gourd in the hut into a calabash, then I shall see for myself if I am now the colour of my father and mother.'

Bahbah, the goat, continued to chew her cud unconcerned, while Bangie sat still with his tongue hanging out and curiosity on his animal face.

Tamba brought out the gourd and calabash bowl and poured the water into the latter, going from under the trees, hoping that the bright sun and water would give him some idea of his blackened face, as it did when he looked down into the big water tank his father and the warriors had made behind the house. But before the bowl of water could tell him anything, he looked up, and had the fright of his life. For on the path leading direct to his little leanto hideout was a picni, staring straight at him. In a flash he thought of all that this would mean. No longer would he be able to keep this, his place, a secret, which until now, had been shared only with his parents, Grandfather Tahta, and his goat and dog.

Now the children of the village would hear about his hut. They would perhaps come all the way up the hill to mock and taunt him as they did when he went there alone to fetch water for his mother. He could not tell how long the picni had been there watching him. She might have even heard all he had said to his goat and dog, and it would make good mocking talk for the children of the village. He saw that the picni was a girl by the plaits as well as by the skirt she wore. He thought she was not big enough to have asked Brer Rat to swap her old teeth for new ones, and that made him feel a little superior. She stood looking up at him or above him, and he, feeling that she was trying to be clever, stood still looking back at her. He remembered that the rest of his body had not been blackened as well, and it puzzled him why she did not laugh at the sight. Just when he hoped she was too frightened to do anything but turn tail, she began to move towards him. He watched in dismay and was somewhat puzzled by the way the girl looked at him, and her strange method of covering the distance of some twenty yards between them. For she did not once look down on where she was putting her feet as she slowly climbed the rise towards him, and she kept on holding out her hand as if to ward off any bushes that might be blocking her path. Yet she must have seen that the track leading to his leanto was clear of bushes, and all the branches hanging overhead were too high to disturb anyone.

He wondered why Bangie who usually barked at even the smallest intruders, including lizards, if they dared to come too near, should now only sit on his hind legs somewhere at his feet without even a sound. He would not take his eyes off the girl to look at the dog, for he felt this picni wanted to win at this game of staring at each other; and he would not allow her to do so, he vowed. If she thought he was going to speak first after she had intruded in his place, then she was mistaken. He felt he knew why she was coming towards him at a snail's pace. She wanted to force him into speaking first, perhaps to ask her what she was doing at his place. Look how many teeth he had given to Brer Rat, and how many new ones he had got in return, and she, by the look of her, had not yet given a single one from her mouth, yet wanted him to speak to her first! Well, he would stand like a warrior keeping guard and give her look for look, and see who would break the silence. Perhaps Bangie also guessed the girl's plans, and that would account for his silence. Good dog, Bangie. Not like that foolish Bahbah who would chew nothing as well as something all day.

The girl stopped now. She stood with her hands a little in front of her, almost looking as if she was seeing something over Tamba's head. He wanted to look to make sure that she had not been staring at some dreadful thing on the rock right behind him, but he steeled himself from the fear by convincing himself that the girl only wanted to make him do that very thing. Then she would laugh at him and say she had fooled him. He would not let her catch him like that, especially because now looking at her, he was convinced more than ever that she had not yet given any teeth to Brer Rat. But he was puzzled and bewildered in spite of this cheering thought. The girl stood still, her head cocked to one side as if she was listening for something. She was about half a chain away now where she stood. He looked at her face. Black, shiny and inclined to be round. Four moundlike plaits with rat-tail ends on her head. The upper part of her body was bare. She wore a skirt reaching her knees, made from lacebark. Tamba, watching the girl, remembered the precious bit of coarse material he wore as loincloth. It was small and dyed brown. Now he wondered if it had slipped in any way as it had done so often when he played alone with his dumb companions. It was all well then, for Bangie did not care much for things on his body himself. He knew that, because once he had tried to get the mongrel to wear a bit of rag as loincloth. But Bangie had got angry and nearly bitten him when he tried to tie it between his hind legs with a piece of creeper. So they had quarrelled and the experiment was never tried again.

Now this was different. This girl who stood so long staring would try to see all the faults and flaws about him so that she could shame him with them when she opened her mouth. But he would not look down or even move his hand from his sides to his waist to see if all was well with his only bit of clothing, for the girl would think, even by getting him to adjust himself because she stared, that it would mean that she had won. He felt something crawling on his bare back and thought it might be an ant. But he steeled himself for a possible bite rather than move his hand to try to brush it off. Just then to his surprise, the girl slowly turned about and began to retreat down the hill. He did not realize that he had swallowed his saliva, and the wrong way as well, until he began to cough. The first burst caused the slowly retreating child to stop dead. Then as he tried to clear his throat she turned, still in that slow way of hers, and with hands in front of her, advanced, looking straight at him. He could not stop coughing, much to his annoyance. The visitor walked up slowly until only a yard or so separated them. Again she seemed to look at him and then over his head, perhaps on the rocks behind him. It made him angry. He could not stop the foolish coughing, the girl trying to fool him by making him think she saw something a little above him, and the way she had stared in silence at him all this while. He was sure she was thinking out another bad name for him in her mind. Perhaps she had heard all the names the picnies of the village had called him and wanted to see if she could find a better one to suit his funny colour and hair—

'What is thy name?'

The question so surprised the boy that it put him off his guard.

'Tamba,' he said before he could think. Then he remembered the hostility he had been cultivating while the intruder had appeared on the path, and decided to be on the offensive right away:

'I knew my ears did not lie.'

She spoke just as he had opened his mouth to say something, and it completely put him off. In fact so much so that he forgot what he was about to say. He did not understand her words.

'How can ears talk, foolish one?'

Anyway, he thought, I called her foolish. It is foolish. Though I know what she means, I shall pretend I do not. She has no right to come to my secret place. To his dismay, Bangie, whom he thought would have agreed to his attitude absolutely, got up, and after sniffing the stranger, raised his head and touched her hand with his wet tongue. In a flash, the girl, without looking down, bent and touched the traitor on his head. The beast to Tamba's disgust began to wag his tail as if he intended to break it off while making little noises and licking the stranger's hand and face. Never had Tamba felt more angry with his dumb companion.

'I knew he was here too. My nose told me.'

This time Tamba did not let surprise or puzzlement get the better of him.

'It is a bad thing to speak lies,' he said heartily.

'I speak no lie, Tamba.'

Calling him by name nearly put him off again but he managed:

'You looked at me. You looked long. Bangie was here with me so you must see him too. How can you say you tell no lie when you say it is thy ears and thy nose which spoke?'

She was still patting Bangie's head and her face was towards the boy as she smiled triumphantly it seemed, showing tiny white teeth and a pair of dimples in her cheek.

'It was my ears and my nose which talked to me about

thee and Bangie. For my eyes cannot talk, they are blind!'

She did look triumphant, as if she had given a riddle and her guest was unable to solve it, leaving her to do so.

Tamba looked at her with utter disbelief.

'How can you say such lies. My mother would have been angry with thee if she was here and my father also, for it is wrong to speak lies.'

He paused, then before the girl could reply, he continued:

'Furthermore, to pretend that one is blind is a bad thing. Once I closed my eyes and walked pretending I was blind, and my mother was very angry and she told me that the spirits might be angry with me if I did this again and perhaps make me really blind, or leave me to fall in a hole, so I never tried it again.'

'But it is true. I cannot see.'

'Once, with my father, I saw a blind man, his eyes were closed. You cannot make a fool of me. Look thine eyes are open and good. And they are looking at me now. How can you be so bad?'

Now the girl left off petting the dog and stood upright. He was the taller of the two by more than an inch. In the excitement he had forgotten until now that he was not like the other people of the village. Right from the minute she spoke he had forgotten. It was her standing close to him now with her black uncovered torso and black hair, while his body, apart from his blackened face and arms, was so different. It made him suddenly want to hide away from her.

'I wonder what she thinks about my colour?' he thought, for he still did not believe her when she said she was blind. And yet he felt puzzled, for he remembered that she was holding her hand in front of her when she came up the path and her bare feet searched the ground the way his had done when he had pretended to be blind that day. But he had never seen or heard of a blind person with two good looking eyes.

'What is thy name?'

He regretted asking as soon as he had done so, feeling that she might not tell him, for he was still suspicious of her.

'Manda,' she said, then added a little sadly: 'But today a boy called me another name which I do not like.'

It seemed she wanted him to ask what was the name, but

he, because he was just a little sorry for her, knowing how it felt to be called names which one does not like, kept silent.

'I like thy name, Tamba. What does it mean?'

He wanted to tell her there and then that he liked her name too, but he remembered that she had told him something which could not be true—pretending that she was blind! Even then he could not bring himself to be abrupt.

'My father said his grandfather bore that name, which his parents gave him because they knew he would be a Warrior-of-Courage.'

'Was thy grandfather a mighty warrior?'

'Yes, like my father,' replied the boy proudly. Then he suddenly had an idea:

'I see a snake!' he cried, feigning alarm. 'Look! There he is!' He pointed to a spot to the side of him, but the child did not follow his hand with her eyes. She stood quite still, but he could see the fright in her face as her eyes stared helplessly.

'I speak a lie. It is not true. There is no snake.'

He himself was in greater panic than the girl as he quickly tried to undo the wrong. He forgot to be shy as he saw the little visitor's lip tremble pitifully as she bravely tried to keep from crying. In a second he had his arm around her shoulder. She buried her face on his small chest.

'Don't bring any more water from thine eyes,' he begged, as he tried desperately to comfort her. 'Look! I shall show thee many things. Grandfather Tahta taught me many things which I shall show thee. I can make fire with sticks as well as knocking iron on flint. Come and see my hut. I will show thee how to boil food without water.'

He chattered away forgetting his resolutions, forgetting she could not see all the things he planned to show her, forgetting the difference in their colour.

It was true to say Tamba was more like his father than his mother, apart from the extra finger he had inherited. Isolated as he was from the rest of the children, he had learned to play by himself and to talk to the mythical characters culled from the stories his mother, father and old Tahta told him from time to time. In his mind his mother was sacred. He felt even at that early age that it was his business to defend her. It was a tradition and an inherited thing peculiar to all negro male children to feel it their sacred duty to protect their mother's name with their very lives. Tamba, by depending so much on his mother for love, comfort and companionship, developed a sense of devotion so strong that to him his mother was a goddess whom all should worship and die for, even as he would be the first to do if the occasion arose. He could not think of himself living without his mother. He never thought her a heroine or capable of protecting herself, not like his god in the form of his father. It never once came to the mind of the boy that he could ever live to be the protector of his father. To him there was nothing which his beloved hero father could not do. When he was at home and the god Hurrican raved, his father could always laugh at the terrible spirit of the wind. For Tomaso was Tomaso—brave, fearless, invincible. The boy knew his mother looked at her husband in the same way and it strengthened his conviction that his god was greater than any other. And of course there was old Tahta there to further the boy's belief in both his mother as a goddess and his father as a god. Day by day, hour by hour, the old man would help the child to think of his hero father as the greatest warrior of all times, and his mother, the spirit of goodness. But if the child made goddess and god of his parents, Tahta made a god of the boy. Every minute the old quackdoctor was able to spare was spent in the company of his beloved Tamba. His small single room hut was only a few chains away from that of his adopted family, and unless he was away on some mission of mercy, or with Tomaso on one of their many dangerous journeys, the old man would always be found at the house of his leader in the company of the albino. It seemed that Tahta felt he had to make up for all the ill treatment and abuses the child had and would suffer. He, wishing to build up the boy into an almost superior being, so as to counterbalance his handicap, taught him countless things he had learnt as a child and a young warrior before he was captured and brought to the island as a slave from his native Africa. He showed him the art of stalking and how to go through dense growth of bushes without disturbing the foliage. He taught him to boil food without water. He showed him how to make fire with flint numerous in the hill, as well as the other way of rubbing sticks together. He taught him how to treat broken limbs of animals, how to know weeds and herbs good and bad, he showed him how to make bows and arrows with bamboo splits as arrows. He even showed him the way of making the tips poisonous, and proved not only that his formula was good, but also that he had not lost his skill with bow and arrow or spear, when he, by these means, killed a coney and a wild pig. The boy lapped up the old man's teaching as a thirsty earth absorbed rain. It was as if the wise old one could foresee the road ahead for his protege and was preparing him for this. Tomaso knew how his son was being taught things, some of which were now forgotten amongst the people of the hills, and, if for nothing else, he was glad that his child was not left to brood on his loneliness.

Lago was hiding in the bushes, waiting for Kisanka to pass back from the village waterhole where she had gone to fetch water. She was anxious that Tamba would not notice that their own waterhole was almost dry, for he would perhaps ask to go as he did when they had the last drought, and she did not want that experience to be repeated. She had taken him herself to the village since then, and she had seen how Lago's poison had worked. For even the wives of Tomaso's special band of warriors had tried to avoid her and her child. She knew it was fear. Lago had told them that it was her albino son who had caused the great sickness four years before, and now they were afraid. They were also afraid that if they were friendly to her and her child, the bullnecked one might be annoyed, and they knew how dangerous it was to court the wrath of their acting chief. For, thanks to the skill of Tahta, the chief was still alive, much to the annoyance of his would-be successor. Furthermore, because Tahta had managed to undermine any little trust the ailing man had for Lago, the chief refused pointblank to either retire or repeal the act which Tomaso had decreed; that a chief must be elected by the people purely on his merits, and not named by his predecessor. But now even Tahta knew that the chief was dying, and unless something unusual happened, Lago would be the next chief. For it seemed none had the courage to be his rival for the post. The people had long since realized their mistake in thinking that the chief who succeeded their beloved Tomaso would make life a bed of roses for them. Indeed, they had suffered disaster after disaster since that night when Tomaso abdicated. Hunger and want was now always with them. Many of the elders of good standing had resigned in disgust when they saw that Lago and his puppet chief had no intention of consulting them on important matters. Rarely had there been a meeting at the cave known as The-Place-of-Talks, and the great clearing opposite was only used when there was some celebration inspired by Lago as a kind of balm to soothe the grumbling population. But Tomaso and his band of warriors were never in want. For while the others went to ruin with their idleness and late night festivals, the ex-chief and his men spent all the time they had when they were not out on some daring mission, to clear, dig, and plant as many vegetables as possible on part of the woodland which they judged most suitable. And as these men on Tomaso's advice insisted on having their usual plots on which their women helped, when others were in desperate need for food, the ex-chief and his men were able to give a helping hand to many.

But now Lago was in ambush, waiting for Kisanka whom he had seen from afar going to fetch water. He hardly knew why he wanted to see her. He knew that she hated him. He also told himself how much he hated her, yet there was never a day or a night when she was not on his mind. He usually told himself that she had bewitched him and that was why he could not forget her. Now, as he waited in the bushes along the loneliest part of the narrow track leading to her exile, he thought of the events leading up to the eve of what might be his election as chief. For, in spite of the grumbling and hard times, he flattered himself into believing that there were many who would support him.

Kisanka was unaware of the ambush until the misshapen figure almost sprang out of the bushes and barred her way. It was a frightening experience, especially as Lago had grown more stooping and twisted than he had been at the Junkunu festival. She had not seen him since, and she wondered how she had not screamed at his sudden appearance. But outwardly she was as calm and as dignified as if she had expected him there, and that he was a dear friend instead of the dreaded Lago. She was forced to stand still, with one large gourd of water on her head and a smaller in her arm. Her skirt was tucked up higher to one side than the other, and the cloth which took the place of a blouse was thrown loosely across one shoulder.

'Let me pass,' she said crossly and scornfully. The disgust on her face cut him to the quick.

'So, there is still pride in thee woman! You who are an outcast, with a picni who is raceless. You, whose husband was the mighty chief, Tomaso, but who is now cast out and must live like the forest dog. What is there for thee to be proud of?' He was close enough to smell the strange thing she used on her hair. He remembered long ago when he had been Tomaso's friend, she had used this thing which Tahta had prescribed for her headaches, which she confessed came on her often since the time when she was tortured on the plantation. Now this pimento smell which he had always remembered, made him suddenly feel as if he was drugged.

'Let me pass, snake. Do you wish to have a twisted neck to match thy body?'

The scornful reference to his physical appearance killed whatever hope he had had of getting the better of the encounter.

'Aye, thy husband gave me a twisted body, but, thanks to thee, I have been repaid!' He laughed harshly. 'You have helped in this matter, O woman! Did you not make him the target for my mocking when countless moons came and went, and you had not given him a child? And when you at last did so, was it not to bring forth a picni which has made him the talk of every mouth? Is not this child of thine feared and made an outcast by every child in the village? Do you think that there is any picni who would want him for a brother? Or any woman child who will want him for her mate?' He came even closer to her now so that his hot breath could be felt on her face. 'Thy child shall die alone, Kisanka! And not even the dog shall wish to die with him! It will be a great day for the picnies of the village when they learn that thy monster who is of no race no longer lives, to bring fear and curse upon them!'

He saw the havoc his words had wrought, for even Kisanka could not keep the terror of the prediction about her beloved child from her face. It pleased him to see that he had wounded her at last. But the next few seconds brought the face of Tomaso, her beloved husband, to her mind, and so strong was her faith in her lord that her fear for her child vanished. Once more the cold calm woman, who he knew scorned him, stood before him.

'Once I fouled thee with my spittle, Lago, and for this I am ashamed.' His face brightened considerably, and thinking that what he had said about her son's future had caused her to change towards him, perhaps hoping he would help her, made him cut in to gloat even before she had finished her sentence. 'So! Shame has at last come to thee for thy insult to me, woman. You seek my aid now, eh? Well, my price will be mighty.' He stopped, because the look of disgust on her face killed the rest of his sentence. 'You did not let me finish, O snake!' she said, almost with laughter in her voice; then: 'I am ashamed because I had honoured thee with my unwanted saliva. It deserved a better fate. Now let me pass, dog!'

The last words were so commanding that the humiliated man stepped to one side of the track for the girl to pass without knowing he did so, and as she did, the full meaning of her words came to him, shaming him even more than the day she had spat on him.

Now, as she made her way with her back to him, he felt that had he a musket or even a machete in his hand, he would have run after her and struck her down. As he had none of these he resorted to words.

'Go!' he screamed after her. 'Go and breed more dundoes to bring more reproach and laughter on thy husband.'

She walked along as dignified as ever with her gourds of water, one on her head, the other in her arm, without once looking back. But Lago's taunts wounded her deeply. Would she conceive again? And would it be another poor innocent infant with this strange colour? Was it possible for her to have another child the colour of the first? What would happen to her husband then? It was true as Lago said, she had brought it all on Tomaso. If he had only accepted Kumse that night long ago when she had brought the girl to take her place and give him a child! If he had not saved her from the ledge of the place where she had planned to go out of his life . . .

From that moment Kisanka began to brood on Lago's wild words: 'To bring more reproach and laughter on thy husband.'

Four

It was a month since that day when the blind girl had first introduced herself to Tamba. Since then she had been as dear to him as his beloved Bangie, and if it were not for the fact that Bangie might feel hurt, he would have admitted that this Manda was very much greater to him than his dumb companion.

To the blind girl, her new-found friend was a god. He filled all the emptiness that was in her young soul until she discovered him. Her mother had died before she could remember her in that bad sickness which had brought banishment to the albino and his parents. She had never known who was her father. Always the old woman who said she was her grandmother had evaded the subject. The child could remember vaguely the things she saw before she became ill like her mother. When she recovered, she was blind. And now at nearly six years of age, she was used to her blindness. Tomaso and Tahta learned of the child and her parents. The father was no other than Lago. The woman was one of a batch of refugees who came to the hills just before Tomaso had abdicated. Lago had claimed her as his. After the mother died from fever, and Lago discovered that the child was blind, he had secretly taken her to an old woman, gave her into her charge, had a hut built far from the village, and there he kept them, charging the old woman to keep his fatherhood a secret. Perhaps he had hoped that the child who was still ill and helpless would not recover to embarrass him, for he reasoned that it would be bad for his name to be associated with an imperfect child officially, though he knew that almost everyone in the village must know sooner or later if the little girl lived long enough.

But Manda did live, and the old woman cut off from the

rest of the village, learned to love the child as if she was really a grandchild. Lago's only redeeming features were that he made no effort to cause the child's death, and he made provisions for their keep just as he had promised the old woman when he made the proposal. So Manda had grown alone in the woods with the old woman, a quarter of a mile from where Tomaso built his house. And now the two had found each other.

Tamba's parents were glad their son had found a play-mate, though a girl and younger than him by nearly two years. Had they guessed that she was so gay, active, and free from brooding, they might have sought her out them-selves as company for their son, but they had left her and her guardian alone, thinking she was a child that needed pity and much guidance and care. When Tamba brought her to see them and they discovered her sunny laughter-filled disposition, they were overjoyed for their child's sake, and for her also; and Kisanka, remembering what Lago had said about the loneliness of her son, prayed that nothing would rob him of the little girl's company. So Manda found a welcome second home. But the adults kept her parentage a secret. Now Tamba was going to the village, holding the hand of his blind friend.

Manda had stumbled up to his house, wanting to find Tahta, for the old woman with whom she lived had taken ill, and there was no one else to send for help. But Tahta was away in the village at the house of the ailing chief. The old man had been reluctant to go, for Kisanka had also been ill in bed for some days now. But Tomaso's wife had insisted that the bushdoctor should go to see the sick chief, declaring that she was much better, and was sure she would sleep well after he had dosed her with a tiny calabash full of his sleeping draught. So the old man had given her the potion, and Tamba had promised to be quiet so that his mother could sleep peacefully. Not that the boy needed telling. For since his father was away he had taken it on himself to be the guard and protector of the house, and as for being quiet, not even the cock was allowed to crow without being chased, and even suffered the humiliation and indignity of cutting his crowing short and scampering away with all the hens looking on.

Kisanka was fast asleep, thanks to the drug which Tahta had given her for this purpose, and her son had to go without asking or even telling her, since Tahta had stressed that she should not be disturbed. His young spirit was heavy as he remembered the terrible way they had treated him twice before when he had gone there to fetch water. But he could not allow Manda to go alone for she could not find the way by herself, and Tahta had to be told that the girl's guardian had taken ill. As he came to the outskirts of the village, Manda grew silent—the first time since they began the journey.

'Tamba.'

'Speak, Manda.'

'Why does thy hand feel like there is fire inside?'

'I did not know of it. Perhaps because we have walked far.'

There was silence for a while as if the girl was pondering the reply, then:

'Tamba.'

'Speak.'

'The village—are the people bad?'

The question took the boy by surprise and he did not know what to reply.

'The picnies are bad. They called me bad names and mocked me when I went there for water.'

Now that he spoke of the incident a slight tremor went through his little body and the sensitive blind girl holding his hand felt it strongly.

'You should not have come then, Tamba,' she cried in alarm. 'Run back.' For now that I am here, I can ask the rest of the way.' She tried to loosen her hand from his hold and pulled back as she did so. But the albino's face was set now with grim determination.

'Come,' he called, tightening his hold on her hand. 'I shall not turn back.' In the short time since she knew him she had learned to understand his intention by his voice. She resisted no further, but now she stumbled as if her bare little feet had lost their eyes also, though the path was now less stony than before. Grimly they went through the village.

They could hear the murmur of voices and bare feet on the hard earth behind them, but one could not see even if she did look back, and the other who could refused to do so. Nevertheless their young hearts pounded the blood into their chests and heads like mighty drumbeats. Instinctively she clung more tightly to his hand, and it seemed as if all his emotions passed through his body into his hand and from there into hers, so that their feelings were almost as one— only that he was the male child of a warrior with aggressiveness helping to boost his courage, while she, the female, had only faith in him to boost hers. The murmur behind them was so close now that they, the followers, had to resort to whispers in order to keep their schemes secret.

Adults, though not many at home at that time of the day, looked through or over their stockade-like fences built for privacy, and frowned at the appearance of the dundoes and his companion. There were some thirty children behind the two now.

'Dundoes!'

The hissing of the name brought terror and anger together to the boy. Manda began to tremble, and Tamba feeling the shaking hand, quickly forgot the insult thrown at him in his concern for his younger companion. In a second the blind girl sensed that her fear was bad for her companion. She drew her hand from his and he started in alarm not knowing her intention, she found his arm and thrust hers under. She had never seen this done before but she felt that walking arm in arm would show their enemies how much she trusted him. He looked at her with admiration for she was trembling no longer. Her round black face was wearing defiance and scorn. Her lips wore a little smile. No adult could look more dignified as this little six-year-old in a skirt of grass. And Tamba rose to the occasion. When the frustrated crowd of children found that their terrorising efforts were ineffective, and ran in front of them to bar their way, the two continued walking; and the children had to make way at the last moment when they saw that the boy and girl treated them as if they did not exist.

'Dundoes!'

'Picni-with-the-old-man's-hair!'

'Black Backra!'

They resorted to name-calling now that they had lost the

first round.

Lago's two sons came to the front, just when their hunched-back father came into view. This time it was Tamba who began to tremble for he recognised the dreaded enemy of his father. A startled look came on the face of the bullnecked one when he saw the girl. But it passed away as he turned to the young bullies of his loins.

'What! Call yourselves my sons and stand shouting afar like barking dogs at your enemy? You Jo! Is not this the dundoes I have told thee of so often? Let him see how a true son of a warrior acts, my picni! Challenge him to wrestle as is the way of our people. Throw him to the number of fingers of thy eating hand and I promise thee a musket as soon as thy shoulder is strong enough. You are more robust than he, boy, and worry not about his accursed eyes, thy father's magic slays his power this moment. Now challenge him to fight or run. Move away you picni; you are a womanchild. Let go of the dundoes' arm.' But little Manda stood firm with her arm locked on to that of her white friend. She could not answer back for she knew that it was wrong to answer an adult, but she felt that it was right to stand by her friend, especially now that he was in danger of being attacked. Now a crowd of people gathered around and Lago once more felt uneasy as people began to ask who was this girl. Most of them did not know she was blind. The boy Jo, some two years older than Tamba, moved forward, encouraged by his father's words and the promise of a musket. His brother, only a few weeks younger, looked envious of the privilege.

Tamba looked for room to pass with his charge, but now the boy Jo and his friends blocked their way.

'God of my Fathers, what do I see?' asked a voice well known in the village. It was old Tahta! He pushed his way through the crowd of people until he had his arms out protectingly around Tamba and the blind girl. Now he looked straight opposite into the eyes of Lago.

'I have heard it said that vulture eats vulture. Now I can nod my head if I am asked if I have ever seen this thing,' said the bushdoctor gravely.

Lago winced for he knew that Tahta was referring to his kinship to the blind girl clinging with fear to her young companion.

'One day thy beak will bring thee sudden death, old man.'

Tahta tossed up his head and laughed scornfully, but his bony hand was on the handle of his razorsharp cutlass in its homemade sheath at his side.

'Thy mouth is a great slayer, O would-be chief!' he cried and the dozen or so adults within earshot marvelled at the old man's daring, for Lago too had his weapon. But after a menacing glare at the bush-doctor, the bullnecked one turned his attention towards the children.

'Come, Jo, show the dundoes the ways of the son of a warrior!' he called to his eldest boy.

'This is a bad thing, Lago,' shouted Tahta in alarm as he realized the other was bent on having his son fight with the albino.

'The picni of thine is older than the other by two years by the bakra counting,' said Tahta almost pleadingly. 'Tomaso's boy has never fought or wrestled before. Indeed he has never seen such a thing. How could he when thy wicked tongue sent him and his parents into isolation?'

Lago laughed loudly: 'Ho-ho-ho! So the son of the mighty Tomaso has never fought or seen a fight, eh? Well it is time he learned, old man. Or should you not have said that he is no male but a woman child, this whitefaced whelp of thy master?'

Despair and anger came to old Tahta's face but he stood firmly between Tomaso's child and the sturdier and older Jo. Tamba stood quietly with Manda clinging to his arm, her face full of anguish.

'I shall not let the child be hurt, Lago, so call off thy bully.' And Tahta drew his cutlass from its shield.

'So!' said Lago also, with his in his right hand.

Women and children scattered as the two stood ready for the death battle. The men looked at Tahta with admiration, knowing that his age was against him, yet never underestimating his prowess.

'I will fight this Jo, O Grandfather!'

The clear childish voice came, and the men ready for battle paused to look towards the speaker. Tamba was trying to loosen his arm from little Manda's frantic hold.

'No, little brother, no. He will kill thee and then I shall have no brother,' cried the blind girl pitifully, and even Lago seemed as shaken as all the onlookers.

'If you die, then I shall die, Tamba.'

This time Manda's voice was low as if she wanted only her friend to hear, while drops of water came from her staring eyes.

'I shall not die, Little Sister!' said Tamba softly as he gently prized the hand of his friend from his arm, and at that moment it seemed to all that the young albino had grown into a warrior. His assurance must have had its intended effect for the silent crowd saw the girl wipe her eyes and let her boy companion lead her aside out of possible blows. Tahta still with weapon in hand watched with a look of pride but not without foreboding as the boy he loved like his own son came forward.

'You must not do this thing, Tamba. There is no shame on thee. The other is older and bigger than thee,' said the bushdoctor as the boy came close to him. Lago, with a sneer on his face, stood with his boy Jo by his side, the latter looking cocky, as indeed he should since he was both older, taller, and more robust, than the coltlike Tamba.

Tahta, afraid for his charge, made one more desperate try as he saw that the child intended accepting the challenge.

'You do not understand, Tamba, my picni! This fight is a bad thing, you will be hurt or you may even die. Is there no fear in thee, child?' The boy thought for a little. 'Yes, Grandfather Tahta, I am afraid.'

'Then, come boy. Take Manda's hand and come, and any who dare to laugh at thee shall answer to me.' And Tahta looked around at the faces challengingly.

'But I shall fight him, Grandfather.'

Before the old man and the now admiring crowd could speak, Tamba stood facing his challenger. Lago, somewhat ashamed, perhaps because of the blind girl's plea, stood silent until his boy and the albino were facing each other. This seemed to rouse him out of his embarrassment for he began to state the rules:

'If one throws the other down to the number of the fingers on one hand, then the fallen one has lost. If one asks for mercy at any time then the other is the winner. If one runs away or refuses to come out again to fight then the other is the winner. All blows are allowed but there must be no biting or gouging of eyes, and no weapons.'

Tahta nodded his consent to these rules for they had always been thus among the Maroons.

Tamba stood, not knowing what to do or to expect, then Jo sprang on him like a tiger. They went down with a thud which caused the terrified blind girl to force her fingers into her mouth to keep from screaming. Tamba was dazed, and the earth seemed to be turning round when he managed to extract himself from underneath his opponent, for it was his body that took the full force from the fall. Jo leapt forward again amidst the cheering of his young companions and the encouragement from his father. This time he took hold of the shoulders of the bewildered Tamba, planted a leg behind that of the other, then suddenly forced the albino backward with all his might.

This time as Tamba hit the ground, Tahta's spirit fell, and he cursed himself for letting the son of his friend have his way.

Manda, not being able to see, suffered more than Tahta and even Tamba himself, as she listened to the cheering for the other boy. Her sightless eyes, grown larger through her terror, stared towards where she judged her companion to be, as if they would penetrate the darkness that had blanketed them for so long.

Tamba took the third fall, and now the triumphant Jo was asking the bruised and bewildered Tamba if he was asking for mercy as he sat on his white dustcovered chest. But the albino, with eyes half closed, partly because of the bright sun above him, and partly from pain and humiliation, neither nodded his surrender or spoke the word. With one mighty heave he managed at last to throw Jo off his chest and so by the rules was allowed to regain his feet. But no sooner than he did, Jo threw him to the ground, for a fourth time.

'The last fall to come, my son,' shouted Lago, almost

dancing with joy.

'Give in, Tamba! Give in, my child,' begged Tahta. 'There will be no shame on thee to give in now.' But as Tamba lay on the ground with the joyful Jo waiting to finish the fight, only one voice penetrated his half conscious mind:

'O Little Brother, you must not die!'

The crowd was moved by the blind girl's agony.

Significantly Tahta drew his cutlass once more, and with death in his eyes came closer to Lago.

But the latter was too excited to see the move.

Tamba came up slowly on all fours to face his waiting enemy. As the albino stood upright, Jo, full of assurance, came forward to meet a terrific right hand which it seemed he could not at first believe, came from the hand of his enemy. Lago's son caught the blow on the side of his ear, and before he could think, Tamba struck again. This time his little fist buried itself on the other's eye, and Jo saw countless stars as he let out a mighty yelp. Now he covered his eye with both hands, one on top of the other, moaning, and the albino, fully recovered, went in again with his fist on his defenceless enemy. Now it seemed that a fit of madness came upon the albino. He remembered all he had suffered from the day he came to the village for water until now. He remembered that this Jo was one of those who led the crowd against him. He struck at the bent face, at the stomach, at the head, at any part of his enemy he thought would hurt most, and, as he struck and Jo howled, he seemed to gain more strength. Jo shouted for mercy but Tamba either did not hear or did not understand.

Tahta was doing a war-dance with his weapon singing dangerously near necks and heads of excited spectactors.

'Flay him son of Tomaso, flay him,' shouted the old man hoarsely, and little wide-eyed Manda knew that her Little Brother was winning.

'Move thy hand from thy face and hit back, fool!' cried the desperate Lago to his son, but the boy was past listening to advice as he covered his face with his hands and accepted breathtaking blows on the rest of his body. At last it was too much. He turned tail and ran half blindly down through the crowded lane, leaving his misshapen father biting his lips.

And when the bruised and redfaced Tamba looked at Jo's brother standing beside his father, the anger and challenge on his face caused Lago's younger son to hide discreetly behind his father.

As Tahta lifted his adopted grandson high in the air then to his shoulder, he hissed to the departing Lago: 'Thy son will be comforted when you tell him how once, nay twice, the father of the boy who whipped him, did the same to thee!'

Lago stopped and scowled and Tahta hastily put down the albino so as to be free with his hands.

'You have courted a kiss from my cutlass often, old man,' said bullneck. 'Take care, or you won't be ready when it is given.'

Tahta grinned toothlessly. 'Go on, mouthslayer, go and see to thy beaten whelp,' replied the bushdoctor, and in spite of the fact that the spectators looked upon the albino with mistrust and even fear, there were many who were glad of his conquest.

But Lago saved his face by another lie which he circulated. 'The Dundoes' evil eye caught those of Jo and blinded him and stiffened his hands so that he could not defend himself. That was how it came about that some talk of Jo being beaten.'

The strange illness of Kisanka preyed on the minds of all, especially little Tamba. He would go about his usual chores, fetching dry pieces of stick for firewood, searching for bark that was used in the making of hammocks and ropes. For the Maroons had learnt the craft of hammockmaking from the original inventors, the Arawak Indians, now almost extinct. Tamba, like all the children of the hills, could twist a rope strong enough to hold a mule, or make a hammock to bear the weight of a man. Even the little blind girl could give a good account of herself in the making of these things.

Manda's guardian died a week after she had complained, in spite of all Tahta's efforts. And after the funeral Tomaso and his ailing wife took the child in their home.

Now she really was Tamba's shadow. For though she kept out of his way when she felt she might not be welcome, she was always there at hand whenever he wanted her companionship. He had long learned to live without anyone but his mongrel or his goat to speak with occasionally, and did not chatter as much as many children. Luckily Manda understood, for she too had learnt to live with only herself as company. She would sit on a stone close to him, feeling for, or making, the knots of the diamond-shaped hammock which Tomaso and his warriors found so useful as a bartering medium with the indentured bakra or the few fortunate negroes who had obtained their freedom. There were many things precious to the Maroons which these neatly made hammocks could buy—cast-off clothing, grains, salt, fish, and precious metal tools, and perhaps lead for musket shot, or a few charges of powder. That was why hammock-making, like the cultivation of allotments, was taught to all at the earliest possible age.

Tomaso made frequent trips to the plains. He would return with things unobtainable in the hills, mostly food and some kind of medicine Tahta had asked him to get for Kisanka.

The sick woman used to make a great fuss of the precious fish, roasted and wrapped in young leaves. She sprinkled some with the luxurious salt her warrior husband had obtained for her at the risk of his life, while begging him not to repeat such a journey on her account. Under the watchful eyes of her lord and the old bushdoctor, she would eagerly place the morsel in her mouth, but after a couple of swallows, she would ask them to save the rest for her until later. Her loved ones would plead, threaten and plead again but they could not get her to eat any more. She would take the potion the despairing Tahta would give her, always drinking every drop, no matter how bitter the taste, or how horrible the smell. But still she grew thinner daily. At last she was almost too weak to walk and Tomaso, himself, grew gaunt and thin from worrying about her. Day by day he would ask Tahta about Kisanka's illness and would only receive evasive answers.

One day after coming back from one of the frequent missions he took to the plains in his attempt to find something tempting and nutritious for his wife, he lost his temper. His two days' absence had shown how quickly his beloved was fading away, and now he faced the embarrassed Tahta just out of earshot of the house.

'Tahta.'

'Yes, my son.'

'What ails Kisanka? She has little fever, she has no cough, and there is no sign of sickness on her body, yet she grows thinner every day!'

'I know, Tomaso. Have I not eyes to see?'

'And you do not think it is a spirit of evil which is causing her illness, Tahta?'

The old man turned his face away from the ex-chief.

'I do not know, Tomaso,' he said at last, looking as if he was anxious to end the conversation.

'You lie, Tahta! You lie!' Tomaso growled in a rage, catching the shoulders of the old one, and forcing him around. But the words of accusation had hardly left his mouth before he repented, taking his great hands from the old man's bare shoulders.

'Oh, my father! Forgive me for this insult. Now I feel that I could cut out my own tongue for the words it has helped my mouth to make. Now the shame because of this talk will never leave my eyes.'

But Tahta quickly assured his adopted son that he bore no malice.

'Nay, Tomaso, blame not thy tongue. Were I in thy place I would have said as much; and more.' He paused and looked down on the ground, then he spoke slowly as if he wished to choose his words most carefully: 'It could be that a spirit of evil is eating up Kisanka, my son, and it could be that I shall never have the power to overcome this evil and so save her from the Long Journey. My snake tells me I shall know soon. My snake also tells me that Kisanka holds the secret of her illness.'

Before the bewildered Tomaso could ply the old man with questions, he was gone.

A week afterwards came the death of the long ailing chief, and Lago felt that he could afford to lie low for a couple of moons, or even more, before he staked his claim to the chieftainship. Pity the old fool could not be persuaded to name him his successor before he died, thought the schemer, and he blamed this on Tahta. Still no rival had dared to declare himself in the running—not even Tomaso, though he had heard rumours that the foolish people were now hoping that the ex-chief would return. Not while he, Lago, lived! he vowed. But in spite of the bright prospect in Lago's eyes, he felt uneasy, for Kisanka was strangely ill and he hoped they would not learn of how he had ambushed her and jeered at her. There was no knowing what Tomaso would do if he thought he had anything to do with it; and now that things were going well, Lago was most anxious to live.

Tamba had crept silently to his little room adjoining that of his parents, careful so as not to awaken his mother whom he hoped was asleep. He had come to get his little knife made from a nail which he had forgotten to take that morning when he left with little Manda for his small vegetable patch. For like all other children of the mountains he had learnt to dig and plant at an early age. Now there were enough sweet potatoes, cassava and ears of corn from his own garden to feed himself and his blind companion for months if necessary. They were allowed to cook their own meals by themselves when they were working away from home, and his knife was needed for preparing their meal.

It was after he had entered his room that he realized that his mother was not asleep, nor alone. He was about to take his knife from off the stool where he had left it when he heard his name called. The voice was that of his sick mother:

'He said Little Tamba would die alone, Tahta! Without even a dog to comfort him! He said the children of the village would be glad. And he called my child a monster! Could this come to pass, my father? Will my child go friendless, unwanted, and alone, to die?'

Tamba stood rooted to the spot, unable to move because of what he overheard. He could not hear what Tahta said, because the blood was pounding in his ears so heavily. He crept out of the house, forgetting his mission. When he was out of sight of the house he began to run recklessly without thinking where he was going. When at last he sat down it was inside his little leanto where he had met Manda moons before. His pink eyes grew big with the thought of death. And being young and healthy, made it even more terrible. He looked around at the place where he was. Suppose he were to die here now, he thought. With no-one near to comfort him. He would first have pain—they say that pain comes before death—and there would be none to hear him cry. Not even Bangie! And where would be Manda and his mother and father? Where would be Tahta? How could they all leave him alone to die? Who told this thing to his mother? Now he was sorry that he did not wait to hear more. But it could not be true! His father was a mighty man who was afraid of nothing. His father would laugh at such talk and say: 'I, thy father, will be with thee always, my picni! And so will thy mother and Tahta. It is foolish talk.' And there was little Manda; she would not leave him to die alone.

He got up, encouraged by the thought of those who stood between himself and loneliness, and his father whom he believed was even stronger than death. As he hurried guiltily to where he had left Manda with Bangie awaiting his return, he thought of telling the blind girl of what he heard, and planned also to ask his father the meaning of the talk and to get his assurance. But when he faced Manda he only pretended he could not find the knife and suggested making do with a worn bit of cutlass. He felt as if he wanted to ask Manda to promise she would never leave him, but did not know how to begin. After they had eaten and sat in the shade of a tree out of the blazing sun, Manda surprisingly enough, in her own uncanny way, felt the change in him.

'Tamba.'

'Speak, Manda.'

'You stayed a long time.'

He did not reply as he stretched out one hand to play with Bangie's ear.

'When you did not come, Tamba, I thought how lonely it would be if you did not want me any more. Then I would wish to die.'

He was touched deeply. He wanted to tell her how much

he wanted her to be with him always, but asked instead: 'Are you not afraid to die, Manda?'

She kept her sightless eyes in front of her as if she was seeing the green leaves of the sunkissed trees moving at the command of a slight wind.

'Yes, Little Brother,' she said at last. 'I am frightened of Death. He is bad. He ate up my mother; and now he has eaten up my grandmother; but when I am with thee my fear is gone.'

As she turned her round little face towards him and gave a dimpled smile, he felt that in spite of the pair of teeth which she had lost only recently, she was as pretty as his mother. It surprised him, for he never thought anyone would be as pretty as his mother.

'Tamba.'

'Speak, Little Sister.'

She felt a sudden warmth at the way he called her Little Sister.

A little time passed before she spoke again, and her face had a serious look now.

'Will you promise that you will never leave me?'

For one wild moment he thought of telling her his own fear since he overheard the conversation between his sick mother and the bushdoctor, but he remembered that she depended on him and thought him fearless and brave, so he only said:

'I will never leave thee, Little Sister!' And afterwards he felt very happy. He laughed gaily as he saw and described the antics of a couple of pitcharies ruthlessly attacking a baldheaded vulture perched on the dead branch of a cottonwood tree. As the luckless bird of prey flew off under the noisy attack of the two small birds and silence returned, Manda said:

'Now you are happy again.'

And Tamba knew that the little blind girl was full of wisdom. But he never asked how she had guessed, nor did he tell her or anyone else what he had overheard, though it never left his mind.

'Tahta.'

'Speak, Tomaso, my son.'

'I am afraid.'

Tahta sunk heavily on a stone in sight of the house. Tomaso, looking taller than ever because of the way he had grown thin of late, stood above his adopted father, his hands hanging loosely by his side, his woolly hair unkempt, spreading wide and high on his head. It was so unlike him to have such an appearance.

'She cannot raise herself out of her bed now, Tahta! I have proven it just now. And Kumse tells me Kisanka will eat nothing and will drink only water. What does it mean?'

'It is bad, Tomaso,' said the bushdoctor in a trembling voice. Tomaso grabbed the old man's shoulder.

'Tahta, my father, do you mean Kisanka will die?' There was a wildness and uncontrollable tone in the voice of the ex-chief. Tahta dovetailed his fingers in his lap and looked on the ground. 'She does not wish to live, Tomaso,' said Tahta at last in a voice as old as the mountains.

For a while only the chirping of birds on the surrounding trees could be heard, and the giant bending over the old man did not realize how much his great hand was biting the bony shoulder beneath it.

'You cannot let her die, Tahta! You hear? You cannot let her die.'

The great knees trembled as he knelt in front of the old bushdoctor.

'My son! My son! I would gladly give my own life to save her whom I love more than my own daugher.'

With a great effort Tomaso managed to control his emotion. Slowly he raised himself to an upright position once more.

'Tell me, O Wise One, why my Kisanka now wishes for death?'

Tahta guessed the effort it must have cost Tomaso to speak so calmly and admired him for it. He prayed to the Great Spirit that the ex-chief would not look into his face as he replied:

'I do not know, Tomaso. Who knows what goes on in the head of a woman? And yet the riddle might not be so great after all. Did not she, when in despair over bearing thee no

122

heir, send for her young friend, Kumse, to take her place? And now has not she sent for Kumse again to take care of thee and little Tamba?'

'Aye, Tahta, but now she is barren no more. She has borne me a son!'

Tahta cursed himself now for promising the sick woman to keep her meeting with Lago and his ominous predictions a secret. He was relieved however to note that Tomaso had not solved the riddle with the clues he had given.

'Yes, Tomaso, I too cannot understand Kisanka's wish to go to the land of her ancestors before her time, since she has borne thee a son. But this I know: none but Kisanka can save herself.'

Tomaso inhaled loudly.

'But she will save herself, will she not, father?'

'I cannot say, Tomaso.'

Silence then:

'Tahta.'

'My son?'

'Are you trying to tell me there is no hope?'

'That is so, Tomaso. We cannot save her, and she has no wish to save herself.'

They stood and sat in silence, each with his feeling of despair, and in the end they parted one from the other with only a touch on each other's shoulder.

Tomaso leaned over the sick Kisanka, his great ebony body dwarfing the thin delicate frame, with the big sad eyes and a face which looked even more beautiful than before, now that she was at death's threshold. He looked down on her face and she, with the eternal light of love in her eyes, looked back at her lord. It seemed that he was fighting to say something, for his lips kept moving and his great chest shivered and vibrated and even his arms which rested on both sides of her bearing part of his weight, did likewise.

'I cannot live without thee, Little Shadow,' he cried at last in a choking voice. 'How shall I feel when the doorway of this house greets me without thee?' His voice was without control now and his whole body trembled with emotion.

'How shall I live when I wake and do not feel thy soft

breath upon my cheek and then to remember that thy face which is dearer than life to me, is hidden under the earth? O, Kisanka, my Spirit! The pain from this thought turns me into a woman. See? Even shame cannot keep the water from my eyes.'

The girl placed her delicate arms around the neck of the shaking giant leaning over her, as the water dropped shamelessly from his eyes to her face.

'Nay!' Nay, Lord-of-my-Spirit! Speak not so!' she cried in a voice shaking with concern. 'Full of wisdom as you are, the eyewater not only blinds thy eyes, but also thy thoughts! How else could such words come from thy mouth? Listen, O beloved Chief! Listen, I pray thee! When the spirit goes from this my useless body, will it not be free as the wind? Shall I need to stand in agony at the door waiting thy coming or the coming of a messenger to tell me of thy end? Ah, my husband, that agony of waiting, not knowing whether the bakra have caught thee in their many traps, or their muskets have found thy precious body! How can men guess the pain of waiting, which is the common lot of the wives of warriors on these hills? But when I sleep for the last time, all this will be gone, O my Spirit.'

Kisanka paused, moved one hand from the neck of her man, and gently wiped the eyewater from his face, her eyes bright with love, drinking in every line on his face as if she wished to store it for the long journey. He did likewise, until every part of his soul could be read in his sorrowful face.

'I shall be before, beside, and behind thee, then, my Lord!' she said softly. 'When a little bird hops, jumps or flies before and above thee in thy travels, that will be my Spirit! When there is danger, if the Great Spirit gives me leave, then I shall find ways of warning thee. When there is a little wind moving the leaves near to thee when there is no wind elsewhere, it shall be my breath making that wind. When a whisper comes to thy ear when there is none to whisper in thy sight, it shall be thy Kisanka's Spirit. And when sleep comes to thy eyes, O Lord-of-my-Spirit, it shall be the bridge by which I shall cross from the Land-of-the-Spirits to the Land-of-Dreams to talk with thee.'

Now the sick girl had a faraway look as she continued:

'When I am not close to thee, then I shall be with our beloved son. I shall pray to the Great Spirit to give me power to watch over you both. Always. What more could I ask, O my Chief? Will it not be a mighty honour to be always close to the two who are more than life to me? Now be grieved only if the belief of our people is not thine also. Has it not been always said that death has no power over our spirits? And even if it had, ours would be too mighty for him, O my husband!'

Kisanka closed her eyes, and it seemed the long talk had exhausted her, but both her arms were once more round the neck of her husband.

'Little Shadow, thy faith and wisdom have humbled me,' said the giant with wonder and admiration in his voice. 'Like fools, we men like to pretend the gift of wisdom comes only to us.' He paused, and she opened her eyes which seemed bigger now because of her illness, and he, looking down at her, experienced again the panic he had a moment before.

'It would make good talk if I could say that thy wise words and hope had taken away the sorrow of parting, Little Shadow,' he cried in despair. 'But though it gives me comfort to know thy spirit will be here with me and our son, I want thee, Kisanka. I want to feel the warmth of thy hands as they are now. The sound of thy voice while I watch thy lips make the words; the heaving of thy breasts; thy laughter; thyself!'

Now he was almost savage with despair.

'Shall I see each little bird and ask: *Kisanka, is it you?* Shall I watch the leaves on each occasion they are disturbed by the wind and cry: *Are you there, Little Shadow?* Shall I always find thee in my sleep, just as I find thee now? God of my Fathers! Would it not be better if I, too, find the Land-of-the-Spirits with thee?'

She, alarmed, tried to raise herself into a sitting position, in spite of the arch his hands and torso made over her. The action made him come to his senses. Gently he eased her back on the pillow.

'Forgive me, Little Shadow. I was wrong. My grief has made a monster of me. I did not mean to frighten thee.' He passed his hand gently over her forehead as he tried to calm her.

'It is little Tamba, beloved!' she said at last, exhausted from her efforts to rise. 'He must not lose us both. I am his mother, and being a boy, his loss will not be half as deep as losing his father.'

Tomaso put his finger gently on the lips of his sick wife. Now his face changed as she gazed, and his look of despair turned to one of hope. He was looking just above her without moving as if he was forcing the mysterious door of death with his staring eyes.

'Hush, Little Shadow. Have no fear. The little one is dear to me. I shall live for him! Hush.'

He sat, half hanging over her with one hand moving gently over her damp forehead until she fell into a troubled sleep.

When the sadness of his mother's illness was too great for Tamba, he would pretend he had something urgent to do and rush outside and into the bushes to cry. His little blind friend would come and sit silently near the doorway every day, and Kisanka would always ask Kumse or Tamba to bring her in. They would stay together for long periods, the sick woman and the blind child, and talk; but none knew what they talked about.

Tamba had been told by his father that his mother would die. He, after his talks with her, felt convinced that if she died her spirit would be with him so that he would be comforted and would not be lonely. It was the belief of the hills, but somehow he could not believe that his mother would really die. It was the only time he had ever doubted his father's words. She had no fever now, and she was so cheerful and happy. After a while even Tomaso began to believe old Tahta had made a mistake. For there were few times when Kisanka was not cheerful. Even when just before the sun went to sleep the old bushdoctor came out of the room and called Tomaso and little Tamba and sent them in for her to speak to them for the last time, they doubted. But at last the father looked down on the frail woman in his arms and at the face of his son standing beside him, and they both knew that Kisanka the wife and mother was now in the Land-of-the-Spirits.

True to Maroon custom, on the day of burial the mourners left the bereaved alone by the graveside to talk with his dead. As the great crowd melted away, and the last sun shone on the tall trees, Tomaso, last of those to say his thoughts, looked down on the earth now beaten flat after the burial and surrounded by a circle of stones. His great frame was almost bony from lack of sleep and despair, climaxed by the death of his Little Shadow twenty-four hours before. Now he looked down hollow-eyed with his great fists clenching and unclenching at his sides.

At last he spoke:

'You have done a bad thing, Little Shadow! You have made me promise not to slay that snake before I knew the poison he had put into thy mind with his lying tongue.' His voice was heavy with anger as well as sorrow. His white teeth were clenched even as he spoke so that the bones of his jaw stood out strongly.

'Not for thee would I have stayed my hand had I known of this thing before thy death, Little One. And even now shall I hold this oath as binding? How can I when he has robbed me of thee?'

The sweat gleamed on Tomaso's brow now as if he had been toiling hard. 'Look at thy son, Kisanka! He wanders about, a lost picni, neither caring to eat, drink or play. His eyes have a look as if there is a fever in his head. I know not how to comfort him, for I too am in need of comfort.'

Now the man turned his eyes towards the trees painted orange by the sleepy sun, and the water rolled down his face effortlessly. He stood like this for a long while, the muscles of his bare torso taut, as if he was pulling with all his strength against an invisible force.

Back came his eyes to the flat new earth with its circle of stones marking the place.

'For one moon I shall keep my promise to thee, Little Shadow! For one moon only. Then I shall break the pledge for it was asked unfairly. The goodness in thee must not be used for saving the life of the evil one. When the young moon comes again I shall seek and find him, Kisanka. Afterwards the vultures will find they can eat what is left of him without the sharpness of their beaks.'

Suddenly the fury of his anger fell from him and he fell to his knees with his head bowed low. And the old man Tahta hiding in the clump of bushes not far away took the opportunity to creep away from the scene of sorrow which was almost sacred.

'Tomaso, my son.'

'Speak, Tahta, my father!'

'The little one: he will not be consoled! He has made a high wall between himself and all, even the little blind one and his dog, and no one can climb over.'

'I know, Wise One, he suffers.'

'He too may wish to die, Tomaso. And for that there is no medicine.'

'It is not like thee to frighten me, O my father! Have I not eyes to see the sorrow of my own son?'

'My son, think not that I reproach thee. Have I not seen thee trying to bring the spirit back into thy son, and yet in thy eyes is a look which speaks of another thing on thy mind since yesterday when we said goodbye to our Kisanka.'

'Forgive me, Tahta. I should have known nothing could be hidden from thee. It is the snake Lago. I shall slay him.'

'And if the wily vulture slay thee in this battle, Tomaso? What will become of thy son who needs thee now more than ever?'

'Such talk will not stay my hand, Tahta, since neither the oath of brotherhood or my oath to her will hold me now. And I shall win.'

'Hush, my son! Be sure of nothing when Lago is involved. He is the father of cunning. Now hear me! I feel it in my bones that there is something in the snake's past of which he is so ashamed that it could destroy him. There is an old man in the village, a great smeller-of-secrets. I do not like these great smellers, my son, but for this cause I shall not hold my nose though the smell knocks me to the ground.'

'Tahta, because of the oath I had taken before you told me what had caused Kisanka's death, I shall keep my promise until the coming of the new moon. After that I shall be hunting a snake.'

'Then give me until the coming of the new moon, Tomaso. Forget the snake until then. Comfort thy son with all thy might or he will die. No-one can break down the wall but thee for he loves thee even more than life, even as he loved his mother. Feed him with the love I know you hold for him for a moon, and his spirit will take courage from thine. That is all I ask, Tomaso. Leave Lago to me and there will be no blot on thy spirit for there will be no need to break the promise you made to thy Little Shadow—not even the oath of thy blood-brotherhood will be able to reproach thee afterwards. Perhaps pity will even come to thy own eyes when I have finished helping him to destroy himself.'

'Pity in my eyes for the monster who has brought sorrow and death to me and mine, Tahta? My spirit! You take my wrath lightly, my father. But I shall heed thy words until the new moon, because my son means all to me, and also because until then I shall keep to the oath. But only until then, I warn thee!'

'Well spoken, my son. Give me until the new moon. I see sorrow coming to the hills, mind you, Tomaso. But did I not warn thee of this long ago when the devil, as the bakra would say, lay close to death? But you would not let me make an end of him and so save us from all these sorrows. I do not know how this badness will come or what shape it will take, but I feel it inside me that this Lago will be the father of it all.'

Tomaso heeded Tahta's words. He took Tamba in hand. He asked Kumse, who was now to be found at the ex-chief's house from the break of dawn until when it was night, looking after their welfare, as she had promised her late companion. Though Manda never complained she felt lost without the company of Tamba. She was wise enough to keep away. Sensitiveness, which is the companion of blindness, told her that her friend wanted to be alone.

Tomaso took his son out into the forest daily, sometimes to teach him new woodcraft, sometimes to hunt the rabbit-like coney, or perhaps the wild hog, fairly plentiful in the hills. Gradually, the boy who loved his father as much as he had loved his mother, began to take an interest in things.

But his sorrow was still great, and the terror of dying alone still haunted him. But he would not even tell his father of what he had overheard. He began to feel once more that his father, so mighty, so confident, would see to it that he did not die alone. And yet he wondered if his father, who could not stop death taking his mother, could prevent him dying alone. But Tomaso's presence tore down the wall which prevented the child from speaking about death and the burden which was on his mind. Three weeks after Kisanka's death, Tamba, alone in the woods sitting by his father's side, said suddenly:

'Oh, my father, I tried and tried and I cannot remember her face! I do not know why. It was as if I would not know her if she was to come back.' And the eyewater gushed from the child's eyes.

Tomaso did not treat him like a baby by drawing him to his great chest. Instead, he sat staring into the semidarkness of the forest beyond.

'I, too, cannot see her face plainly now when I look, Tamba,' he confessed softly. 'But this has not brought me despair. It is because we crave so strongly the face of her whom we love why the mist comes to blur our eyes, my child. But that face is carved big and strong like the head Subengo, the village carver, made out of wood.'

Tomaso thought the boy would not understand; and he felt that his explanation was not adequate; but Tamba, hearing his father confess to having a similar experience as himself, did not care about the reason for this. His father was no longer remote, to be worshipped from afar. His father felt as he felt. It was the beginning of a new bond.

'I wished to die when death came to thy mother, child, and then I remembered she had left me a son of whom I am proud. Death is a monster, child. A monster whom none can fight. He comes, and his shadow darkens the door of the hut. No-one can pass. Life is like the spark which comes when we strike iron against a piece of flint stone. It can go with the puff of a little wind, and it can stay to blaze into a great fire, Tamba, my son, until Death blows on it with his bad breath and drives it out. But Life has a twin brother called Spirit, who sticks to his brother as a man's shadow clings to him under the fireball on a treeless plain . . . And when the monster Death blows at Life with his bad breath, Life runs and hides into his shadow and twin brother Spirit. And now Spirit is bigger and stronger because of this, and he is not afraid of Death. He laughs at the monster and calls him bad names and Death gnashes his great teeth, and goes mad with rage, for though he can blow out life from our eyes, he does not really kill it altogether. And when it finds refuge inside the body of its twin brother Spirit, in place of the body of man, Death cannot harm it, until perhaps if the Great Spirit of Spirits wills, and Life returns once more into a new body. So there are many who have been here before and live again, my son; only they cannot remember, just as you cannot remember what had happened before you came from thy mother's belly. Perhaps thy mother shall come back again as a little picni, who knows? But you and I shall not know it. Perhaps she shall live like one of the many Spirits around us, whom most of us cannot see—giving us warning dreams, guarding us.'

After that talk, Tamba and his father became one in spirit. His fear and sorrow were still there, but controlled. How could it be otherwise when there was such a new strong bond between father and son? He began to eat well again, and before the new moon returned, to Manda's joy, she was called to share her friend's companionship with Bangie, the mongrel.

Five

Tomaso looked up from his thoughts before the dying fire in the little shack which served as a kitchen. The flickering light gleamed on the comely figure of a young woman bare from the waist upwards, who had appeared as silently as if she was a spirit.

Kumse was some four years younger than the late Kisanka, fairly plump with a round face quite pleasing to the eyes. Her hair was pulled on top of her head and tied with a string as was the custom. Her skirt of coarse material reached nearly to her knees. Her breasts were in unity with her shapely body—largish, firm and youthful.

'Kumse? Why are you still here? Soon the cock will crow for the coming of a new day,' cried Tomaso, with a look of surprise on his face.

'You too are not yet in thy bed my chief though the night is far gone.' Her voice was soft and warm though there was a touch of nervous embarrassment there also, and she kept her head bowed. Tomaso too was embarrassed.

'It is a custom of mine to use the silence of these times for the working of my mind,' he said, but guessed that she would know he could have fed his mind with work in bed. A sudden thought came to him and he looked straight at her after feeding the fire with a couple of pieces of bamboo which the flames immediately appreciated.

'Did *she* make thee promise to come to me, Kumse?'

The young woman looked up, and the whites of her eyes looked extremely white in their very dark settings. The question took her by surprise and she looked confused.

'Sometimes the comfort of a woman's body can soften one's sorrow, my lord.'

She looked as if the shame of her words would bring water

to her eyes, and Tomaso guessed that she had only offered herself so brazenly because Kisanka had asked her to do so; but he guessed rightly that had she not loved him she would not have agreed.

'The new moon is not yet here since I have lost her, Kumse! Would you have me come to thee when I have not yet forgotten the gentleness of her arms?'

He knew the rebuke was harsh and saw her flinch as if he had struck her, and though he had his reason for hurting her, he was ashamed of the pain he had caused. Now he stood up, his tall figure nearly reaching the thatched roof of the little kitchen.

'I have never offered or given myself to anyone, my lord Tomaso—except the time when I came to thee at Kisanka's wish, and you did not take me.'

If he had any doubt about the hurt he had caused her, there could be none now.

'I am keeping the promise I made to her. She had hoped that this would console thee.'

'Ah, thus I prise the story from thy lips, my child. I knew that only a promise to her could have made thee so bold.'

The anger which had come to Kumse's face after he had scolded her went and again shame was uppermost.

'I would not have offered myself to thee so soon had I not promised, my chief, but I cannot swear that my spirit was not full of hope and not only for thy sake. Nor that many moons hence I would not have asked for my own sake in spite of my shame.'

The ex-chief looked down on the girl with admiration.

'In not pretending it was all for her sake you have shown there is truth in thee, child, and think not that I spurn thee. It is a mighty thing you have done this night, and you can feel thy promise kept.'

He put a hand on the girl's bare shoulder, and tilted up her chin with the other hand. The light from the fire showed on her polished-like-ebony face, and he could see the light of love there. He did not love her yet he could not let her go without a promise for the future, for what he saw there made him feel that she would mate with no other man.

'Perhaps when the moon comes and goes many times,

Kumse, and if there is no warrior big enough to fill thy eyes and time has softened my sorrow, I shall speak with thee. And if there is a look on thy face which can be interpreted as now, then I shall test thy words!'

Kumse laughed softly and somehow the laugh stayed with him long afterwards. 'There are so many ifs in this promise of thine, Lord Tomaso! It is like a fence with many gaps,' But the way she said it made him feel that she would be always waiting.

'I shall come to do the necessary as usual for thy house, my chief—*if* you will allow me,' the girl added mischievously.

'*If* you will come, Kumse, I shall thank thee,' replied Tomaso, surprised to find laughter in his voice.

After she had insisted on going home alone, Tomaso left to himself, wondered if Kisanka as well as Kumse had not foreseen that his reaction to the latter's advances would have been just as it had happened, for though he had refused the girl's offer, the incident had caused a distraction for a little while from his brooding. He went to bed a while after, feeling that his Little Shadow was somewhere in the dark corner of the house looking very pleased with herself.

Lago anticipated his succession to the chieftainship by getting an elaborate stool made by the village carver. It was carved in one piece and took the shape of an elephant with a kind of bowl-like seat on top. He was secretly worried because of the death of Kisanka, and what Tomaso might do to him when next they met kept him awake most of the nights. Yet the thought of being a chief still had its charm.

The would-be chief had also built himself a new house, far from the road and neighbours, perhaps having in mind surprise attacks on his person; for he knew that he had more enemies than friends. It was when he had placed himself comfortably in the new chair that he looked up and saw that he was about to have an unwelcome visitor. As he was out in the yard in full view of the man coming up the new stone-strewn path, it was impossible for him to get out of his chair without being seen, and he, recognising his visitor to be no other than his enemy Tahta, feared that the biting tongue of the old bushdoctor would make something unpleasant of a scuttle. So he sat, pretending to be unruffled by the approaching visitor.

'Greeting, O great Chief of all Maroons!' cried the old man with mock courtesy, bowing low. 'I would fall on these bony things the bakra call knees, but there are so many sharp stones, my chief. It is indeed sad to see a path so smooth to the eyes on yonder hill opposite should be so stony and rough when we come closer.'

Lago, knowing the wily Tahta, guessed rightly that there were other meanings to seemingly harmless words.

The old man continued blandly: 'But my Lord-who-sits-on-a-stool-of-asunu, I thy lowly slave, would be willing to kiss thy great feet with this toothless mouth to show my devotion to thee.'

If wrath had a face, then Lago must have posed as the model for its creation as he was now.

'So, this is thy mission, old chicken-neck?' he sputtered. 'Did my so-called blood brother ask thee to do him this favour of mocking me, since you are old and long past fighting age?'

Tahta looked almost genuine in his humility; only the hawk eyes in the wrinkled face spoke differently. 'Nay, nay, my lord the king! Pardon me, O merciful one! I am so tied up with confusion, not being certain if thy true title is king-chief—or—traitor! Perhaps my lord will guide me in this matter.'

There was a puzzled frown on Lago's brow in spite of his wrath. He began muttering to himself: 'What word is this? Traitor! This is not a Bantu word? It is no title amongst our people and yet I feel I have heard it before.'

He leaned forward on his seat, his eyes now mere slits as he hissed to Tahta standing some three yards away:

'Open thy mouth while you can, old fool, and tell me the meaning of this word traitor. I warn thee, thy age shall be of no interest to the mouth of my cutlass. Now speak!'

As Lago roared out the last words he stood up, his great arms seeming ready to grasp and crush the little bush doctor to a pulp. But Tahta never moved back a step. His little black eyes still gleamed with malice. Yet he managed to look pained. 'How suspicious is my lord, the king-traitor! I, an old man, call on thee to pay tribute to the mighty, and to ask the Great Spirit to bless thy reign as king and traitor of the Maroons of all the hills, and my lord thinks evil of my words! traitor is a title, my lord! It is a title the bakra give to those who are to be lifted high to the sky! It is a mighty title my chief! Mightier than to be called asunu, or elephant, as the bakra say it.'

But now Lago's hand was on his forehead like a man trying to remember something. Still Tahta rattled on: 'I would not like to call thee asunu, great one, since that name has been used to praise a . . .'

'Cease thy chatter, talking bird,' growled Lago, still looking as if he was trying to remember something. 'I do not like this word *traitor*,' he said slowly. 'I know thee too well to think that you would call me names which are good. Perhaps I shall find someone who will tell me the true riddle of this word, then, by the Great Spirit, you will know how Lago treats those who throw insults at him. If this is an insult!'

Tahta feigned fear by cringing at Lago's words. 'How could I insult my chief, my king, my traitor?' he asked, holding out both palms imploringly. 'Now I came in peace to pay homage, and I have done nothing but offended my traitor chief. I am covered in shame. I must depart before thy wrath overflows, O mighty traitor.' The old man turned shaking his head sad-like though his eyes gleamed with malice. In the meanwhile, Lago, with furrowed brows seemed to have thought of something. 'Stop, old man!' he cried, just as Tahta seemed about to go away.

Now Lago stepped towards the old man. The place was silent at that time of day and there was no-one about.

'I am remembering this word *traitor*. It is a bakra word. It is coming back to my head,' he continued softly, looking down on the ground with furrowed brow.

It seemed that the old man either did not know how near he was to danger or did not care.

'Yes, old man, I remember. I saw the bakra kill one of their own people once when I was a boy slave, and they had called him a traitor!' Quick as lightning the bullneck's hand shot out and grabbed the skinny arm of the old one.

'Traitor! Did you call me traitor, old man?' he hissed

between his teeth, with one great hand biting into the arm of the quackdoctor, and the other on the skinny throat. It seemed he would have killed Tahta then and there, but as his hands closed around the unresisting man's throat, a thought occurred to him and he quickly let go of this, but not the old one's arm.

'Why have you chosen this word, fool? Speak with one tongue and no riddles or thy death will not be easy.'

The calmness and unresisting manner of old Tahta shook the other, even in his mad anger. For it was plain the former had no intention of running away or even resisting. Lago's anger began to evaporate, and fright and alarm began to take shape in its place. 'Why have you chosen this word?' he asked again, but now his voice was a little cracked. Both the hunchback's hands were clasped in a vicelike grip on Tahta's arms, as he stared down into the wrinkled unperturbed face. Searchingly Lago gazed into the mocking eyes.

'You know!' he whispered at last, fearfully, then quickly looked up and around, as if he were afraid there might be an eavesdropper.

'Yes—traitor!' hissed the courageous old man. Lago struck him a terrific blow on his mouth with his hand, which sent him to the ground. The old man sat up and slowly wiped the trickle of blood coming from his lips with the back of his hand. Lago stood looking down with his hands hanging by his side, as if they were too long to be on his misshapen body. Tahta sat where he fell, with his eyes fastened on the face of the would-be chief. At last he spoke.

'Now thy fear has escaped from its cage, O chief!'

There was neither hate or malice coming from the voice, and because of this Lago felt that whatever the old man had to say would be a prophecy.

'This fear shall now grow big like a mountain and have the strength of many asunus.'

As Tahta paused, the frightened Lago looked as if he would ask forgiveness for the assault, for it was looked upon as a bad thing to raise one's hand to the aged, but the old man had merely stopped to wipe the blood away from his lips once more, and continued talking, before the other could find words for the apology.

'Thy fear shall sit on thy shoulders, Lago, and it shall disguise in thy shadow, so that there will be no knowing which is which. In thy bed it will be also, and thy eyes will search every face on these mountains to see if thy secret has come to their ears. Yet you will not know who learns of thy treachery and who does not.'

Now the speaker slowly raised himself up. Lago took a couple of steps backward as the old man stood upright, as if he was afraid of being struck in return, but now his face took on an ashy appearance, and his eyes could not look anywhere but into those of the bushdoctor. Now Tahta's voice was almost a whisper: 'There is something we call *cocobeh* in the Bantu language, Lago—the bākra call it leprosy. Live, Lago! Live and be treated even by thy own sons as one stricken with *cocobeh!*'

Lago flinched and licked his dry lips, his eyes bulging with fear. 'Aye, even thy enemies shall pity thee, O traitor, and thy own mouth shall call the monster death as if he were thy greatest friend,' said Tahta relentlessly.

Then as the terrified Lago opened his mouth to say something, Tahta spat with contempt, turned and walked down the hill, leaving the bullnecked one to collapse in his new chief's chair like an empty sack.

From the minute Tahta left Lago, the spirit of fear came upon him. He looked into the faces of people and saw, or thought he saw, accusation there. As the days went by, he would peer in every face suspiciously, and after passing would turn to see if he was being watched. Most of the time his very strange action caused people to look back after passing him, and of course that convinced him more than ever that everyone knew that once he had betrayed his countrymen and women to the bakra.

He was convinced that Tahta would tell them that he spoke for fear of the ants' torture. He saw the end of his dream because of this secret past of his. Tahta, now that he was sure that his hunch was right, played on his enemy's nerves without mercy. He made great lengths of bamboo into speaking tubes, hid for hours in the thick branches of trees along the path leading from Lago's home, and from there the night wind would whisper: 'Traitor' in a ghostlike manner almost in the ears of the frightened man. And always a sudden smell of that strange pimento concoction which Tahta had prescribed for the late Kisanka's headaches would come after the whisperings, so that Lago was convinced that the Spirit of Kisanka was taking its revenge. And, when people asked each other why Lago was acting so suspiciously and jumpily, Tahta, if he was near, would merely hint that it was something dreadful he had done to his fellows on the plantation which now confronted him. The whisper went from mouth to mouth as the days went by, and now Lago's two sons were being made to suffer for their father's past. Boys older than themselves began mocking their misshapen father openly, and, once, the one called Jo overheard the talk of Lago's shame being passed from one adult to the other.

The boys knowing that their father was being looked upon as a coward and a traitor, tried their best to avoid going out with him, or even meeting him openly. This hurt Lago more than anything that anyone could have done to him. In his near madness he began to think of something which would wipe out the shame on the faces of his boys, and perhaps win the people over to accept him as chief. But he could hardly plan when his sleep was disturbed by the word *traitor* and he awakened in the dark to find the room reeking of the thing the dead Kisanka alone used to use for her headaches. The sweat would stand in great drops on his forehead and his head would grow as large as a mountain as the ghostlike whisper of 'Traitor' would come from somewhere in space.

He had a plan, he thought. He would show the people of Twin Sisters that he had courage in spite of what they were saying about him. Since the fall which had resulted in his semi-deformed body, he had not been to the plantations on raids. He had planned, and even directed two from afar, but all had agreed that because of his unusual physique, he would be easily spotted as a stranger in the plains, and the bakra would capture him. Now he would go to the plant-ations—alone. He would show them all that he was no coward, for he would return with people whom he would rescue single-handed. His sons would look at him once more with respect, and the people would have to admit that whatever he had done when he was young could be forgiven because of his daring. If he brought it off they might even think him greater than Tomaso. For he, the ex-chief, had no such handicap as a twisted back . . . He would not tell them his plans. He would say he was going on the long and dangerous journey across the island to the biggest of the Maroon settlements over in the Cockpit mountains. They all knew such a journey would take at least one moon, not because of the distance, but because of the route and the danger of being captured by the bakra soldiers.

So Lago announced his departure to talk with the Maroon chiefs of the Cockpit mountains and departed, and among the uneasy ones were Tahta and Tomaso, for these two, knowing the man, did not believe his story. But they never guessed that Lago was desperate enough to plan a one-man rescue of slaves from the plantation.

When Lago was caught by the bakra, they acted wisely, knowing that every slave was a friend of the Maroons. They kept the capture a close secret. The three slaves who did see were taken away and locked up in the militia camp. So the people of Twin Sisters never knew that Lago was in the hands of the bakra.

It took the bakra a full week to break Lago. First they tried two days without a bite and little water. After that they brought him hunks of meat soaked in brine and roasted, then soaked again in brine. The starving man wolfed up the lot. He was given more until he could not swallow another bite.

'Water!' he cried to his jailors. But instead of the liquid to quench his terrible thirst, they placed him in a smaller cell with the flat roof only a little above the height of a man with the relentless tropical sun beating down making even his chains hot. But no water!

'Water! Water! Water!' he cried until he was hoarse, but since he would not tell the secrets they wished to know, such as the unguarded route to Twin Sisters, they left him there until he became almost raving mad. Later they took him out into the barrack yard after seeing that no slaves were present to recognise their capture. They lashed him mercilessly, and afterwards rubbed the open wounds with saltpetre. He fainted but he did not speak. They prised open the palm of his hand and dropped liquid boiling lead in it. His scream went up to the skies, but he still shook his head when they asked him questions, and even they looked at the misshapen figure with admiration. Just before dawn they took him in a cart to a lonely spot and he sensed that for him this was the end.

At first he could not see properly as the morning light had not yet reached the lowland, but when they took him nearer and the daylight was upon them he could see.

Only the shape told him that it was a man lying staked out on the ground covered by countless ants. Only the hair made it possible to guess that he was once black. Yet there was slight heaving on various parts of the naked body to tell him that life had not yet gone completely. As Lago stared, his eyes grew until it seemed to the watching bakra that they would fall from their sockets to the ground. The slave who was now food for the ants had dared to catch hold of his master's foot to save himself from a kick while he was lying on the ground. His master had fallen and bruised his behind, and as a result, and as the law allowed a master to do whatever he wished with the life of his slave, the bakra chose this punishment which he hoped would be a lesson to others. The one bakra whom the Maroons called 'Man of God', had protested again, but he was tarred and feathered by his fellow bakra for his continued interference in the normal affairs between master and slaves, and as he had no legal right to do so, he was entirely in the wrong.

So now, after nearly ten hours of slow death by the ants, another stood staring down with horror at the fate which would also be his unless he talked.

As the sun touched the tip of the mountains, the watching bakra saw the bare lacerated torso of the captured Lago begin to pulsate visibly while countless pinhead-like drops of perspiration appeared. The pulsations grew harder and harder as the fascinated eyes of the man stared down on the slightly moving thing beneath him. Soon Lago's body reaction to the horror before his eyes became a kind of St. Vitus dance, only more powerful. The watching bakra knew that it would not be long before the man between them would tell them what they wanted to know. But it was when they laid their hands upon him to prepare him for the feast that it happened.

'I will tell! I will tell!' he shouted in Bantu, then in his terror, fearing they might not understand made him remember the broken English every slave, and ex-slave, knew. 'Ah-will-talk-Massa! Ah-will-talk,' he screamed. After that they could not stop him talking even if they wished. There was nothing he did not tell. They took him away from the scene and ordered that he should be fed and treated well in his confinement. For they wanted him to lead them by the secret route which he told them of, and there were other services he could render for sparing him from death by the ants.

It took the bakra a week to have everything prepared, including four cannons, a dozen imported Mosquito Indians, and a pair of slave-hunting dogs. They picked the best of the militia for the trip and from a Man-of-War in the harbour at the time came fifty sailors to make up the invading army.

Slaves necessary to help with the guns, kegs of powder and other heavy equipment, were chained together so that it would be difficult for them to run away when they reached the hills.

Lago too was chained like a dog on a lead. They did not want him to run away, or even to commit suicide—yet. Afterwards it was agreed that it was the best kept secret of the island. For none of the Maroons in any of the hills heard about the capture, and apart from Tomaso and his band of warriors, the people of Twin Sisters slept in that calm which usually comes before a hurricane.

The eketeh and the talking drums were telling the people of Twin Sisters that the bakra were coming towards the foot of the hills to attack them. Warriors jumped to the call. They poured from every part of the village at a trot towards the foot of the mountain, and the drums and eketeh told of their coming:

'We hear you. We come. We hear you. We come,' said the instruments.

Now many remembered how careless Lago and the last chief had been since Tomaso had abdicated. Warriors found supplies of powder badly distributed so that some posts had none, and the same went for balls for the muskets. New bows and arrows had not been made for years by some of the warriors, and some could not even find a workable one. Did not Lago say these were unnecessary weapons since they had muskets and the bakra would never come within spearthrow? Only Tomaso's Spirit Men had insisted on being always prepared with bows and arrows, spears and even battleaxes. It was only because it would have been courting death to laugh at these men why those who agreed with Lago had not laughed at Tomaso and his men for their old-fashioned, over-cautious ways. True they were equipped with muskets too, but why worry about spears and so many bows and battleaxes, when the bakra would never break through the Maroon guard at the foot of the hills and so reach the forest where such weapons might be useful? So thought and reasoned many, though most of the oldtimers who saw service under Tomaso felt uneasy and longed to be under his command. But Tomaso and most of his men were not there. The ex-chief had gone to the plains to kill three birds with one stone—to get food for their muskets, information about Lago, and, if all was well, help some slaves to escape with them back to Twin Sisters. Kumse was left to look after Tamba and Manda.

Thanks to old Tahta, Tamba could make out a few of the words the talking drums were saying. He stood with his little blind friend and the young woman Kumse at the door of his house peering in the darkness with his head leaning on one side so as to hear the drumtalk better. He translated enough to convince Kumse that danger had come to the hills. As the boy realized the significance of the words, he wished that his father was there in the hills instead of somewhere in the plains.

He was sure he would not have been frightened. He hoped that Manda and even the young woman Kumse would not guess how frightened he was, for he was the man of the house, the only one now that his father and Tahta were absent, and he felt it was his job to protect them.

The sun was just going to sleep when the eketeh and the drums stopped their talking. Tamba went for his bow and arrow, his bit of machete and the bag he used when he went to hunt coney or birds. They stood at the door as the night came down, watching down towards the village beneath them a mile away, and listening for sounds of musket-shots. Tamba wondered where the spirit of his late mother was at the moment. Was she watching over them there? Or was she by his father's side ready to warn him of danger? Bangie, the mongrel stood before his little master and his companions, hoping they were about to go on an adventurous trip perhaps.

Night had come. Kumse persuaded Tamba and his blind companion to go to bed. She told them what to do in case of an attack. Tamba should take his little bag in which she had placed some cassava bread, meat and a few other things, along with his gourd full of water, and make for his little leanto which he had in the woods, taking Manda. She would find a way of getting help. She made him promise not to leave Manda, not that this was necessary, and said she felt certain that before the night was over his father would be back, or on the hillside winning the battle. She assured them that the bakra could not pass the warriors on the foot of the hill to reach the village. But like all the other people of the hills Kumse did not know that not only had Lago been caught but that he had talked, and had told of the secret, unguarded route, where even mules could climb and which would bring the invaders right above the village. She did not know nor did the people until it was too late that the bakra's appearance on the broad foot of the hills was to draw the warriors to defend this position, while the real invading force came by the secret route. Tomaso and his men would not have been caught so easily, for in the first place, the warriors on guard on the secret route would have given the alarm. But Lago and his puppet chief had long abandoned this precaution. So while the warriors gathered to look down on the numerous well-lit tents the bakra pitched at the foot of the mountain just out of distance of the muskets of the defenders, the real invaders crept down through the secret route unnoticed, with Lago chained like a dog to the saddle of an officer, and the chained slaves toiling under blows with the guns and the food for such weapons.

Tomaso and a party of his Spirit Men were in hiding in the woods above the main road leading to the village and militia barracks. Twin Sisters were some forty miles away, and the fifty-odd men were divided in four groups spread out within signal distance of each other. Tahta was as usual with his ex-chief, who had to be persuaded to rest and doze, for they had travelled all night through the mountain, and now the sun was high.

Suddenly Tomaso jumped from his bed on the bare ground, his face full of bewilderment and alarm at the same time. But in a flash he realized where he was. The ever alert Tahta looked at his adopted son with a question in his eyes.

'We must go, Tahta! We must go back quickly,' Tomaso whispered, unusually excited. 'We must call our warriors and run like sky-fire,' he continued hoarsely, and for a moment Tahta thought his companion was ill in the head. Tomaso guessed by the other's eyes that he was under suspicion. 'No, Tahta. My head has no fever and the sleep is gone from my eyes,' he said earnestly, holding tightly the bony arm of the old man. 'It is my Kisanka, Tahta. She told me and I could swear I was only half asleep then, my father, for I could still hear thee humming the Song of the Eketeh under thy breath.'

Tahta's face cleared, and now he looked towards their companions resting a few yards away, ready to summon them. There was never a doubt in the bushdoctor's mind now. If Kisanka spoke to Tomaso whether he was asleep or not, whatever she said would be the truth. Every Maroon on the hill would have felt the same.

'Come, my son! I shall call the others. A good spirit like our Kisanka does not speak with two tongues. Nay, waste not time to tell me the dream, vision, or whatever it may be. That we can speak of when we are on our way.'

Within ten minutes the message to return to the hills in

haste was relayed to the fifty-odd warriors resting about the hillside, and so well trained were they that not even the Mosquito Indians, whom the bakra imported to track down runaway slaves, would have been able to follow the trail they left behind as they headed with all speed towards their mountain home.

'She stood there, Tahta, and I did not know she had gone to the Spirit Land, so true she was to life.'

Tahta breathlessly grunted to show he was listening as he trotted behind his former chief. But Tomaso knew that the old man would make the forty mile journey back to Twin Sisters with the same pace and endurance as any of his young warriors, in spite of the fact that they were most of the time following a rugged trail and almost jungle thickness not daring to follow the road below where the bakra patrols might appear any time of the day.

'Speak on my son, I listen,' encouraged Tahta between breathing.

'It was as if she had been running, Tahta, for I could see her breasts heaving hard when she came up to me, and when she came closer I could feel her breath on my cheek, and the thing she used to use to bathe her forehead—that which you made for her, seemed to be right in my nostrils.'

Tomaso broke off as he discovered that the talking had slowed up his running a little. Not before the miles-eating pace was under way again, with the warriors stringing behind in a close line, did the leader speak again:

'*Go, Tomaso! Go like the wind to the aid of our people,* cried my Kisanka, Tahta! As plain as I am saying it. *Lago has talked! Look well when you reach the hills, My Spirit, or you will fall in the bakra hands! Go now, Tomaso! Go!*'

Again Tomaso realized that his men were right up behind him and his old friend and he set the pace again before he spoke:

'I still cannot believe it was a dream, Tahta, and I know there is danger. Kisanka would not lie.'

Tahta's breath came from opened mouth as well as nostrils. 'I too know that thy Kisanka's warning must be heeded, Tomaso,' he panted, drawing alongside his leader now that the path was wide enough for this. 'And yet, how can this be? None of our spies have seen the accursed Lago taken. Also, those who send word to us do they not say a band of bakra soldiers have taken the other road which leads to the Maroons of the Cockpit mountains, which is a great journey from Twin Sisters?'

Tomaso thought a while before he answered.

'Perhaps the bakra are wise, Tahta. Perhaps they wanted to fool our spies so they go towards the other side of the island and when they make fools of us they turn back and fall on us, just when we think them elsewhere. Perhaps they now know it is wisdom to keep a captive from the eyes of our people on the plains and might have hidden Lago in their barracks.'

'Spirit of my Fathers! Tomaso, my son, there is wisdom in thy words! Woe! We are lost if that snake Lago falls into the hands of the bakra. He will talk, Tomaso. Remember how he had talked before and had caused Kisanka to be tortured? And yet he kept the secret of his treachery until I smelt him out with the aid of the old village news-smeller? The dog would talk even after his head was chopped from his body. How I wish I had slain him when I had him at my mercy on the day he fought with thee, Tomaso!'

The sun was just going to sleep when Tomaso, with his warriors close behind on their bellies, peered down on the plains below. From where they were they could see the tents and accoutrements of war which could leave no doubt in their minds that the bakra had tricked the slaves who served as spies, and had doubled back from the route they had taken.

The ex-chief and his men were still a good distance away from their own mountain. To reach it they would have to make a detour, for they could not go down on the plains as the bakra soldiers stood between them and the known entrance to the inhabited hills. Tomaso also guessed that every single able-bodied warrior was now massed behind trees and boulders, ready for the bakra soldiers whom they were certain would try to fight their way to the foot of the hills. The ex-chief judged that the invaders had about two hundred men on the plains. He wondered why they had not attacked before nightfall, which would have been the natural thing to do. Instead, they had camped just out of musket range from the foot of the hills. Why? he asked himself. Then he remembered something! His spies had told him that there were two lots of bakra soldiers! One lot was dressed in soldier clothes of bright colours, and another was not so well dressed and had left long before the well dressed band, yet all Tomaso could see were the brightly dressed soldiers. Where were the others? Another thing! This did not look like the mighty band of men his spies had told him they had seen marching out of the town. Tomaso remembered again the words of Kisanka some hours before. He gathered his Spirit Men about him, and with fear clutching at his spirit, prepared to lead a breakneck dash into the hills, knowing that time was against them reaching the village before the bakra.

'Tahta!'

'My son?'

'How are thy breath and body?'

'My feet are moving as fast thine, my son! Why ask?'

'We cannot go by the Place-of-the-Big-Jump, or any of the other paths Lago knows of.'

'That is true, Tomaso. The bakra soldiers might be there waiting.'

'He does not know of the cliff with the hanging rope, my father, so this will be our route to our village. I placed a new rope there last moon and no rain has come since to make it weak.'

'Aye, Tomaso, but there will be rain tonight, I can smell it, and my nose can also smell blood, my son. Fear is eating up my spirit for the blood I smell seems like that of our people.'

For the bakra who manned the cannons, it was like knocking sitting hens off their eggs. All they needed to do was to point the guns from their perch overlooking the village towards the places where the fires, recently used for preparing late meals or perhaps merely to give light to those who were sitting up discussing the present situation, were. After that the touching of flame against powder was all the invaders needed. The night was pitch dark, the clouds heavy with the threat of rain. Out in the distance there were occasional flashes of lightning and the usual rumbling accompaniment.

The flash of the first cannon, the roar of the echoes around the sleeping village brought terror and bewilderment to the unsuspecting inhabitants. The first cannon ball scored a direct hit on one of the many wattled and thatched houses, and within minutes, there was nothing but flames. Now the great death-dealing weapons roared one after the other on the terrified villagers below with the cries of the dying mingling with those of the frightened children.

The bakra guns made fire of the wooden and thatched huts. It ate up many women and children and the old men who had long passed the age for fighting. Nevertheless only the wounded and the children screamed. The women sobbed inside themselves as they tried in vain to help the old warriors to load their long useless muskets. They tried to gather the children, scattered and trembling in terror. They herded the youngsters they could lay hands on and pushed them out of the battered and burning village into the darkness of the forest. Once a stray ball from the cannon above them struck a tree under which the crowd of children were hiding, and there was a terrible scream as the ricocheted ball crashed in their midst killing many and wounding many more.

Thereafter the terrified children lost all sense of reason. They dashed into the darkness of the hills, not knowing where they were going, fearing only the blazing village and the destructive thunder of the thing above them. Many died as they went. Some fell over cliffs or into sinkholes in the dark; some died from sheer terror. Others lay with broken bones, moaning into unconsciousness. A few escaped to wander aimlessly and hopelessly into the heart of the hills as water began pouring from the skies.

When the sound of cannonfire came to the ears of the defending warriors watching the bakra camped before them on the plains, the guardians had already decided amongst themselves that this was one of those periodic raids the bakra usually made without daring to reach any part of the mountains.

Finding the invaders out of range, they settled down for the afternoon and night, feeling that, as usual, the bakra would wait for daylight before venturing closer. They had heard of these cannons, and most of them had seen these weapons, but the bakra had kept such heavy stuff for pointing at the sea in case the Spanish bakra returned to capture the island, though some were to be seen at the barracks of the militia.

At first they thought the sounds reaching their ears were peals of thunder heralding the promised downpour. And when they discovered that this was man-made thunder they were hearing, they thought the bakra wanted to confuse them by attacking some part of the mountainside which was almost inaccessible, and, thanks to the echoes, this illusion lived for some minutes. But to the amazement and consternation of all, they finally became convinced that the original sound was not thunder. Not many minutes later the glow from the fires three miles up into the village told them their fears were confirmed. There was a great cry: 'The bakra are attacking our village! They are killing our women and children up there! We are betrayed!' The bakra tried to add to the near panic and confusion by attacking from the plains, though it was too dark for them to see their targets. It was a foolish move, however, for the near-panic warriors half killed the natural instinct to climb back to their village and die by the side of their young ones, for now they felt they could perhaps get their revenge on the hated bakra by staying where they were. A cry came from the lips of all:

'If only we had Tomaso as our leader! Tomaso would have led us to victory even now! Where is Tomaso and his Spirit Men? Perhaps they too have been caught into the bakra trap. We are doomed but we will fight to the last. Let the bakra come. It is Lago who is the cause of this. We have been betrayed by Lago.'

Kumse was just halfway to the village when the shattering blast from the bakra's cannons shook the hills and brought terror to her as to all who heard it. For neither she or the people of Twin Sisters had heard these sounds before, and the echoes made it seem that the whole mountain around them had exploded. Luckily she was on the opposite direction to which the cannons were aimed, but she could see the skies lighted up as the village began to blaze under the still mysterious earth-shaking sound. All the young woman could understand was that the terrible sound was the cause of the fires in the village. Faint screams came to her ears and she thought of her young charges she had left behind her in the house of the man she loved, and turned back, feeling it would be better to be with them, giving them assurance and comfort, for even though they were far from this mysterious thing which was shaking the earth and causing fire in the village, she was convinced that the terrible sounds must be loud enough even there to cause the children to feel frightened out of their wits.

Kumse, like all of the mountain people depended on memory and bare feet to locate and follow the narrow stony bushlined paths leading to home, so though the night was starless and the darkness seemed thick enough to be felt, she had no trouble to follow the path back. She was naturally afraid of evil spirits, but the feeling of having the spirit of her best friend protecting her was there to counteract her fear, and the thought that she was doing something for her idol by going back to look after his child, made her feel that if necessary she would even go down to where the terror was still shaking the mountains. She was nearly home when there was a lull in the earthshaking noise, and her ears picked up the sound of someone approaching, and the murmur of voices.

She was just about to call out joyfully, thinking it was Tomaso and his Spirit Men who were coming, when the call froze on her breath. For the Spirit Men, whose group included her own father and a brother, and all warriors with whom she was well acquainted, would not have walked like a band of asunus in a frolicking mood, nor would their efforts of low talk be so meaningless.

Fear took hold of her, but she did not panic. Was she not the daughter of Jomo whom Tomaso swore was as wise in bushfighting as the best of the Spirit Men? Was not her brother Quako, though younger than her, already famous as one of Tomaso's fearless fighting men? She would stop trembling. Whoever they were, they did not know she was hiding by the path in the darkness. But it was bad to wait, for it seemed they were trying to find Tomaso's home, and if they were not Tomaso's men or men of the village, then they would mean harm to whoever they found. She remembered the big noise and now she realized that there were faint sounds of musket fire in the direction of the woods near the village. It could mean one thing. The mighty sounds she heard had come from the big thunderstick her brother had told her he had seen on the plains on one of his trips with the Spirit Men. He said it could shake the earth when it spoke . . . She reasoned the bakra must have beaten the Maroons at the foot of the hill, and now they were destroying the village.

Kumse thought of all this as she waited to get more proof of the visitors. But for the last few minutes she heard no sound. It seemed whoever it was was now at a standstill. She wondered if they were listening and if they had heard her before she had them, but dismissed this thought at once for she had made no sound since she noticed the noise of their approach and their low talk. She waited for half a minute more and now she did not know whether the intruders were still there or not. Now she was not sure they were not Tomaso and his men, nor was she sure that they were not her own people perhaps hiding from the bakra. Yet she must go back to see to her charges.

She remembered her warrior brother telling her how part of their training for bushfighting was to make a hiding bakra reveal his position by throwing a stick or stone in the opposite direction. The Maroon warriors never fired at a sound such as this would make. Her brother swore that the bakra always did since they felt every sound in the jungle meant danger. She found a stone, stood up, and threw it far from her in the opposite direction.

Seconds later two blasts came almost deafeningly not many chains away from the girl. The echoes had not died when she began to run towards the house, for now she was sure by the gunfire that the intruders were those whom the people of the mountains feared more than death—the dreaded people known as whites to the outside world, and bakra to the Maroons.

Tamba was still awake when the mighty thunder-noise

began. So was Manda.

This night both lay side by side on the floor in Tomaso's part of the house as Kumse had suggested, so that they could keep each other company. Tamba had on a kind of nightshirt of coarse material and the blind Manda a smock made of cloth. They were both frightened, though at first they had mistaken the noise for thunder. It was only when the skies above the village became ablaze with fire and smoke that Tamba realized they were wrong. He had heard about mighty thundersticks big as little picnies from both his father and Tahta, but he could not understand how these could be in the village. Did not his elders say the dreaded bakra could not pass the warriors at the foot of the plains unless they managed to kill all the Maroon warriors guarding the whole area? Yet if it was not the mighty thundersticks of the bakra, what could it be?

He was standing at the doorway pondering these matters in his mind when Manda, at his side, spoke:

'Tamba, Little Brother!'

'Speak, Manda.'

'I have never heard the thunder so bad. It shakes my inside.'

'It shakes my inside, too, Manda.'

'Is there rain in the sky, Little Brother?'

For a few seconds Tamba wondered why she had not spoken of the glare of fire in the village, until she asked the question, then he remembered she was blind. It had often happened like this, and always after such forgetfulness he would feel a great pity for her, and there would be tenderness and absence of scolding for whatever she did even if it was something which would have otherwise annoyed him. Now he took the little hand in his.

'Little Sister, there is rain in the sky, but I do not think the thunder is because of coming rain.'

Manda stood silent, and the mongrel Bangie, seeming agitated, as well as afraid of the sound, stood in front of the two, unable to make up his mind whether to run back inside the house or bark defiance at whatever it was. He compromised by taking a couple of steps backwards until he bumped into his master's legs. Full of embarrassment, the animal tried to save face by making a half-hearted growl before he discreetly squatted where he was.

'Little Brother!'

'Yes, Little Sister?'

'What is it? Is it the bakra?'

'I do not know, Manda. It could be.'

'If it is the bakra, would they find us here?'

'No. We will go into the bushes with the string bag and my gourd if we hear them coming this way. We would hide in my little hut and they could not find us, for my father said that the bakra cannot see in the dark as well as us.'

Manda did not tell Tamba that she was afraid. Tamba did not tell Manda that he too was afraid. For he reasoned that if the bakra were attacking the village and his father did not come, then they were in great danger. But the boy gathered the string bag in which the thoughtful Kumse had placed cassava bread and smoked pork wrapped in green Badu leaves, and placed it close to the door, along with the small gourd full of water and his machete.

The two were sitting by the doorway, now half asleep. The light in the house was dim as usual, being a little piece of wood made like a flat cork with a wick made of wild cotton floating in a tiny calabash of oil made from castor seeds.

Suddenly the blast of two musket-shots shattered the uneasy stillness which came after the roaring cannons. Manda grabbed her companion's hand in terror. Bangie growled his alarm as the two stood undecided what to do. Then their ears caught the sound of running feet. Tamba grabbed Manda's hand and they dashed across the yard after taking the bag, gourd, and machete, they had ready. A few minutes later, Tamba could see a shadowy figure dashing into the dimly lit house, and heard the call which he immediately recognised as the voice of Kumse. The frightened young woman was glad to see her charges as they came out of their hiding.

Quickly she told them of her experience and suspicion, and promised to try to find Tomaso. Tamba begged Kumse, either to come with them, or to stay with Manda, and let him try to find his father, but she refused, getting impatient at the time lost arguing. Then she pressed each to her breast lovingly and sent them away. As the darkness swallowed up the two children with the dog, Kumse blew out the improvised lamp. Seconds after she did so there was a blast of muskets with a cry from the attackers to surrender or be killed, only Kumse did not know what was said, for the language was that of the bakra. She crawled on all fours from Tomaso's room through Tamba's, then into the nearly finished annexe planned for Manda's comfort, and, with one great intake of breath, dashed through this exit, expecting every moment to be blasted by the attackers. But, to her great relief, she reached the protected darkness of the nearby forest before the bakra discovered the escape and began to fire indiscriminately.

Now she dared not follow the path which would take her again to the village, but she was determined to find Tomaso if he had returned to the village. She was encouraged by the sound reasoning that Tomaso was important to the bakra, and they had not killed or captured him, to their knowledge, or they would not have sent their soldiers to attack this lone house. She remembered one of the secret places the ex-chief used at times as meeting place for his men, for she had taken supplies there on her father's instructions. There was always a guard there, for it was a cache for the arms of the Spirit Men. She thought that if she could find her way in the darkness and reach this place, the guard might be able to tell her something. She could hear the sound of musketshots and knew that all the way to her goal would be full of danger. Just then the long spell of drought was broken by a great shower of rain, and as the large drops fell from the trees above to her bare torso, she felt for and found a creeper with which she tied her soaking skirt of rough material at the waist so that it now reached high above her knees.

The tree-tops grew bright suddenly and she looked back to find the skies alight from the glare of a fire. It was from the house she had left not long before.

Half an hour later a great pair of hands dragged her to the ground.

Tamba heard the musketshots, and his heart jumped so that

he stopped his running suddenly. He was thinking of Kumse back where the terrible sound came from. He felt he should not have left her side though he was afraid. Then he thought of Manda. Had he stayed, she would have stayed too. But as he hurried along holding the arm of his young companion, his spirit was back there with Kumse. Perhaps they had shot her, and she was now lying dead or perhaps wounded! He loved Kumse. She was good to them and his mother had loved her like a sister. What would his father have done in his place? Manda stumbled along by his side saying nothing, but feeling most of Tamba's thoughts through his fingers. They had reached the little leanto hut when Manda whispered:

'Tamba, Little Brother!'

'Speak, Manda.'

'Do you think they have killed her?'

'I do not know.'

'Could you know if you went back to look?'

'Without you, Manda?'

'I would not be afraid for myself, Little Brother, only for you. I could stay here and wait with Bangie.'

Now conflicting thoughts tore at the boy's mind. Perhaps the bakra had caught, wounded or killed Kumse. If she were dead he could do nothing. But if she were wounded, she might be lying there alone with no-one to hear her cry or to give her a calabash of water which he was told all wounded people craved. If she were captured perhaps he could find some way of helping her to escape out of the bakra's hands. His father would have tried to know what had happened to the brave woman were he in his place. How could he stand before his parent and say he did not know because he did not go to find out after he had heard those musketshots? And yet he did not want to leave Manda alone. She was blind and would fall over some precipice or into some sinkhole if she were to try to find her way further into the forest. And lastly he was afraid!

'I cannot leave thee alone, Manda,' he whispered at last, just as the rain began to fall.

'But I shall sit here until you return, Tamba, if it is in thy mind to go.'

156

Now the boy felt that unless he went his companion would know he was afraid, though he was genuinely thinking of her welfare as well.

'Perhaps I could go to the edge of the woods towards the house and listen, Manda,' he said half reluctantly, for he felt that the girl was hiding her fear of being alone. He rose to go, then he remembered that Kumse had pushed a little bundle of cloth with the other things in his string bag. He found it with his fingers, and recognised it as a small piece of material he often used as a loincloth. There was a larger piece also, perhaps intended for Manda. Kumse was wise, he thought, for the rough shirtlike material he was now dressed in could be a nuisance in a jungle full of thornbushes. He told Manda of his find, changing his shirt for the smaller cloth. As he changed he sensed that Manda had been doing likewise. The water from the holes in the leanto poured on their bodies now almost as bad as if they were outside. Suddenly, Tamba gave a gasp and his thought of going to find out Kumse's fate became out of the question. For in spite of the rain, the trees around the hillside were lighted up by a great blaze which the boy knew for certain was in the direction of his house. At the said moment, Bangie who was somewhere about the children's legs, growled, and before Tamba could get hold of him, the dog rushed forward into the darkness barking furiously. The next moment there was no doubt about what Bangie had been barking at. For a great roar came from another dog somewhere in the darkness, and Tamba knew that he and his blind companion were in fearful danger.

After the one-sided battle came the rounding up.

The bakra soldiers found the big artificial cave, known as the Place-of-Talks, just right for their plans, with its great clearing before the entrance quite adequate to take the captives and to hold them there, not only by their ring of armed soldiers, but also with the threat of two of the four cannons pointing towards them from the mouth of the cave. It was a godsend this cave, for were they to place the cannons in the open, the downpour of rain would have played havoc with the powder. Now the kegs of gun-food were stored right behind the gunners, safe and dry.

Away from the explosives was a small fire. Further along at the other end of the cave were the officers in charge of the invasion, and near them, still chained like a dog on a lead, and looking as if he did not care whether there was still breath in his lacerated body and hollow cheeks or not, was Lago.

It was during a lull in the rain, that the bakra heard the sound of some kind of horn. They remembered Lago, who had told them everything they wished to know since the affair at the ant-feast, and now they called on him to translate the signal someone a long distance away seemed to be sending.

Lago read the faint message of the eketeh.

'Stay where you are, warriors! The bakra wait on the hillside to slay you . . . Stay where you are . . .'

The bakra asked anxiously the meaning. Lago looked up on his captors and they could not see the hate in his eyes which had sunk so deeply inside his head, and the pitch-dipped torches lighting the cave were flickering.

'Eketeh tell de warriors dem mus' all surrender, mas'er,' said the hunchback in broken English.

The bakra were satisfied. All was well. Only one thing more they wanted, apart from capturing the trapped warriors near the foot of the mountain—and that was their former chief. For they had heard of Tomaso and guessed that his capture would completely demoralize the captives sitting in the rain-swept clearing guarded by a crescent of soldiers, as well as the cannons trained on them from the mouth of the cave. Lago had told them where Tomaso lived. They had sent four soldiers with two imported Mosquito Indians and a slave-hunting dog to try to capture the ex-chief if he was still at home—or his son.

Now the bakra thought of a better idea. They would send Lago to find or capture the man he had told them was his enemy.

They took the chain off the wreck which was once the bullnecked one. They told him what they wanted of him. They threw gold coins at him, promising twice as much if he returned with Tomaso dead, and four times as much if he was still alive. For he was better alive for what they wanted to do. They called the guards and told them that if their captive returned with the former chief they should let him through to their headquarters in the cave, no matter what the time might be.

Lago picked up the money and a whistle they gave him to use in case he needed help. The only piece of clothing he had on was a pair of coarse, wet and dirty trousers, frayed at the legs. He showed his teeth like a tiger and the bakra accepted it as a grin of pleasure.

Painfully the man the whole village knew betrayed them walked through the crowds of captives. As he came past the struggling fires which were permitted because they helped to light up the clearing, some of those miserably sitting around them warming their wet bodies recognised him, and a great murmur went up from the crowd. But the guards were told to expect this, and they used their musket-butts on those who would have laid hands on the would-be chief. Only when his escorts had set him free into the pitch-dark woods was he sure there were none to see him.

A great weight fell from the water-laden tree on to the *thing* moving beneath. Hands like steel found the throat of the victim as both crashed to the ground.

The body underneath did not struggle. Indeed it was as if it was defenceless—even lifeless, so easy was the capture.

The aggressor explored his victim's body swiftly. Satisfied that there was no lurking danger in the form of a weapon, the attacker spoke, at the same time releasing the throat from the mighty pressure his hands had exerted:

'So! The spirit has gone from thee, O betrayer of women and slayer of picnies!'

There was no answer but the swift intake of breath convinced the speaker that his captor recognised his voice.

'Aye, snake, whom I once called bloodbrother, it is I, Tomaso! Come where there is light, for I wish to see the white of thine eyes before the vultures vomit over thy poisonous flesh.'

Tomaso kicked at the wretched man so as to give him a start. The sky had cleared now and there were stars enough for the trained eyes of the ex-chief to see his enemy's outline.

Apart from the startled gasp, Lago said nothing, even when Tomaso caught his wrist, twisted his arm near to breaking point, and frogmarched him further into the woods.

'Did not I say there would be pity on thy face when I had finished with this snake, Tomaso?'

Startled, the leader took his eyes off the man sitting bent almost double at his feet. A bamboo-fed fire lit up the rocky recess of the cove in which the men sheltered, and showed plainly the bare torso of the captive as well as the dozen warriors standing around.

They were well secluded from the bakra soldiers here, for the captured village was more than a mile away and cliffs and woodland of jungle thickness were between them as well. Even then Tomaso had made certain of preventing surprises by having his warriors posted all around the place, and others were in strategic positions all along the possible route to this meeting place.

The embarrassed Tomaso was just about to reply to Tahta, for it was the bushdoctor who had read the leader's face, when the man on the ground wearily raised his haggard, unshaven face and turned his sunken, bloodshot eyes towards the old man. His voice was hoarse and cracked. 'Aye, old man, you have tasted revenge. Think not that I seek thy pity.' He turned his head almost defiantly towards Tomaso standing almost behind him. 'Finish thy work and have done, blood brother! I wait.'

Saying this, Lago allowed his head to drop once more, so low, that his chin rested on his chest. It seemed to the onlookers that he cared not whether his head would be chopped off that moment or the next. And looking at his lacerated body, it seemed to even such hardened warriors that death would be a relief to him. For the terrible journey back to the mountain had earned the miserable prisoner more lashes, and the wounds he had from the beating and saltpetre administration earlier, had not taken kindly to the journey through the jungle. The thornbushes had seen to that. And later the rainwater and his recent capture had helped to make the wretch an object for such pity as Tahta had caught on Tomaso's face. The leader ignored his enemy's invitation to have him dispatched to the Land of the Hunters. Instead, he turned towards his well-disciplined companions.

'I have seen the position the bakra soldiers have taken from a tree not a stone's throw from the Place-of-Talks. It is as my mind saw it beforehand. The bakra leaders are in the Place-of-Talks. The thunderguns are at the door of the cave, but partly sheltered so that the rain may not wet the powder. I saw a glow so there must be fire inside the place, and since the thunderguns are in the doorway pointing at the people, the kegs of powder must be inside, for they would not want this to be wet.'

Tomaso paused, and the dozen men nodded admiringly at their leader's reasoning. Tahta, who had hardly taken his eyes off Lago since Tomaso flung him into the cove at their feet, noticed now that the prisoner was taking great interest in Tomaso's talk. If the leader noticed this, he ignored it and continued.

'All we have planned before can take place. If I could send word to our captured people so that they may not be frightened at what they will see and hear, it would be good. But this cannot be, for the newstaker would have to be captured and I cannot spare any from our warriors. There is much for all of us to do!'

Now he turned to the mulatto Jacob. 'Have you the things ready, Jacob?' he asked.

'Aye, my chief!' cried the lieutenant, promptly displaying the uniform of a bakra soldier. 'There is a stain, but it is small, my leader; furthermore, the light will be bad.'

Saying this, the man hastily donned a uniform, which immediately transferred him from a wild-looking, half naked, bare foot jungle fighter, to a bakra soldier, in a bright, if somewhat tight-fitting, uniform.

'Speak quickly if you approve, my chief. I am in haste, for I am longing to free my toes from these feet jailhouses in which I have placed them. My Spirit? How can a bakra climb these mountains and fight with these things on his feet? I would rather walk on maccka even if there were nothing else covering the earth!'

The men laughed at Jacob's boot discomfort, but nevertheless, looked admiringly at the man who could, within minutes, change from a warrior of the Maroons to a bakra soldier.

Tomaso nodded his approval as he turned to the old man. 'Tahta what of the things I asked?'

The bushdoctor begrudgingly took his eyes off the interested Lago.

'All you asked for has been done, my chief,' he cried, hastening to bring from a corner two items. 'Here is thy bamboo tube made like something-which-will-make-a-noise-when-blown, here is the cork on one end with a string attached.' He handed a four foot bamboo the thickness of an infant's wrist, with smaller pieces inserted at one end like a mouthpiece, and a wooden cork with a string on the other, to Tomaso who nodded approvingly.

'This is the little gourd, my chief, packed tight with gunpowder as you ordered. I dried the gourd over the fire, so the powder is dry and that which is in the bamboo tube also is dry.'

Now Tahta handed his leader the small, corked, water-gourd, housed in a net of bark.

'We have emptied every powder horn, Tomaso, the gourd is greedy,' said Jacob.

'It is luck that we shall not be using our muskets this night,' replied the ex-chief grimly.

'There is a keg of powder hidden in a thick cloth by the root of the great cotton tree behind the village.'

It was Lago who spoke and now all eyes turned to him with a look of surprise, disbelief, and suspicion.

'Aye, more of thy treachery, snake?' asked Tahta with a sneer.

Lago winced, looked angry and opened his mouth to speak, but thought better of it.

Again Tomaso ignored his enemy and went on to discuss his plans.

'Once more I shall speak of what is to be done.'

Every face in the circle of warriors looked grim, now that their leader was giving his final orders. He turned to the uniformed Jacob, who now had his musket in hand.

'Jacob, you in the clothes of a bakra soldier must look as if you had captured me, and must be behind me with thy musket pointed at my head. We will pass the bakra, I, with this gourd full of powder, and I shall hold this bamboo thing in my tied hand, allowing it to draw on the ground when I reach the Place-of-Talks where the bakra officers and the thunderguns and kegs of powder are. I shall make a line of powder from this bamboo by standing on the string first, as I walk from the guns to the fire. This will pull the cork at one end. You, Jacob, my brother, must go like the wind when you see my hand on the gourd, for the powder inside will make merry when I smash it on the bakra fire, and powderkegs in the Place will surely join in.'

As Tomaso paused, Tahta, vibrating with emotion, could contain himself no longer.

'I shall not let thee do this thing, Tomaso! I shall not let thee feed thyself to Death!' he cried, clenching and unclenching his bony fists. A babel of voices joined in:

'Let one of us go in thy place, chief! You are worth many of us!'

'I will gladly go in thy place, Tomaso.'

'And I.'

Each warrior vied with the other for the grim task the leader had reserved for himself.

Tomaso raised his hand for silence.

'My brothers,' he began earnestly, 'my head grows big at your offer. But even if I did not wish to go myself, none could take my place. Think well. Have not the bakra for many moons been offering bags of gold for my capture? Do they not say it will be easy to know me because of the extra finger on my hand? Who except I and my—my son on these hills has an extra finger?'

The men knew that the thought of his son's whereabouts was heavy on the mind of the speaker now. He shook his head as if to clear his thoughts before continuing:

'When Jacob, disguised like a soldier, walks into the bakra's mouth this night, they will look on the man who calls himself Tomaso, but it will be the extra finger they will take as proof that it is indeed I.'

The men hung their heads for they now saw that only Tomaso could make the sacrifice.

'Let me speak!'

The voice, rasping and ghostly, came from behind them. In their excitement even Tahta had forgotten Lago. Not that he could have escaped, for he would have to pass them to do so and there were other warriors alertly watching from the shadows of the trees around the cove. Nevertheless, they were startled when they looked back and saw him standing grim and hunched with the flickering flames playing about his deepset eyes and mud-spattered hair and body. There was an angry murmur of protest at the demand, but Tomaso held up his hand for silence.

'Speak!' said the leader coldly.

As the prisoner stepped forward out of the shadows and came closer to the firelight, it seemed to the watching men that the tall shadow his misshapen body cast on the wall was no other than Death. They shivered without noticing.

Hoarsely, Lago began:

'This plan of thine needs another if it must come to pass. Let me be this man.'

The listeners gasped at what they felt was indeed impudence. Tahta, as usual was the first to say what he thought.

'I would rather bed with a snake than trust thee, traitor!' he snarled, almost dancing with fury.

To everyone's surprise, Lago showed no anger. 'Old man,' he called almost mildly, 'this bakra word *traitor*—if I wear this name because of what happened on these hills between thy leader, his kin, and I—perhaps I should not murmur.'

The warriors all looked at one another, unable to believe their ears.

'Of the other things I have done, the bakra word is a bad fit,' continued the prisoner.

'Ah!' put in the bushdoctor. 'The riddle is plain. The smell of Death has come to thy nostrils, traitor, and it brings such fear that you have even given up mating with the woman called Boastful.'

The old fire came back to Lago for a moment. 'I first named thee Talking Bird old man, now I am sure that was thy name at birth.'

Tomaso anticipated Tahta's hand moving towards his

cutlass in its bark scabbard. Lago stood unperturbed.

'Come to the end of thy talk, evil one, I have little time,' said Tomaso sternly to Lago.

The prisoner obeyed. 'They sent me from the Place-of-Talks to find thee. They threw gold at me and gave me this blowing thing around my neck. This would serve as a pass and also to call the bakra soldiers if I need help. Now if I return with thee, they will think I have captured thee and thy plan could not fail.'

The warriors around Tomaso spoke in fury.

'Trust this dog?'

'The one who betrayed our people asks this?'

'What fools he must think we are!'

Tomaso held up his hands and the tongues grew silent.

'There is something in thy talk, traitor,' he said, looking thoughtfully at his enemy. 'But you who have given your own friends, aye, even your own picnies, to the bakra thunderguns, you who speak with countless tongues would have me put myself in thy care? Am I not thy greatest enemy? Talk quickly, dog, I have no time to waste on thee, but know this, whatever be thine answer, I shall offer thee nothing, not even thy life!'

Lago laughed bitterly. 'What shall I gain by betraying thee, blood brother?' he asked. 'Go with the bakra back to the plantations as a slave, or even a free man with fingers pointing at me as the one who sold his people? Or if this plan of thine works well and the bakra are driven from the hills, what would be here for me? Would anyone wish to live if his own picnies flew from him as if the disease called *cocobeh* was showing on his face?'

Lago saw that his words had made a favourable impression, for no Maroon cared to live if his children despised him for something he had done. Dramatically he prised open the palm of one hand with the other for their inspection. They looked and saw the havoc the molton lead had created when the bakra had him prisoner. They had already seen his body. He looked into the faces around him until his eyes met his blood brother's:

'If I go to the Land-of-the-Hunters through the door of the Place-of-Talks, perhaps some of the shame will go from the faces of my picnies, if they still live,' said he, almost to himself.

Tomaso pondered long. 'Aye, I think I will use thee after all, my blood brother,' he said, at last. 'It will be better than slaying thee myself.'

Lago looked almost pleased.

'I thank thee, my blood brother,' he said softly.

It was while they were discussing details, now including Lago in the suicide party, much to Tahta's dismay, for he felt certain the prisoner would trap them, that a warrior appeared, escorting Kumse.

Kumse had escaped her attacker. When the hands closed on her throat bringing her to the ground, she fought bravely, but it was no use, and discovering this, she had the good sense to relax suddenly.

Her attacker took one hand from her neck and explored her body for weapons. It was then he discovered that she was not a warrior but a woman. Feeling certain that the opposite sex could be no danger to him, especially when unarmed, he took the other hand from her throat, though he still sat astride her.

Now that she could breathe properly, the smell of rancid palmoil told her that her attacker was not one of her own people mistaking her for an enemy, as she thought at first. The shadowy figure above her was just about to raise himself upright when she brought her knee up with all the force she could muster. The move not only threw the attacker off balance, but also gave him a painful jab in his belly, causing him to fall back with a grunt.

Kumse was up and gone like the wind in the darkness before her assailant had properly recovered, thereby giving her a few yards start, but the man—one of those Mosquito Indians the bakra imported from the island of that name to help them against the Maroons, was like Kumse, a native of the jungle, giving him the same advantage of seeing in the dark things and movements which would be lost to a bakra. It was when her ears told her that her pursuer was almost upon her that she heard an 'Aah,' followed by a crash behind her.

She did not stop her dash through the trees until a call in Maroon language came from behind:

'Cease thy running, I have killed him!'

She almost fainted with relief, for it was the voice of her brother who was one of Tomaso's Spirit Men.

Tomaso heard the news about his son and the boy's little blind companion, from Kumse, and his spirit went low.

'You must make haste to save the little one, Tomaso!'

'Take me with thee, chief! We shall find him and his blind sister.'

'The bakra know about the boy from this snake Lago, my chief! They seek to capture him to use as bait for thy surrender. See? The dog of a traitor hangs his head. He knows I have guessed the truth.'

This last was from Tahta, and the men turned to look at the prisoner and knew Tahta was right without asking for confirmation. Tomaso's hands clenched and unclenched as he thought of the choice before him. The warriors stood silent, knowing of the battle raging within their leader's mind. Tahta, watching with as great an agony as his friend and leader, drew a rasping breath which sounded like a sob as he anticipated Tomaso's verdict.

When at last the giant spoke, try as he would, he could not keep his voice under control.

'My brothers,' he began: 'You, Quao, you, Chaka, you, Quako, all you warriors, are there any among you who are not fathers, who have not mothers, sisters, brothers? Are your feelings for your kin less than mine? Yet since we returned from the long journey, since we heard the noise which told us the bakra thunder-guns were eating up our people, have one of you asked to go to find those who hold your spirits in their hands? There is no Spirit Man who does not cry inside himself as he thinks of those who may have passed into the Hunter's Land without saying a farewell dehdeh.'

The warriors kept their eyes down as Tomaso paused.

'My son, aye, and my daughter—for the little blind one is now also part of me—they, like your sons, your daughters and the rest of your kin must wait until this thing which might save the whole village is done.' Now the great voice grew soft.

'If Tahta, my father, as well as I, obey the call of the great eketeh to the Hunter's Land, then, when the battle is over, I ask you, my brothers, to search for my picnies, and if they live, leave them in the care of Kumse and her kin. This is all I ask of you.'

The hardened men wiped their eyes shamelessly.

'Thy son and the blind one shall be our picnies also, Tomaso! We swear,' they cried.

Kumse could not speak. Neither could Tahta.

Quickly the ex-chief tried to erase the sorrow from the minds of his men, reminding them of their duty and the task he had for them:

'Forget not my plan for this fight,' he cautioned. 'There will be no muskets for you this night. The bakra will find to their sorrow that rain in the forest is no food for muskets. Use your bows and arrows, your spears, your blowing darts. Strike silently. Let the bakra in the forest look for the one who struck, and find nothing! Let them find death from the trees under which they pass, behind the rocks, at the cave mouths. It matters not if some escape but first they must know what it is to fear. Let them feel that the hills are our mother, the rocks our father, the trees our brothers, the sinkholes, gullies, and even the snakes, our kinsmen. Let them know the night is our friend and the darkness our clothing. This fight is not ours alone, it is for the Maroons of the Blue Mountains, the Cockpits, and for our brothers on the plantations. If the bakra win, no Maroon will be safe on any of the hills, no slave on the plantation will feed his spirit with hope. Every warrior must fight as if he were an army. There are many amongst you who are fitted for my place, should I, Jacob, and Tahta fall. There must be no fight for leadership. Choose well. Now the time is nigh. The bakra's eyes will be heavy.'

It was after these instructions that Kumse, wanting to do something useful, heard from her father how Tomaso wanted the captured villagers to know of his coming, and what to do when he came, but could spare none of his men. She begged to be allowed to take the message. Tomaso refused at first, but allowed himself to be persuaded, stipulating that the young woman should be protected on the journey, and the warriors should see that she came to no harm until she allowed herself to be captured.

That was how it came about that just before midnight a bakra soldier caught a young woman, prowling just on the edge of the clearing where all the men, women and the children who had not been sent into the bushes by their elders, were sitting on the rainsodden ground under guard.

Later, even the wounded, and those who silently wept for their lost children and their dead, looked as if the spirit had come back to them at the news which passed from mouth to mouth . . .

'Tomaso will come!'

Tahta had managed to persuade Tomaso that since Lago was to be included in the party going to the Place-of-Talks, he also should go along with Jacob and the chief. Since everyone seemed to feel that only thus could Lago be kept from being treacherous, the leader had consented, stipulating however that the old man should stay outside the cave, or failing this, to make his escape with Jacob at the arranged signal.

The four now stood in the dark just before reaching the clearing where the bakra soldiers and the two cannons from the mouth of the Place-of-Talks pointed on the mass of huddled captives.

Tomaso had his hands apparently tied, with the gourd filled with gunpowder slung by a string over his shoulder and the powder-filled four foot bamboo under his arm. Tahta had nothing except a little reed and a tiny bag at his side. Lago had the whistle the bakra gave him to use as a pass or to obtain help, hanging around his neck. Jacob was in the full dress of a bakra soldier, including musket, and to the mulatto's disgust, the pair of feet jailhouses, as he named the late soldier's footwear.

It was Lago who broke the silence:

'This is our last meeting, blood brother. Our last talk also. I ask two boons as parting gifts.'

Tahta was outraged. 'Know this, traitor-dog,' hissed the

bushdoctor, 'I still suspect thee! Know also that I shall always be behind thee with this, my reed of poison dart, ready to send it into thy neck should Jacob's musket fail.'

Lago breathed hard as if he was angry, but he only said to Tomaso, 'There is little time, blood brother, so if you will ask this talking-bird to close his beak, I will speak.'

Tomaso anticipated Tahta's move by finding the old man's arm and restraining him.

'Speak,' requested the leader coldly.

'This I ask,' began Lago. 'Let me take the gourd and bamboo to the Cave—alone. I have been there this night, and know where the powderkegs are, and where they have made a fire.' He drew in a deep breath then continued. 'One other boon I ask: The little blind one whom you have taken—tell her not that I, whom you call traitor, was her father.'

Tomaso thought for a little then asked: 'Why this concern for my life from thee, my worst enemy?'

Lago let out a strange giggle. 'Perhaps my thirst for revenge on the bakra is much mightier than my hatred for thee, blood brother,' he replied softly.

To Tahta's and Jacob's horror, Tomaso replied: 'You shall have the things you asked of me, Lago, but I shall be at thy heels all the way. As for the little blind one—' the leader's voice grew soft. 'Jacob and Tahta have given their promise to save themselves, and they will not speak of thy secret since they know it is my wish. Now here are the gourd and the bamboo. Let us go. The sleep must be great in the eyes of the bakra soldiers.'

Lago said nothing more, but took the loaded gourd and bamboo, and the four began the last steps. But all the way Tahta whispered in Jacob's ear.

They came to the clearing where pitch-drenched torches as well as wood fires threw light on a great arena. The crowd sitting on the wet ground saw when the bakra soldiers challenged them. They saw Lago gesticulating almost wildly, and the bakra soldier examining Tomaso's hand with the extra finger, and though the whisper they heard before told them that this should be a fake capture organized by the brave Tomaso himself, they were now doubtful, seeing that Lago was playing the leading part. Kumse had been instructed not to give any details, but only to say that when they saw Tomaso under capture they should not worry, and when there was a loud explosion in the cave, the men should rise and overcome their guards, and the women and children should take to the forest and wait there for the call of the eketeh.

Now as Lago satisfied the guards and the four passed through, the crowd grew as angry as a disturbed hive of bees. There was hissing and cursing, and before the group reached the entrance to the Place-of-Talks, two bakra officers, hearing the disturbance, came out in the open to investigate.

By now, almost everyone was convinced that Tomaso had been outfoxed. The officers being told of the reason for the noise, quickly returned to the man-made cave to make ready for interrogating their most valuable capture.

Prisoners and guard were a couple of chains from the entrance of the cave, when Lago suddenly began to run forward fiddling with the string at the end of the bamboo tube as he went.

Tahta quickly put his poison dart tube to his mouth and blew, but the distance between himself and the running man was too great and he missed.

Tomaso sprang like a hound after his enemy, but a bakra guard crashed his gun-butt on the ex-chief's head just as the latter reached the cave entrance. Tomaso fell on his face and lay still.

Bewildered at the turn of events, Jacob, forgetting his role as a bakra soldier, crashed his musket on the side of the head of the soldier who attacked Tomaso. Tahta, now in despair, grabbed the nearest soldier and brought him to the ground seconds before, it seemed, the whole mountain above them was exploding.

. . . Thus Lago had redeemed himself.

Six

Tamba, hearing his beloved Bangie in a desperate fight which by the sound of the growls, convinced him that the intruder was a bigger animal, remembered just in time that the other dog might have a master too, and that master may have been the one who had set his house on fire and the enemy which Kumse had seen. Though terrified, he felt it was his duty to see if he could save his friend, almost forgetting his little blind companion standing trembling beside him. The rasping bass growls from the other animal could be distinguished plainly from the tenor-like howls, barks and yelps from the brave little Bangie, and Tamba could judge by what he heard that his dog was getting the worst of the fight. He felt the hand of the trembling Manda and knew that his knees were also doing the same thing; and with a tightness in his throat he grabbed the bag with his things, felt for and found his machete, and with his companion's hand firmly in his, crawled out from under the back of his little leanto, and dashed into the woods beyond.

He could see the glare and smoke coming from the place where his house once stood, and the thought that he was without a home, perhaps without a father or even a relation made him weak with fright. Suddenly a musket crashed behind him and there was a great yell from a dog. Tamba was sure it was Bangie.

He stifled a cry for his dog as it came to his lips, and another thundering crash flaring from somewhere closer behind them made him realize the danger which threatened them.

He began to run, pulling Manda with him, forgetting for the moment that she was blind. Not that sight would have helped her for the night was still pitch dark, and more rain was threatening.

Now as they reached unfamiliar parts of the forest and the crashing sounds of pursuit were still there each time they listened, Tamba grew desperate.

He did not know where he was going. The darkness seemed full of mysterious shapes which made him feel that their flight was hopeless and would end in the arms of the dreaded bakra. Sometimes he stumbled; sometimes Manda did. The only thing he knew was that he was going away from familiar ground, and that they were going higher. Once, when he felt that neither he nor the terrified Manda could go any further without resting, he brought her to a halt in a clump of almost inaccessible bushes. They crawled under, until they lay panting and wet on their bellies deep among the bushes. For a while they felt safe and Tamba even thought they might try to return by the route they had come if they could find it, when they heard the baying of a dog, deep and throaty.

Tamba had heard tales of slave-hunting dogs from Tahta, and now that he felt that these were the kind of dogs he heard barking it made his teeth chatter. Manda had kept silent all this while, except when she wished to let him know she understood his orders.

Now he felt they dare not rest too long, for though the sound of the barking hound was not very close, from what Tahta had told him these dogs could follow a scent even more than Bangie could.

They crawled out of the thicket and began to go further into the forest as fast as they could, and every time they stopped to listen they could hear some sound or something like the movement of animal or man to terrify them.

They would stop to rest, only to jump up, afraid of some new sound in the dark around them. Once Tamba stepped on nothing and went crashing down a sudden slope on the mountainside, pulling Manda with him. Luckily the place was without stones and they ended up in a great line of giant ferns in a gully. But they had the frightening experience of being parted, and when he, by whispering her name from time to time, found her, he knew by the sound of her voice that she was crying.

It took him an hour or more trying to find his machete and the bag, and while they were searching in the gully of ferns, they froze to a standstill as they heard someone calling, and saying something in a language they could not understand. They had given themselves up for lost when the voices began to recede. After a while the voices died away and the two lay trembling, cold and muddy where they were. Not long afterwards there was a flash of light and a thundering sound some distance away. As they clung to each other and listened, they thought they could hear the wailing cries of people.

'It is the bakra,' said the albino to his companion in an awed whisper. 'Their mighty thundersticks have eaten up all our people, there will be none left after that noise, not even my father!' And for the first time since the terror began, Tamba broke down and began to sob.

'Do not shed eyewater, Little Brother, cried Manda pitifully, well knowing that she was doing the same. 'We will stay in the forest, you and I, and the spirits of my mother, thy mother, and thy father, will take care of us so that we may not be lonely,' she ended between sobs.

Tamba, hearing the confirmation of his suspicion that his father was now a spirit, felt all was lost, but he could not allow the little girl who had just changed teeth to be braver than he. He wiped his eyes and began to pretend that all was going to be alright.

'Yes, little Sister, the spirits of our parents will look after us. We shall try to find the Place-of-the-Big-Jump, and cross the great log there, since our village is no more. We shall cross over to the other mountain and there we shall find a hiding place,' he said.

So they sat in the ferns in the darkness, wet and miserable, leaning on each other, and in their weariness, fell asleep, until a sound of thunder woke them up hours later.

Once again Tamba went on hands and knees, feeling on the ground for the things he had lost, with Manda crawling behind, holding tightly on to one of his feet so as not to lose him.

He almost sobbed with relief when his searching fingers

came upon something flat and cold which proved to be the blade of his machete. But the bag and the rest of the things, including their change of clothing, could not be found and the sound of musket shots made him give up the search and make for the higher part of the hills.

The great number of roars which destroyed the Place-of-Talks had not died down, nor had the dust from the explosion settled before Kumse was on the spot where she had last seen the man she worshipped felled from the blow of a bakra's musket.

Crying for help, the frantic girl dug with her bare hands the debris which, she guessed, hid the ex-chief. Handicapped by the darkness now that the torches which had given the light to the man-made cave had disappeared with everything else, she was forced to depend on her fingers for information. The soft touch of a human body came to her hands after a while, and now she felt relief and dread together as she searched for information in the darkness, holding her breath as she did so.

The pandemonium which followed hard on the heels of the explosions was now taking a definite pattern. The people of the hills turned on their guards, and even those who were expected to retreat to the forest as instructed, ignored the order in their thirst for revenge on the invaders.

The soldiers who were too deep in the circle of prisoners to escape when the explosion occurred had no chance to let off a musket before they were killed. Those on the fringe managed to fire into the crowd but had no chance of reloading before they were brought down with either wood taken from the fires or with bare hands. A few fled into the woods only to undergo the terror of nights in a jungle with their comrades sent earlier to ambush warriors whose retreat from the foot of the hills never came, thanks to Tomaso's message.

The Spirit Men were to wait for the leaderless invaders, and afterwards to play cat and mouse with them until the luckless soldiers, many of whom had never set foot in a woodland before, wished for death rather than the unseen terror which for three days and nights thinned their numbers with noiseless and mysterious disappearances and death. At the end of that time those who still lived and eventually reached the plains, did not only show signs of starvation, thirst and privation, but each had a vacant stare which bore convincing proof of the unbalanced mind.

Tomaso's strategy had won.

'A light,' cried Kumse as she passed trembling fingers over the body half covered with debris. Now the people, rid of their captors, turned to rescue their saviours, yet felt that their task was a hopeless one, for the lighted torches they seized from the tree-bordered arena now showed the complete destruction of the artificial cave, and were it not for Kumse, it would have been hard to tell where the entrance was once situated.

The young woman had found Tomaso, and willing hands gently cleared away the rubble from his broken body. None knew if there was still life in him or not. They found Tahta next, and though his breathing could be heard he was badly hurt, and by the signs they saw, they knew that one eye was completely damaged. Next they found the brave mulatto Jacob still in the uniform with the despised feet-jailhouse on his feet. There was no doubt in the people's minds about their brave Jacob. He had gone to the Spirit Land. Lago was left where he fell, if there was anything left of him. So were the bakra officers buried in the cave with him. It was the hope of the people that even the spirit of the late bullneck one would not escape from the demolished Place. The rain poured as if the skies were shedding eyewater as the people lifted their wounded and their dead to new grounds.

It was morning when the children found the path leading to the Place-of-the-Big-Jump. Tamba had been there with his father as well as Tahta and knew that he only had to go some distance up the path to find where the gully curved and the narrow gap where the crossing log would be found.

He felt frightened at the thought of crossing the fifty foot span by edging his way astride the wet tree-trunk with the terrible depth of the gully beneath, and of Manda, clinging close behind. If they ever lost their balance, he wondered, but decided he would not think of that now, as he came round the curve to the Place.

Leaving Manda to wait behind a rock, the boy advanced alone cautiously, to find out if there was danger ahead. Suddenly he stopped dead, staring down, feeling that he could not make a cry come out of his throat even if he tried, though he pushed his fingers hard in his mouth so as to prevent such a possibility. His pink, white-fringed eyes grew big with terror and it seemed his bare feet were spiked to the wet ground.

Afterwards he could not tell if he saw that the log was no longer across the gorge before he saw the thing, or after. All he knew was that nothing would make him forget what he saw lying not far from the place he had hoped to cross.

He lay with his face up with eyes and mouth as if he was struck in wonder at the sight of the sky above him. His body had clothing on it which the boy had never seen before. There were big heavy things on his outstretched feet. But what struck the petrified albino with horror was that the thing lying there was not like any man he had seen in the hills, for his face was of the colour of bleached bark-cloth, and the hair on his head was like the beard of corn.

Though the sight of a dead Maroon would have frightened him had he come across such a body suddenly, this fright he had was twice greater because he was seeing one of the dreaded people whom he and his people associated with slavery, torture and death in all their tales.

And now to see this awful bakra in man's most frightening state—rigid, wide-eyed and open-mouthed in death—caused the boy to have a fright bordering on insanity.

Suddenly he felt as if the things which pinned his feet to the ground were lifted. With the fingers of one hand still in his mouth he turned from the horrible sight and ran. Now that he began to run his feet seemed to have wings, and in his imagination, the dead man was close on his heels trying to catch up with him and drag him down. He stumbled and fell flat, and was up in the blinking of an eye, with both hands now ready to save him from further falls.

When he reached the rock where he had left Manda, it surprised him to look back and not find the dead man close behind him. Manda must have heard him running for when he reached her side she was standing with his machete in her hand, and her sightless eyes big with fear. Tamba grabbed her hand, 'Come! We must go. This is a bad place and they have taken away the log so we cannot cross there,' he panted as they ran.

The terror of his experience was still dominating his feet as well as his mind so that he forgot to make allowances for the blind girl, and she took two bad falls before he realized the panic in his behaviour.

Ashamed, he stopped to allow her to rest and to describe vividly what he had seen. Only then did it occur to him that his colour was not so very different from the dead man he had left, and the thought that he might have looked just as horrible made him almost hate himself. Manda must have imagined all the terror Tamba's experience had evoked. For she looked just as terrified as if she had come across it herself. They climbed up the steep rocky forest above as if both the living and the dead were at their heels at the same time. There was now no doubt that the bakra were somewhere beneath them. They heard shouting several times in the language not of the Maroons; and musket fire became more numerous as time went on. It was when Tamba made a difficult climb, and turned to help his blind friend, that he found she was not there.

Alarmed, he called her name softly as he scrambled down to where he had last left her, but there was no Manda.

'Manda! Little Sister!' he called as loud as he dared, but there was no answer. Desperately he searched the clump of bushes and behind rocks, working his way down as he went, and now he was sobbing as he whispered her name.

He remembered at that moment the talk he had heard his late mother having with Tahta: 'Would die alone . . .' It was coming true, he said to himself. Bangie gone, now Manda! Yet it was the thought that his blind friend was lying somewhere at the foot of one of the rocks injured and alone which drove him almost mad with fear.

Then he saw it.

The head of woolly plaits tangled and untidy now, barely showing above a rock he had just passed. Within seconds he had her hugged close to his bare white chest.

'Manda! Oh, Little Sister! Why did you run away?' he asked crying still.

'I only hid because,' she blew her nose before continuing, 'Because you could go better without me.'

And then her women's poise left her and sobs shook her little body as she clung to her friend.

'You must not do this again, Little Sister,' he begged, comforting her with a tight embrace.

'You must promise that wherever I go, you will follow, and we must never leave each other as long as we live.'

He waited breathlessly until she replied solemnly in spite of her sobs:

'I shall not run away from thee again, Little Brother. I shall never leave thee.'

He looked down on her bleeding toes, her fingers with their nails split and bleeding, her body marked with the cruel clawlike maccka. And he remembered the way his whole body itched because of its contact with bushes whose leaves were noted for this kind of discomfort to the human body, and he wondered if he could ever be as brave as she was.

Once more they made for the rocky slopes, keeping in line with the gorge in the hope of finding a negotiable place.

Seven

Jomo, father of Kumse, who was trained to take the place of Tahta in case of emergency, sweated in the morning sunlight as he, with the assistance of his son and two of the other Spirit Men, worked on the two unconscious men in their hastily erected hut in the centre of the clearing. Outside a crowd stood, squatted or sat, in spite of the wetness from the heavy rains. They talked in whispers as they waited. Only those who had their own wounded to attend, their dead to be buried, or their lost children to find, were missing.

In the distance the faint sound of musket-shots told the waiting crowd that the Spirit Men had not deserted their duty in order to find if their families were safe. Tomaso had set the example for them when he had refused to change his plan to go to his son's rescue instead. Now the warriors he left behind had listened only for the explosion which told them that the plan to blow up the Place-of-Talks had not failed. They did not know whether their leader and his aides had been killed as expected. They only knew that each had been given the task of terrifying the bakra so that those who escaped their spears, their poison darts, and their arrows, would be henceforth afraid of the hills.

They did not fail. Every warrior determinedly carried out Tomaso's order. The bakra soldiers, fighting their way through the terrible jungle, sometimes created their own end by falling into one of the many sinkholes which dotted the hills, or some walked suddenly into space and to their deaths hundreds of feet below. They would wrestle with giant creepers trying to find a way out of the maze in which they found themselves trapped, using their muskets to beat down the things around them, knowing all the while that somewhere in the denseness beyond, beside, or behind, black faces were watching and waiting—playing with them as it were. They sometimes made great headway, it seemed, until they discovered that they were back at the spot where they had rested an hour before.

When their terror at being lost in the jungle was relieved by the sight of a track seeming to lead down to the plains, a sudden sound would make them turn terrified faces and hastily discharge their muskets from where they thought the noise had come. But instead of a black body no one was in sight and they would find a young tree or a sapling still swaying, even though there was no wind. Later, when they tried to discharge their muskets, the powder, damp from rain and contact with the wetness in the forest, would fail to ignite, and the thought of their one and only protection being useless up there among the watching warriors and treacherous jungle would cause fear to eat them up. They would try to break out of the nightmare by running in different directions. Then, as they scattered, the silent Spirit Men would strike with arrows, spears, or poison darts, from the branches of trees, from behind rocks—or from out of the very earth, it seemed to the bakra soldiers.

Later the Spirit Men could afford to merely drive the invaders out of the hills.

After Kumse found her wounded chief in the rubble from the Place-of-Talks, they had to use force to separate her from him. She would not have left otherwise. Now she waited with the crowd in the morning light to hear if the man she worshipped silently still had life in his broken body. She said nothing as she stood waiting, the bare upper part of her body as well as the torn cloth she wore around her still muddied and stained from her fight earlier with her attacker and later from her contact with the injured leader.

Jomo came at last to the door of the hut, weary, gory, and downcast. The crowd grew so silent now that it was hard to think they were not statues.

Jomo looked on the vast throng and wet his lips desperately as if he wished he had not come out to face them. Kumse could not bear the suspense of waiting until her father spoke.

'My father!' she called out hoarsely. 'Is there life?'

The crowd held their breath to hear the answer. It did not matter that there were two wounded men there in the hut. They loved Tahta. But it was after Tomaso Kumse had asked, and Tomaso was the reason for their silent waiting these many hours.

'There is still life!'

The words from Jomo's mouth had not come joyfully, but a mighty sigh of gladness echoed over the vast clearing like the murmuring of the wind.

'He lives! He lives!' they cried.

Women wiped their eyes with the ends of the wet muddy cloths tied around their bodies. Men blew their noses lustily as water welled in their eyes.

'What of Tahta?' they asked now, feeling guilty of the neglect to the brave old warrior.

'He too has life!' replied Jomo promptly, and there was another murmur of joy at this news. Only Kumse stood silent from the time she had asked the question. Her young face bore an anxious look as she watched her father. Again it was she who led the question: 'Will he live, my father?'

The harassed man turned almost angrily on his daughter.

'Who am I, child?' he asked evasively. 'How can I say when I have not seen such injuries before.'

Kumse realized she had placed her father in an embarrassing position when she heard the confession. But her fear for the man she loved drove her on even at the cost of being disrespectful to her father—a grave crime in the eyes of every Maroon.

'Thy words do not go with the look on thy face, O my father!' said the girl in a voice clear and strong. 'I am thy child and I will bow to what chastisement you may give when this talk is done, but now, O my father, I must know the meaning of the fear which I have never seen before on thy face.'

The girl's bare chest heaved with emotion as she spoke, and the crowd's joy suddenly turned to consternation as they realized that all was not well. Jomo knew that he could no longer evade the truth by pleading ignorance.

'It is the truth when I say that I cannot tell, O my people,' he said, avoiding his daughter's eyes. 'Our chief has suffered many bad things to his body. There is a mighty cut on his head. There is bleeding from inside his body when he coughs, and the hand—that which bears the extra finger, we must take away, for it is crushed, and there cannot be much blood left in his body.'

A low moaning sound came from somewhere deep in a human chest, and none could tell from whose it came, but the great crowd took up the moaning notes as despair took hold of them.

'I shall go to him,' cried Kumse, moving forward towards the door. Two warriors who were helping the sick in the improvised hospital tried to bar her way. Not a word did she speak as she fought with them.

'Let her go!' murmured the sympathetic crowd.

'Let her go,' echoed her father resignedly, moving out of her path.

'Forgive me, O my father,' she begged softly as she passed into the hut.

Kumse was there to help when they took away the crushed hand. When they thought he was dead it was her face against his which detected the slight breathing. When he first opened his eyes she was the first to see. He seemed to have mistaken her for another and had whispered, 'Little Shadow!' and it was her ears which first heard this sound and when again he whispered 'My son, my son, Tamba, where is he?' but which she was unable to answer. And when, at last, he lay calmly asleep, only then did she whisper:

'I have helped to bring thee back from the monster, O keeper of my soul. Had I failed, I would have followed.'

But moons later, Kumse was not only to regret that she did not let Tomaso die, but she was to be the one to make the suggestion!

They slept in the shadow of the rock where Manda had been hiding until the sun was in the middle of the sky. The great fire-ball peeped out every now and again above a sky still heavy with rain.

Tamba sat up, then went to a clear part of the hillside to look down on the woods beneath, and saw to his alarm that there was a group of children almost beneath him, and climbing up in his direction. He knew that they saw him because they could be seen pointing to where he was.

It seemed his white body must have alarmed them at first, for some had turned back and begun to run down the steep incline, but one of those still pointing said something and this halted the retreat.

By this time, Tamba had told Manda what he had seen and she did not appear as alarmed as her companion at the news. It was when the group of children drew nearer and the albino could see them clearly that his alarm became greater, for two of the boys he could make out were no other than Jo and his brother, the same with whom he had fought that day in the village nearly a year before.

Manda, too, was frightened and begged her companion to flee. But it was too late, and now that they were nearly at the summit of the mountain and the vegetation was sparse and low, he knew that he would be spotted wherever he hid, especially because of the colour of his skin. So he stood by the rock almost defiantly, holding his machete in one hand and the arm of the blind girl with the other.

They came to within a chain of the two before they stopped. They were eight, five boys and three girls. The boys had on what might have once been shirts of coarse material but were now wet muddy rags hardly worth wearing. The girls wore smocks which were in no better condition. To Tamba, they looked cold, weary and frightened, and he couldn't help wondering if they had seen the dead bakra also. He was watching his old enemies, Lago's two sons, as they whispered among themselves, and stared back at him. After a while they all sat down on the wet ground where they were and Tamba, seeing that they had no intention of advancing further for the moment, began to explore his surroundings with his eyes.

Suddenly the sound of musket-fire came to their ears from the lower part of the mountain.

Tamba was moving upwards with his blind companion before the echo of the shots died away. He glanced back to find that the eight had also decided to do likewise. The two climbed the rest of the hill as fast as their weary legs and arms would take them, for now the incline was so steep that they had to travel on all-fours most of the time. They knew that because this part of the mountain was almost bare they could be spotted at a distance and Tamba now regretted that he had ever been unwise enough to rest where they did. Looking back he could see the sons of Lago climbing up behind them with the rest of the children stringing out in single file behind the brothers.

Of the eight, Jo and his brother Dan-Dan were the oldest at eleven, which was two years more than Tamba's age. The ages of the rest of the children ranged from nine to ten, so Manda at seven was the youngest of the climbers.

No other sound of musket-fire came from the woods beneath the fugitives, and at last they were on level ground right at the summit. Tamba and his blind friend decided that it was best to put as much distance between themselves and whoever it was who had fired the musket. If there was any hope in the albino's mind that the bakra had not captured or killed his father as well as the village people, the sight of the terrified picnies wearily stumbling behind, banished it completely. He wanted to ask them about their experiences, about his father—to be friendly with them, but they never came near enough. And every time he stopped, they would all halt abruptly, and if they found themselves closer than perhaps a chain away, they would step back and wait until he began walking again.

The strange procession went on. The sun, or what little peeped out upon the earth through the day, was now blacked out completely by fast-moving clouds, and the flashes of lightning and thunder warned the refugees of a new downpour. They had barely reached the more wooded part of the forest, still going towards the opposite side from which they came, before the rain began to lash down mercilessly. Hungry and worn out from their experiences. with feet full of broken prickles from the cruel maccka thornbushes, Tamba sat down pulling Manda down beside him. He saw the weary look on the face of his friend as she sat tiredly beside him, and in that moment he forgot the eight who had now shortened the distance between them and were squatting not more than half a chain away. Night was coming quickly, and the rainclouds foretold that it would be starless. Telling Manda to wait there, the albino got up, taking his machete with him.

The eight seemed to shrink away and huddled more closely together as he came towards them. But if he noticed their attitude he ignored it. Passing them without as much as a glance, he went along as if his heart had not been beating as if it would burst out of his chest, until he came to the root of an aged cabbage-palm tree, under which he had spotted many pieces of canoe-shaped bark and limbs it had discarded over the years. The light was still good enough for him to see the group watching as he chopped off useless parts of the palm limbs, taking back with him a load of the skinlike husks as well as some of the solid parts of the branches. They watched silently as he drew the branches along until he brought them to rest where he had left Manda.

He made three trips, looked around again and saw two large dead branches of wood not far away. These he also fetched in a short while. By this time the rain was pouring down in bucketsful through the tree tops. Soon the albino had a rude leanto erected. It was a crude bower, leaning against the side of a great broadleaf tree, but it protected the two from the fierce downpour.

They huddled together under the makeshift shelter and soon sleep came to their weary eyes.

Next morning they tackled the precipitous descent down the rough mountainside. Tamba went first, digging footholds along the route with the point of his machete and directing each step of his blind companion. It was a dangerous task and a nerve-racking ordeal, but they managed it and at last they were at the bottom of the gully, trembling and triumphant.

Tamba looked up and saw the boys Jo and Dan-Dan examining the places as if they were wondering if they, too, could also descend in that manner.

Tamba did not wait to see what would happen. It was easy to find a negotiable place on the other side of the gully, so as to reach the foot of the other mountain, and after splashing through muddy rainwater they climbed out of the dreadful gully and made for the hills. But they had not gone far before weakness and hunger overcame them so that they were forced to rest. The rain, which was merely a drizzle since morning had stopped now and the sun came out uncertainly. They found a few off-season plums and a soursop, and, as they were too weary to go further, they lay under a huge cotton-wood tree and rested. They must have slept long, for when Tamba opened his eyes he saw the eight children squatting a respectable distance away, watching him. Angrily he told the wakened Manda that he would have it out with them for following him in this manner. He got up, and as he advanced towards the group, the girls moved to the rear of their companions looking frightened, while the boys seemed as if they too would have run off if it were not for the shame of it. The brothers, Jo and Dan-Dan stood up looking with hostile eyes on the albino. The latter remembered the fight in the village with Jo and wished now he had not followed his impulse to challenge them. But he felt he could not stand this silent trailing any longer.

'Why do you follow us?' the albino asked the group in a clear, strong voice.

Nobody answered. Manda's grip tightened on her friend's arm.

'Why do you follow us?' he asked for the second time.

'We are not following you,' replied the boy Jo, looking guilty.

'You are!' declared Tamba.

'We are not!' denied Jo, a little more courage in his voice now.

'We can go where we wish.' This time it was Dan-Dan who spoke. He was slimish with a long face and cast-eyed.

'Yes, we can go where we wish,' agreed Jo, glad of the help. The other children looked on sullenly.

'Then if you can go where you wish, why do you follow us?' from Tamba.

The brothers did not have a ready answer to that question.

'And you are afraid of us!'

It was Manda who spoke this time, and one of the three girls gave the answer: 'We are not afraid of you, blind picni, only the dundoes, for they say he is a witch.'

The accusation, coupled with the names 'blind picni', 'dundoes' and 'witch' made Tamba angry now.

'You call us names and say I am a witch, but you follow us like dogs!' he cried. 'You cannot even do things for yourselves, and even my Bangie could do things by himself!'

His anger frightened them and they drew back from his white face with the strange eyes flashing in anger, his machete tightly gripped in his hand, and Manda holding on to his free arm.

Jo and Dan-Dan as the oldest of the gang knew that they must find some face-saving excuse for following the boy who was supposed to be a witch, for it was their father and they themselves who had circulated this slander.

'We have no machete, that is why we follow you!'

It was an inspired bit of excuse and the minute it came from the mouth of Dan-Dan, Jo seized upon it, and all the others followed suit.

'Yes, we follow because we have no machete.'

'One cannot travel without machete in this place.'

'If we had machetes we would not follow you.'

It seemed they partly convinced Tamba and his blind friend that this was the reason for following them, and he took Manda's hand, turned and walked away without another word, certain now that they would be always following and that his machete was now the most important thing, and must be guarded night and day.

Strangely enough the other children from that moment began to look upon the old, worn machete as a symbol of authority, or even power. The feeling grew in their minds so that within a few days they were looking at the albino as they would at a leader they hated, feared, yet at times, admired.

Tamba, conscious of the feeling of dependency on his machete, if not on himself, saw to it that all his plans were broad enough to take in his uninvited guests. And, thanks to his early woodcraft training and his years of isolation in the forest, he was able to astound them with his knowledge and skill. He searched for and found caves where bats had dropped hundreds of luscious naseberries gathered from trees perhaps miles away. He showed them that the parasite wildpines usually held enough rainwater at the roots of their long machete-like leaves, to quench the thirst of a mountain traveller. He made fires by striking the back of his machete on flinty rocks, catching the sparks on dry nests of rotting wood and leaves, and when that was not possible, from rubbing wood together. And although the rest of the children had heard of or seen some of these things done by their elders, the albino's remarkable bush-knowledge and the way he performed these miracles brought the curious crowd nearer and nearer, so that within a couple of days they, though apparently still afraid of him, no longer kept to themselves all the time. But Jo and Dan-Dan were at the same time losing their influence on the children they led, and jealousy took hold of them—especially Jo, and when he was forced to admit that he could not do some of the things which the albino did, he never failed to remind them that all these were possible to the albino because he was a witch. Now that they were all on speaking terms, Manda and Tamba heard the story of the terrible night in the village from their fellow refugees, and since the latter had left before the counter-attack by Tomaso and his men, they had no idea that any of the villagers were left in the hills but themselves. So it became necessary for them to live by themselves in the forest, they thought. It was not uncommon to hear someone weeping in the dark, remembering his or her experiences, or perhaps mourning the loss of loved parents.

And so they were always on the lookout for somewhere where they could live without wandering all over the mountains as they had been doing for a week. They had found several caves, but they were either too small, too fouled by hundreds of bats, which had made them their homes through centuries, or, they were too easily located for safety. For the children always took the precautions necessary to keep their presence secret, in spite of the fact that they were miles away from their former home and the mountain on which they were roaming seemed as if it had never before had the invasion of human beings.

Then Tamba by accident found the ideal place. Climbing a tall tree to gather fruits he looked down and saw a kind of sunken garden some four hundred feet wide, overgrown with tall ferns and creepers covering the sides of the enclosure completely and making it a perfect hideaway.

He knew that they had found a new home at last and unselfishly the two thought of the others.

By nightfall all the wanderers were sharing the excitement of a new home together. True, water was from a tiny spring, more than a mile away, and must be fetched with gourds. And Tamba had warned that soon fruit would be scarce, and the birds would be finding new feeding grounds. But they were too happy to mind this.

They had ample room around the great basin for their comfort, and the dry shelters under the shadow of the rocks, large and high enough to be called rooms, would protect them from rain and sun. They used the largest as a kind of communal kitchen. Here they would tell tales before the fire—tales which always included the legends of Tomaso's raids on the bakra slave plantations. In the telling they would forget that his son was sitting quietly in one corner with the head of the faithful Manda in his lap. She was always with him, unless he was on a hunt for food, when she would share that part of the shelter allotted to the girls.

A new village was springing up away from the ruins of the last one. The survivors had chosen the site near the one their beloved Tomaso had once chosen as his exile. They had mourned their dead and their missing children. They had searched and had found many bones and relics which had made it possible for most to be identified. Tomaso's Spirit Men had hunted time and again for his lost son and his blind companion. But they had given up hope now, just like the parents of those children whose bones they could not find. There were sinkholes and cavities enough to swallow a crowd of children without trace on Twin Sisters. They knew this only too well. As for the little ones, Tamba and Manda, they had only continued searching, even when the moon had come and gone to more than half the fingers of one hand, because their chief was still lying sick in mind and body, and old Tahta with one eye missing had insisted that they do so, until at last he too felt that it was useless.

The truth was they had found bones which could have been those of little Manda. And even if they had not found one which Tahta had said would be identified easily because of the white hair on the skull—they had found the boy's dog shot. Had they not found his shirt and Manda's smock not far from the string bag which Kumse swore she had given them with cassava bread? And by the signs they had not eaten the bread. Last, but not least, the log which would have given them the means of crossing the great gorge to the other mountain had been destroyed on Tomaso's order before the great explosion. Then how could children of that age escape to any of the other mountains? But in spite of these reasonings they had searched the sister mountain and the others, and had returned empty handed.

And their chief with one arm cut off lived only with Kisanka in his mind, said the people. He remembered nothing of the fight, or after. He answered yes and no and ate without knowing that he did. The blow on his head, though healed, had killed all but the woman he called Little Shadow from his mind. He thought all was well with everything. He did not know that the people now swore that as long as there was life in him, they would have no other chief. They would follow Tahta's instructions, but no chief would be elected.

It was the Spirit Men who had vowed this, and the people had enthusiastically agreed. Now the giant, mere skin and bone, sat or walked slowly around the new house they made for him, with the faithful Kumse always by his side and the one-eyed Tahta, still weak from his brush with death, following behind as if he was afraid that his chief would fly into the arms of the monster Death if he were left alone. And the man, once noted for his wisdom and leadership, now stumbled along weakly, living with nothing and no-one else but his Little Shadow.

So the villagers talked and shook their heads sorrowfully behind their chief's back . . .

'Oh, Little Shadow, wipe the water from thine eyes.
'How can a man live without his shadow?'
Kumse wiped the water from her eyes at the giant's words,

and Tahta leaning heavily on a stick, with one eye bandaged, looked the picture of misery.

Time and contact had reduced the fear of Tamba as a witch in the children's minds in spite of the jealous brothers who did their best to keep it alive and to blame him for whatever misfortune they had. Now the ribs on their naked torsos could be easily counted. Their eyes were deep in their bony faces; their heads looked abnormally big in contrast to their meagre bodies; their bellies were the shape of the watergourd.

Manda's physical appearance was the best amongst the ten; next were the other three girls in the group. Their skirts made from leaves of dwarf-palm could stay tied for long at their waists. Not so Tamba. The responsibility of leadership as well as his habit of giving the blind girl extra bits from his meagre share of the food they had, had made him into a walking skeleton. Were it not for the fact that Manda had at last discovered by her fingers her friend's condition, and now insisted that they must eat together with her feeding him with each morsel, he might have died.

Tamba had reacted almost violently to the suggestion at first, not only because he wanted to continue to give the blind girl the bigger share of their food, but also because he thought his enemies would mock him for allowing himself to be fed like a baby. And it was only when Manda insisted that this agreement would prevent her from starving herself, that the albino was forced to agree. But no one mocked, not even the brothers, who themselves now brought little gifts to Manda, as if they wished to help to make up for her sacrifice.

The brothers did not know the blind girl was their half sister, neither did the others, yet there were times when the two would show a certain amount of tenderness and concern for her. But it was hard to tell whether it was because she was brave, blind, and the youngest, or that instinct of being a blood relation was responsible.

But there were times when they would be very angry with her, such as when she would counter their attack on her idol by relating the story of the beating Jo had from the albino that day in the village and the way his brother ran away. The story never failed to reach eager ears and the two brothers knew that the rest of the children enjoyed the telling, no matter how often. One of the brothers' tricks was to try to turn the tables on Tamba, pointing out a stain or dirt mark on his white body and accusing him of putting it there himself because he wanted to change his colour to black.

Remembering how often he had wished this, and how he once attempted to do this with charcoal, never failed to make him blush, then his tormentors would notice the sudden redness and call the others' attention to 'see how the dundoes was changing colour like a lizard'.

Of late they had not gone as far as usual into the forest, since they had heard the faint sound of musket fire. That was three months ago but they all felt sure that the bakra were still searching for them, so they were careful not to make a noise, or go too far from the basin. They did not know the muskets had been fired by the last party of their own people searching for them and hoping by this means to discover if they were about before abandoning the search.

Only Tamba had dared go any distance away, and he had only done so because there was no longer any paw-paw on the nearby trees, nor were there any mangoes, naseberries and the few fruits that were then in season in the nearby hills; nor had they caught a coney in their traps for over a month; and even the birds were few of late.

Once Tamba returned from his lone trip with a stringbag half full of unripe fruits and also had a frog in his hand. He did not know if frogs could be eaten or not. He had not seen such large frogs up in the hills where he lived before the invasion of the bakra. Only tree toads were plentiful and he had caught and played with these; but not frogs.

But when he took the frog into the basin, the children not only said it could not be eaten, but told him that it was said the milky liquid which came from its body when frightened could cause cocobeh.

At the mention of the word for leprosy, the albino hastily released the frog and washed himself thoroughly.

And the talk swung to the dreaded cocobeh. Most of the children told tales they had heard about this plague. One told the story he heard from his mother how one stricken with the disease would find his fingers and toes falling off one by one after a while and there would be no sign of blood, even when the member dropped off suddenly.

Others told of the custom of people committing suicide on discovering they were stricken with the sickness; others, of the custom of a tribe to stone to death any leper who came close to their village.

Tamba vowed to himself never to touch frog or toad again.

The moon had come and gone to the number of the fingers of one eating hand since the bakra came and were driven back from the hills. Tomaso's gaunt body seemed to be off-balance because of his missing arm as he moved slowly about the yard of his new house. The blow on his head had taken many things out of his mind, such as the great battle, the death of Lago, or even that his son was missing, or that his wife had died, though often he would speak to an unseen Kisanka about the child, either as if he was still a baby in arms, or as if the albino was somewhere in the bush playing by himself as of old. He spoke of little Manda once or twice in the same vein. Always it was to Kisanka he spoke. When others addressed him, such as Kumse or Tahta, he answered briefly.

Today the usual crowd of villagers came as they had been doing since his illness, bringing gifts and to voice their gratitude for saving them from the bakra. As usual Tomaso's mind seemed far away as they talked, and it was more to Tahta than to him that they repeated their gratitude.

'We shall have no other chief but Chief Tomaso, not as long as he lives!' vowed a grateful villager.

He was one of those who had formed the deputation which once came to tell Tomaso of his banishment.

The leader, who had been sitting on a log, head down, slowly looked up on the face of the speaker, and the embarrassed man, seeing the flashing eyes in the gaunt face, stepped back as the other rose to his feet.

A dead silence came to the spectators as they watched.

'Once you drove me and my Kisanka from the village because of the thing you believed about our son.'

His voice was hoarse and deep, and his hearers could not

tell whether it was because of his months of near silence or bottled up anger, which made it so.

'You have fed your picnies with this badness, until they are filled with nothing else', continued Tomaso. 'They have mocked my son, fouled him while you hid behind fences saying "he had no right to come to the village".'

The spectators, shocked at the suddenness of the long unbroken silence and the shame from the just accusation, stood dumb, as the sick man paused for breath.

'Hear me now!' continued Tomaso, relentlessly. 'My son has not changed the colour of his face since you drove us from the village. Go back to your huts and tell your picnies that what you taught them was a lie, that he has the same blood, the same laughter comes from his mouth, the same water in his eyes as they, and only when I have seen with my own eyes that they, the little ones, have taken to my child, only then shall I, with my Kisanka, and the two little ones, come back to your village, and I be your chief once more. I have spoken!'

As soon as the last word came out of his mouth, another look came into the ex-chief's eyes. The crowd knew this look which replaced the one of recognition now. They had seen it there since their leader regained consciousness after the battle. The eyes now looked at something none of them could see. To Tomaso, the crowd was no longer there. Only his Kisanka, and perhaps his two faithfuls, Kumse, and the tough one-eyed Tahta, were hovering somewhere around him and his beloved.

'Ah, Little Shadow,' he called softly, staring vacantly before him. 'It will be good to see the laughter in thine eyes in place of eyewater when we stand together and watch our Tamba with the little blind one going to the village to play with the picnies there without fear.'

Slowly the sick man eased himself down to his seat on the log without once taking his eyes from whatever scene his mind must have created.

'You must not go from me, Little Shadow. You must grow well and strong again.' He leaned his head to one side as if someone was whispering in his ear: 'No! No, my Spirit!' he cried, shaking his head. 'How often have I not told thee a man cannot live without his shadow.' Feeling that they were listening to something too sacred for their ears, the crowd tiptoed away, their bare feet making hardly a sound on the grass around the new house as they went, leaving the ever present Kumse and the faithful and courageous one-eyed Tahta, with their leader.

When the last of the visitors had disappeared and Tomaso's talk to the unseen Kisanka continued, Kumse drew Tahta some distance away almost out of earshot.

'Tahta!'

'Speak, Kumse, my child.'

'Will he ever be as he was before? Will he remember that she has been eaten by the Great Monster?'

The young woman looked into the old one's eye as if she would see the answer there. He, knowing this, quickly looked down, for he did not wish to kill her hopes and yet he could not lie.

'Would it not be better if he remembers nothing, child?' he asked kindly.

'How could such talk come from thee, Tahta? Is it enough just to draw the air through the nostrils and push it out again?' The girl's breasts heaved almost violently as water welled up in her eyes, and her hand went up to her face in a vain attempt to hide her emotion.

'Would it not be better if you make him a potion which would send him to the arms of his Kisanka?' she blurted out in her anguish.

Tahta turned on her wrathfully. 'What talk is this, woman?' he asked loudly, and for a minute the angry sound brought a puzzled look in the wandering eyes of their leader, but the next instant the sick man was once more with his Kisanka.

Kumse was aware of the badness in the thing she had suggested even as it came out of her mouth. She realized also that Tahta might think that what she said was out of jealousy.

'O, Tahta, Father of Fathers, pull this bad talk of mine out of thy ears,' she cried, kneeling and grasping his hand. 'You are full of wisdom. Look inside of me and see if there is badness in me?' Now she was almost in terror as it came to her that Tahta might in future prevent her looking after Tomaso.

'Cannot you see that for him I would gladly die? Cannot you see that if he had wives as many as leaves on yonder tamarind tree, I would not care? If he never breathes into my face, I would be satisfied as long as I can eat him with my eyes, and my ears can hear the music of his voice?'

She was almost hysterical now. Forgotten was the fact that Tomaso was sitting only a few yards away on a log with his head almost buried between his knees. Even Tahta forgot his leader at that moment. But it did not matter whether they did or not, for it was as if the sick man was deaf and blind, or in another world.

The water fell from the young woman's eyes, one drop after the other, as she bent low to hide her face.

Tahta roughly tilted her wet face so that his one good eye could see all that was there.

Kumse closed her eyes at first out of shame, then, almost defiantly, she lifted the lids and tilted her face further so that the old man could read what he wanted to know.

Tahta looked at the eyes staring back at him for a minute or more, then his hand released her chin, but the face still looked upwards at him as if it would never again return to its normal position.

'It is bad to give without hope of getting in return, child!' the old man said, frowning.

'Nay, Wise One! Nay!' cried Kumse, without hesitation. 'It is bad to give with hope of getting returns, for such is not true giving!' she finished.

'Aye, child! Thy answer pleases me! For I was but testing thee!' said Tahta. Now he looked towards Tomaso sitting on the log talking and smiling once more to himself. 'Perhaps I was angry with thee because thy voice was an echo of what had hatched and grown in my own mind since the day I saw that our chief could not remember,' he mused, still with his eyes on the sick man. 'The mightiest warrior that ever lived, now talking and smiling like a little picni!' His voice was hopeless now as he continued: 'Today they came, the people of the village to pay him homage. Aye, they now build their village around him in the place where they once drove him to hide with his kin. They did not laugh when he spoke many foolish words among the wise ones, for the memory of his mighty deed which makes him a picni still stands fresh in their minds. And perhaps they guessed that my hands would have squeezed the breath of any who had laughter on their faces. But though they did not laugh yesterday or today, what will they do tomorrow when dust begins to cover the deed of his? Will they not pity him at first? Will they not say he was once a mighty warrior who fought against the bakra and drove them from the hills, but now he is without understanding and cannot remember so there must be pity for him?'

Tahta had worked himself into a rage as he opened the secret of his mind to Kumse. Even then he seemed to have forgotten that the girl was still by his side as he thought of the future of his leader. He spat as if the faces which pitied their hero were there before him. 'Their picnies will come up when the ananse's web has hidden the bigness of what our chief has done. They will laugh at the one-armed, old man who does not remember and sees the dead as living. They will wonder if there was truth in the story that this Tomaso who talks strangely was really once a mighty warrior.'

The thought of such a possibility suddenly overwhelmed the one-eyed Tahta. 'Aye, it is better that we should die,' he said resignedly.

'It is good to hear thy *we*, O Great Father!' said Kumse humbly.

Tahta glared at the girl. 'Think you that I would wish to live after the going of Kisanka, the little one, and now my chief?' asked he, scornfully. 'Nay, child! The calabash from which my master would kiss the Monster Death, would also wet my lip,' he said decisively.

'Aye, Tahta, you have looked deeply into my face, but the look has not been deep enough!' said Kumse softly. 'I know this, because now, even with thy mighty wisdom, my mind is still a riddle to thee.'

Tahta turned an amazed face to the girl. Then understanding came. 'Aye, child, thy rebuke is just,' said he with shame. If it be thy wish and I deny it of thee . . .' but he knew the answer the girl would give before he asked.

'Then I must find my way to the Great Forest alone, O Tahta!' Kumse replied with a sad sigh.

There was a long silence while the two looked at the golden hills, then at the gaunt, one-armed giant, still deep in his talk with the unseen.

'There has been one who was like no other on these hills, Kumse. There will never be another like Kisanka!' said Tahta, shaking his head.

'Was she not nearer to me than a true sister, O Great Father?' asked the girl in a hurt voice, but it was as if the bushdoctor had not heard as he turned his one good eye on her:

'Also,' continued the old man slowly, 'On these hills *lives* a woman which is like unto no other!'

Before the meaning of the riddle came to Kumse, Tahta was walking away towards the forest.

They heard what they thought a miracle—the squealing of a pig. Tamba rushed towards the spot where he had set his trap. He arrived just in time to see the sapling which was part of his trap snap, and a young wild pig heading for the thickets with the cord and half of the sapling trailing behind. Desperately the boy threw himself forward to grab cord and wood. After that the fight between boy and pig was fierce and desperate. Bushes were violently flattened and furry dust from strange creepers showered down as Tamba hung on for dear life. Just when he felt he could hold on no longer, help came in the form of the other children and the fight was over.

Bruised, exhausted but triumphant the albino and his companions sat down later to the best meal they had since they came to the forest.

But he felt feverish and burning after the excitement and went and lay down, asking to be called before the sun went to sleep.

Manda felt worried because it was not like Tamba to lie down when they had so much to do, but she remembered his fight with the pig . . .

She called him when the sun felt low on her face.

He came out of his quarters and saw them actively preserving the rest of the meat by smoking.

They all looked up as he came among them.

There was a sudden silence. The children got up and crowded round him, looking at his body, especially his face, neck, and shoulders. Bewildered he stood watching their faces. Manda, conscious that there must be some great reason for the sudden silence, stood listening.

'*It is cocobeh! He has cocobeh!*' cried the girl Akua fearfully.

The mention of the dreadful disease froze the albino where he stood. The crowd of children began backing away with horror on their faces—all but the blind girl. She stood as if the meaning of the word for leprosy was too big for her to understand.

'The frog! It was the water from the frog!' cried Dan-Dan, and the other children nodded slowly in confirmation.

Tamba whispered dazedly, almost to himself:

'Cocobeh! Cocobeh!' as if he had lost his senses. Slowly his hand moved up to the place on which most of the horrified children had focussed their eyes—his face. His shaking fingers reached and touched—a lump. The trembling white fingers passed to another and another. He knew that his one hope was gone. These were not bruises or bumps obtained from his struggle with the pig.

'No! No!' he cried in agony while the children looked on from a safe distance, with terror in their eyes.

'Tamba! Little Brother?' It was Manda, feeling the air with her hands, a dreadful look on her face.

The sight of his beloved friend coming towards him awakened the boy from his petrified state.

'No, Manda! No!' he shouted as she came forward feeling for him with her hands.

'What will you do, Little Brother? Do not go away and leave me!' the blind one cried in a broken voice as she frantically groped for the touch of her companion. But Tamba was backing away now. She sensed it, and grew desperate. 'Do not leave me, Little Brother! Do not leave me or I will die!' She listened, trying to follow the sound of the albino's bare feet as he backed away.

'No! You must not come, Manda, Little Sister! You must not come!' His voice broke as he turned and fled towards the lowest part of the basin. Manda tried to follow, moaning pitifully. 'Do not leave me! Do not leave me!'

The sound of her cry caused the boy to halt as he was about to climb over the top of the basin, just as the blind girl crashed headlong on a projecting rock and lay still. He stopped and instinctively turned to run back to his friend's side. But stopped himself, and with a terrible cry of 'O, Little Sister!' he fled with eyewater streaming down his face. He did not know where he was going. He did not care. He felt Manda must have been killed by the fall. Nothing mattered any more. What his mother had been told was true: *'He would die alone, friendless, even without his dog.'*

The last rays of the setting sun showed him the mouth of one of the caves they had rejected as a home because of its exposed position. He did not realize he had run that far. He would go in the cave and die there, he thought. It did not matter that the cave was dark and smelt of bats' manure. It did not matter now that he had cocobeh. Manda was dying or dead.

As he sat down on the ground in the semi-darkness, he thought of the spirits of his mother and the father he thought dead. Where were they? Had they deserted him too? Even Tahta's spirit? He was not even afraid of the many evil spirits which must be around him in the dark cave. Even the bats coming and going with flopping wings and horrible screeching noises did not disturb him. He wondered how long it would take him to die. His eyes burnt; so did his body. He wondered if his fingers would fall off one by one if he lived long enough. Those were the fingers which held the frog when it spilled the milk water. His faced burned, so did his eyes.

He heard voices calling his name far away, and he remembered where he was, and what he was, and would not answer.

'They have come to stone me to death,' he said to himself. Then he wondered if they came to tell him of Manda's death.

He could not resist finding out.

He was surprised to see that light was coming. He did not know he had slept that long. The voices came nearer. He could make out Jo's, then Dan-Dan's, but he could not make out the difference between the rest of the boys.

Perhaps they were calling him to stone him to death because they felt that unless they did he would sooner or later contaminate them!

He could still hear them calling, and this time it was a girl's voice, though not Manda's.

They were loud in their calling now, and the echoes went over and around them as they called:

'Tamba, where are you?'

'Tamba!'

'T-a-m-b-a!'

'T—a—m—b—a!'

He must know about Manda—if she was buried, and where. He got up and moved nearer to the entrance of the fairly large cave. He would not go outside and they were somewhere by the side of the cave and he could not see them.

'What have you done with Manda?' he cried, dreading the answer, and when it came loud and clear, his heart jumped with gladness, yet he regretted asking.

'Oh, Little Brother, I am here,' answered the voice he would have known among countless children.

'Go back!' he cried, going further into the semi-dark cave. Now the knowledge that Manda was alive brought on the depressing thought of dying. But he knew that a leper must die alone.

After a while he thought they were there no longer. They must have at last persuaded Manda that it was best to leave him where he was to die, he said to himself hopelessly.

She came through the opening with her hands stretched before her, and even in this tense moment the albino remembered when she first came to his leanto holding her hands before her.

'No! No!' he cried as she advanced into the cave, with the rest of the children crowding the doorway.

'You must go, Manda! Go! All of you, or cocobeh will

come to you also!' he cried in panic.

The girl made no answer, following in the direction of his voice, while he tried to dodge her outstretched hands.

'It is bad, Manda! Cocobeh is bad! It will kill!'

His voice broke with the last word and this time he failed to dodge the groping hands of the blind girl. With a cry of triumph she held him with all her young might while she rubbed her face and body frenziedly against his in spite of his struggles, and as she released him and stepped back triumphantly, the rest of the children solemnly followed each other into the cave: Jo first, next Dan-Dan, his brother.

Tamba realized what they were about to do only a few seconds before it was done. He opened his mouth but no words would come as his old enemies grabbed his hand and carried on the same ritual as the blind girl. Stunned he stood with his back to the wall, while one by one they came, took his now unresisting hand and rubbed it on their naked bodies. The girls were the last to come, and when they had taken part in this ceremony of their own making, they sighed as if they had just got rid of a heavy load.

It was the boy Jo who broke the dead silence that followed. 'Now there is no need to run away, Little Brother,' he said softly. 'For now each one of us has rubbed ourselves on thee!' he said triumphantly, yet they all shivered in spite of the pride on their faces as they thought of the disease to which they had committed themselves.

They began furtively to look at their hands and arms as if they now expected to see the beginning of the dreaded thing, or perhaps to see if all their fingers were still there after the contact.

'We shall go back together now, Little Brother!' cried Manda joyfully, as she felt for the unresisting hand of her bewildered friend. 'I had promised Ka Kisanka that I would not leave thee alone!'

She paused, remembering how she had run away from him on the first day of their flight. 'That did not count, for it was for thy sake,' she continued as if Tamba had reminded her of it.

Suddenly the narrow entrance to the cave was darkened.

Tamba looked up, and what he saw froze whatever he was about to say on his lips.

'Death in the shape of my father has come for me!' he whispered in awe.

All except Manda turned to look, and when they saw what was holding the albino petrified, they too crouched back in terror:

'It is Death!' croaked a voice, and the others pushed themselves against the far corner of the cave as if they would force an exit through the solid wall. For silhouetted against the brightness of the morning sun, staring at them in the dimly-lit cave was a gaunt figure with one arm missing, muttering words, to someone beside him.

'I thank thee, Little Shadow,' muttered the silhouette in a dreamy unnatural voice. 'I knew you would not lie!' the voice concluded.

Now the children shook as if they were attacked with ague for there was no-one beside the silhouetted figure!

Tamba gripped the hand of the blind girl standing bewildered beside him, and she could feel the trembling of his body as she pressed against him.

'They have come to take me—my dead father and mother!' he whispered hoarsely, but almost as if he was resigned to this fate.

The children felt faint with fear. Manda, now understood part of what was happening and she too felt the cold sweat of fear on her brow.

'I have come for thee, my children!' said the silhouette at the door, still in the same dreamy unnatural voice, and Jo bit his lip hard to prevent a scream, while one of the three girls beside him slid slowly to the ground with a sigh; but the others were too frozen with fright to notice.

Then out of the sunlight appeared another figure, smaller in size. He whom the young ones thought to be the monster Death turned his head slowly, and wiped his face just as slowly with one hand.

'My father, have I been asleep?' And now the voice was no longer dreamy—only bewildered! 'I came with my Kisanka. She brought me here! But where is she now, Tahta? I can no longer see her!'

The silent unbelieving children stared at the drama before them, still feeling that there were no flesh and blood men at the cave entrance. All but Tamba and Manda. They instinctively knew that life was in the two before them. They did not understand how this miracle had happened. They only knew that rescue had come. That they would once more live under the care and loving hands of adults. No more fighting to keep life in their emaciated bodies. No more wandering in the wilderness, homeless, hungry and afraid. Those two quick minds digested these facts within the minutes it took a man to regain his memory, and an older man to understand the miracle. The rest of the children were still under the spell of fear.

'My Father! Grandfather Tahta!'

His mad rush towards his elders with Manda's hand in his died even before it started. For within that second, he remembered. The rest of the picnies were just on the threshold of belief that the two blocking the entrance might be really flesh and blood, when a broken, despairing cry came from the lips of the albino.

'No, Manda! We must not go to them! The cocobeh!'

A low moan came from the children as they heard the cry. Tomaso—for it was indeed he, was still brushing the cobwebs from the mind which had fallen asleep since he had been rescued from the debris after the great explosion. But now the cry of his son awakened him completely.

'Tahta! It is the voice of my son!' cried the chief, advancing.

'No! No, my father!' screamed Tamba almost hysterically. 'You must not come! I have cocobeh! And the others have mingled with me!'

The last words ended with a great sob. It was as if his father had not heard. He walked forward with his one good arm and what was left of the other, opened wide as if he was about to gather unto himself all the children of the world instead of ten.

Tahta was by his side now. Between them, they, with one move, included every occupant of the cave in the protective enclosure of their arms.

Not until they were able to stem the flow of eyewater did

the bushdoctor ask about the leprosy. He took the child out to the doorway of the cave, and examined the angry lumps he found on his face and body, in the sunlight.

'This is no cocobeh!' cried the bushdoctor with confidence and relief. 'These bumps come from being dusted with the fur-dust from the pads of a bad creeperbean called cowitch. I have seen it happen once to a bakra.'

It took but a few seconds for the children to realize the meaning of Tahta's words. They stood with their big heads, sunken eyes, lean bodies, and bellies inflated with wind, only half believing it was real—this thing which would mean the end of their misery—until they felt the warmth of the morning sun on their faces. Then they knew it was not a dream.

Manda, the baby of the group, forgot dignity as Tomaso bore her in his arm. Tamba looked up at his father and knew that he need never fear of parting from his blind companion.

Tahta, after blowing his nose mightily, lifted a bull's horn, converted into an instrument, and loud and strong came words from its mouth:

'*We have found our lost picnies, O people! And our mighty chief remembers once more!*' said the talking horn, and after a little while an answering talk came from another eketeh from far away.

It cried: '*We hear you! We hear you! God be praised!*'

The Jumbie Bird

Ismith Khan

The tragic story of an East Indian family stranded in Trinidad, betrayed by the authorities and discarded by Mother India.

No-one can escape the sinister call of the Jumbie bird, a ghostly message of death. It haunts the childhood world of Jamini: his fierce, proud grandfather, Kale Khan, a born fighter who dreams of returning to India; his father, a struggling jeweller; and the doomed relationship with his childhood sweetheart, Lakshmi.

The Jumbie bird returns, a symbolic and fearful omen, as Kale Khan prepares for his final battle.

'A new and exciting voice . . .
exotic and baroque . . .
moves with its own poetry'
Caribbean Quarterly

Longman Caribbean Writers Series

ISBN 0 582 78619 3

Listen, the Wind
and other stories

Roger Mais
edited by Ken Ramchand

An important selection of short stories by one of Jamaica's greatest writers, Roger Mais (author of *Brother Man*, *The Hills were Joyful Together* and *Black Lightning*). The collection has been edited by one of the Caribbean's leading scholars, Kenneth Ramchand, professor of English at the University of the West Indies, Trinidad. It includes work that has never previously been published, as well as many of Mais's best-known stories.

Longman Caribbean Writers Series

ISBN 0 582 78551 0

Plays for Today

Edited by Errol Hill

Three outstanding plays by three of the Caribbean's greatest playwrights brought together for the first time in one volume.

Ti-Jean and his Brothers was Derek Walcott's first venture into musical plays and is still his most popular work. A lilting St Lucian folk-tale, it tells the story of a poor family who dwell on the edge of a magical forest haunted by the devil's spirits. The brilliance of Walcott's writing draws us into the realms of fantasy where the actual and the miraculous collide.

Dennis Scott's *An Echo in the Bone* is set during a traditional Nine-Night Ceremony held to honour the spirit of the dead. Shattering sequential time in a series of dreamlike episodes the play takes us back to the time of plantations and slavery — and the savage murder of the white estate owner. Who killed Mr Charles? The answers lie deep in the racial memory, they 'echo in the bone'.

The giddy atmosphere of carnival is the setting for Errol Hill's *Man Better Man*, a rumbustuous, colourful comedy musical about stickfighters. With dance and song the battling troubadours and the calypsonian weave a tale of bravery, superstition and fraudulence. When first performed the *Times* described it as 'a blazing electrifying feast of rhythm and colour'.

Longman Caribbean Writers Series

ISBN 0 582 78620 7